I am forced to swallow hard and regain composure.

I move the camera from my face and try to look at something, anything else. Anything but Ethan Wyatt's face—a tender face now warped and twisted with a look of repugnance . . . and disgust. Directed squarely at *me*.

I feel slightly ashamed to be holding this camera, and hyper-aware of the weight of it dangling from my neck.

Gazing down at my feet, I inhale deeply and try to steady my nerves. . . .

As I turn back toward Ethan Wyatt, I see nothing but a dying wisp of smoke rising from the ashtray.

The automatic doors slide open and he stomps back into the airport. I force my feet to follow him, but when I get within range, my knees go a little funny. They're jittery, weak. . . . I should sprint out in front of him and get a shot of his face. I should. But, I can't. He would look at me again, and for some reason that terrifies me.

Accidental

IT

Girl

doWn tOwn press

New York   London   Toronto   Sydney

An *Original* Publication of POCKET BOOKS

DOWNTOWN PRESS, published by Pocket Books
1230 Avenue of the Americas,
New York, NY 10020

Copyright © 2006 by Sarah Castellano and Emily S. Morris

ISBN-13: 978-0-7434-9924-8
ISBN-10:   0-7434-9924-7

This Downtown Press trade paperback edition October 2006

10   9   8   7   6   5   4   3   2   1

POCKET and colophon are registered trademarks of
Simon & Schuster, Inc.

Manufactured in the United States of America

For information regarding special discounts for bulk purchases,
please contact Simon & Schuster Special Sales at 1-800-456-6798
or business@simonandschuster.com.

For

Katie, Mary, Samantha,
Stephany, Joshua, and Jeremy,

our intrepid siblings.

Acknowledgments

One thousand thank-yous go to our brilliant agent, Wendy Sherman, who somehow manages to keep us calm and encouraged—while being the most quietly glamorous woman in Manhattan. Many thanks also to Michelle Brower, who does so much for us behind the scenes, not the least of which is sending us checks. We cherish your correspondence. Our most heartfelt gratitude to Amy Pierpont and Megan McKeever for reams of good advice and very generous selective amnesia. (Yes, the first draft was *that* bad.) And to Shari Smiley and Jenny Meyer for all their lobbying and negotiating. Last, but certainly not least, on the business front, we thank Anne Dowling—publicist extraordinaire—for all her hard work, for accepting our many "inspired" ideas cheerfully, and for always going above and beyond the call of duty.

Giuseppe, there are no words to describe how grateful we are for all you do. You are an amazing husband, friend, and designer. Thank you for letting us look over your shoulder and monopolize your time and talents. Sarah would like to thank

Acknowledgments

Giuseppe for being an absolute gentleman in the face of her craziness. His unwavering love and encouragement is overwhelming. Emily would like to thank Tony for having a very sturdy shoulder to lean on, and for putting up with her many book-related mood swings. All the contributions you make to my happiness, sanity, and well-being do not go unnoticed—I promise. Jen Bittle, your wildly enthusiastic and optimistic view of our work and dreams is a constant source of encouragement. We love you dearly.

Julie Tripi, thank you for your friendship, support, and phenomenal party planning. Someday we hope to be able to pay you with, you know, actual money. Many thanks also to Lauren Flower for helping us get libbystreet.com off the ground. Also, Susie Foster, Nate Trier, Jimmy Hoover, Lisa Moore, Jay and Laura Cooper, and Jay Bittle, for their love and support.

Finally we would like to thank our families, Brian and Rocky Bushweller, Randy and Shawn Morris, Kate, Mary, Sam, Steph, Josh, Jer, and their families, for their unflinching, irrepressible belief in us and the many wonderful ways they show it.

—Sarah Bushweller and Emily Morris,
("Libby Street")

Accidental IT Girl

Prologue

People hate me.

Some of them openly *despise* me.

I'd bet a couple dozen would cheer if I were maimed.

People. Hate. Me.

For some reason when I meet someone for the first time, I feel compelled to tell them this. "Hi, my name is Sadie Price. Yeah, great to meet you, too! People hate me." I've gotten pretty good at suppressing the urge to say it out loud, but it's still there swirling around in my mind. I'll shake a person's hand, exchange the usual pleasantries, and look from the outside to be a completely sane person—while a part of me silently repeats the words, "People hate me. People. Hate. Me. Peoplehateme."

I think the reason this particular little neurosis developed is that it's not some imaginary thing. The idea that people hate me is not the invention of an irreparably wounded self-esteem or chemical imbalance. I am not some terminal wallflower who feels unworthy of kindness. I'm no paranoid agoraphobe with an irrational fear that people are judging her. I am a twenty-eight-year-old woman whose longest and most satisfying relationships are with a four-thousand-dollar camera, a fully restored 1979 Camaro (a gift from my father), and a lovely man called Antoni who works in the shoe section of Bergdorf's. I pay my taxes—approximately on time. I've spent Thanksgiving and Christmas Eve for the last five years at a homeless shelter on the Lower East Side. I'm blonde and blue eyed (like your local TV weather girl, not Marilyn Monroe). I'm a college graduate with a BA in fine arts. I'm somebody's best friend. And, I am a paparazzi.

People do, in fact, hate me.

When I first started out in this business the people-hating-me thing really rubbed me the wrong way. The same kind of rub as, say, a dislodged underwire gouging into your skin. While you're forced to do jumping jacks. On a trampoline. In those days, when I met someone I would make excuses, "Yes, but I'm not *that* kind of paparazzi." I'd give them a well-rehearsed briefing on my degree in fine arts. I'd tell them that I was really known for my stripped-down black-and-white portraits, and that these portraits were praised by my subjects for their beauty, and by professors for their technique and artistry. At my lowest point, I even went so far as to recount—word for word—an article in the alumni mailer about how my fellow classmates had voted me Graduate with the Most Potential.

My best friend, Brooke, was the first person I met who greeted the news of my occupation with anything but suspicion and ire. Her first words were, "How completely fascinating! A paparazzi, huh? Give me all the dish." It was then that I realized practically everyone in the industrialized world has an opinion about the paparazzi, and in the eyes of most people *every* paparazzi is *that* kind of paparazzi. These opinions are so well established that they will prevail no matter how I might try to explain myself. This realization, despite the fact that it was an embarrassingly long time coming, was a pivotal moment in my life . . . and my popularity at cocktail parties.

I now understand that *all* the people in the world don't actually hate me *personally*. The more rational part of me gets that only *some* people hate the *idea* of me—they hate the job, the institution. Yet, even in the face of these strides in amateur self-psychology, the *peoplehateme* repeating part of my brain absolutely refuses to make this distinction. So, hi. My name is Sadie Price. People hate me.

CELEBRITY SUMMER

As temperatures rise across the nation, Hollywood is preparing for a much-needed jolt. Recent lackluster box office tallies are projected to bounce back in the next few months as this year's crop of larger-than-life action pix and heart-string-plucking indies draw moviegoers out of the heat and into theaters. "This summer looks to be our best in a number of years, possibly our best ever," says industry analyst Gordan Sterne. "We're anticipating record numbers." And the suits aren't the only people feeling cheery about this summer's prospects.

Several publications have crowned this the Summer of Celebrity as the film industry emerges from the doldrums and money and champagne once more begin to flow freely. One well-connected insider declares, "The party atmosphere is back in force. People are beginning to feel that the worst is over. The sweet smell of change is in the air. It's all about L.A., Vegas, Miami, and New York. We're back!"

CHAPTER 1

Do you think I have too much facial hair?" asks Luke as we stroll our way up Broadway toward midtown Manhattan. "It looks like you just shaved," I reply.

Unable to resist the impulse, I stop, close my eyes, and arch my neck up to soak in the warm golden sunlight filtering between the skyscrapers.

This spring was frigid, with bone-chilling rains and blasts of icy air streaking between the high-rises. The few warm days in April felt like fall, not spring. But, not a moment too soon, the cold has broken. Today, the sun is spreading its warmth unimpeded in a cloudless sky. You can practically hear the city sigh with relief. At long last, it is molting season in Manhattan.

Businesses and restaurants emerge from hibernation, their wares creeping out onto the sidewalks. The people of New York peel off their protective layers, shedding sweaters and jackets as the day progresses. Even the most jaded New Yorkers look skyward, not at the buildings, but to confirm, "Yep, look at that—

the sun." In a couple of months the streets will reek of urine again, and the oppressive heat and humidity will force us all to cram into any air-conditioned nook we can find. But, right now, this city is extraordinary.

Luke tries again: "In *general*, do I have too much facial hair?"

Squeezing my eyes closed even tighter, I enjoy the sun-induced tingle on my cheeks and draw in a gulp of the fresh, increasingly humid air.

"Sadie," he prods.

"Hold on," I reply. "I'm having a moment."

Luke huffs before going silent—except for the impatient tapping of his foot.

I take one more deep breath, then open my eyes. "Okay, you're asking if—in *general*—you have too much facial hair?" I ask sardonically.

Though I'm a rather Amazonian five-foot-ten, I have to get on my tiptoes to properly inspect his face. Luke is built like a tree—strong, sturdy, and undeniably vertically oriented. His sinewy six-foot-six frame always manages to dwarf everything around him. Luckily, that includes me. Next to him even the tallest, most gawky girl can feel delicate.

"Again, I say . . . you just shaved," I quip, resuming our stroll. "Did some mean girl tell you that you were too hairy?"

"No. It's just that, like, Conan O'Brien . . . he's all pale and Irish like me. But he always looks so *smooth*."

Pale is a bit of an understatement. Occasionally Luke's pasty Irish pallor gives him the eerie look of semitransparency. Fortunately for him, his blazing red hair and deep green eyes round out sweet, unassuming good looks. He also has the kind of smile that sears itself into your memory, so that whenever you think of him, you only remember him smiling.

"What about, um . . ." I try to think of ruddy, hairy Irishmen to compare him to. Not having much luck. "What about Albert Finney?"

"You think I look like Albert Finney?" he asks.

"I don't know," I reply thoughtfully. "Yell 'Punjab, bring me the autocopter.' "

"I'm serious, Sadie," he retorts.

"So am I."

"Is that from *Annie*?" Luke asks.

"Yes. Say it," I reply.

"No," he snaps back.

I shrug my shoulders at him. "Okay . . ."

"Fine." Luke rolls his eyes. "Punjab, bring me the autocopter."

"Huh," I huff.

"So?" Luke asks.

"No, you don't look anything like Albert Finney. But I just made you say 'Punjab, bring me the autocopter.' "

"Nice. Very nice," he says, trying not to smile.

"Thank you."

We turn the corner at Forty-fourth Street, nearing our destination—one of New York's finest hotels.

Luke and I met through work. He is one of the many autograph hounds who wait patiently outside restaurants and hotels for the celebrities I photograph. I would call his autograph-seeking a hobby, except that he makes almost as much money hawking signatures on the Internet as he does from his day job waiting tables. You see, Luke is not just your average, run-of-the-mill, psycho superfan. He takes his collection very seriously and is extremely well connected. With a minimum of effort, he can tell you where to find anyone in Manhattan—provided they are, or have been, famous. He also helps me sometimes by acting as a decoy, keeping an eye on the competition.

"Check it out," I say, discreetly pointing ahead as Luke and I near the hotel.

A very large, very militant-looking individual waddles into view—the evil Phil Grambs. I cautiously peek over Luke's shoulder and see Phil adjust his camera and dig into the fanny pack that is part of his uniform. The fanny pack sort of emerges from his back like a tumor, as the straps are wedged somewhere between his belly and his pants. I think this particular vast, fur-enshrouded enclave could also be the final resting place of Jimmy Hoffa—and possibly Atlantis.

"Yeah, you're going to need backups," Luke grumbles.

Phil spins toward us with his ears pricked up like a dog.

My heart rate doubles in an instant. I grab Luke by the arm and yank him behind a newsstand before Phil can spot us.

"All right," I say, getting into commando mode, "you position yourself with Phil, act like you're just waiting for an autograph and talking on the phone to someone. Just do what you do best—"

"Loiter."

"*Exactly,*" I reply with a wink. "I think the target will be coming out the side door and through the alley; I'll wait there. But if he comes out the front door you can tell me. Oh, and keep an eye on Phil—tell me if he does anything strange."

"Okay—"

"No, on second thought, just tell me if he tries to go anywhere." Pretty much everything about Phil could be perceived as strange.

"Aye-aye, Cap'n," Luke says, mocking me.

We plug in our cell phone earpieces, and I quickly dial Luke's number.

"Got me?" I ask into the little mic dangling around my chin.

Luke replies with a nod.

"Okay, you first," I say.

Luke skulks out from behind the newsstand. I peek around and watch him walk casually over near Phil.

I wait a few seconds before sneaking onto the sidewalk and darting quickly around the corner. I slip into a back alley that dumps out a block or so from the hotel's main entrance.

For the record, when people say they hate the paparazzi, they're talking about Phil Grambs. He's practically a legend in this business. A legend like Godzilla, or Dracula . . . or that guy with the hook who terrifies the teenagers at Makeout Point. He is loud, vulgar, and cruel to those he photographs. He's also a scheming, conniving weirdo. I would say he was born without a heart, but I know for a fact that he's had quadruple bypass surgery—he showed me pictures. Call me judgmental, but I can't stand the guy. He's one of those people who deludes himself into believing that he's a real part of the film industry, that somehow his physical proximity to the stars makes him famous, or at the very least, *worthy* of fame.

Phil is also one of a rare breed—he actually *intended* to be a paparazzi. Generally speaking, this is not the kind of career you spend your life dreaming about and preparing for. It's the kind of thing you bump into by accident. You're not watching where you're going and, boom—you smack face-first into it. Sometimes you get lucky and it just breaks your nose. Other times, it flattens you, but good. You come to and find yourself five years older, eating greasy nachos on the bumper of a Con Ed truck while your best friend gives a detailed description of his extensive Wonder Woman action figure collection—directly into your brain. These things just happen.

". . . the thing about the so-called realistic invisible plane replica is the thing's supposed to be *invisible,* so can any physical representation of it really be considered realistic?"

I can't say that I've spent much time grappling with this particular philosophical issue, but if I don't say something Luke will surely segue into his treatise on the "so-called realistic" Wonder Woman wristbands. I say, "Well, since you put me on the spot . . . if the replica isn't actually invisible, the claim of realistic does seem—"

"Hey, Sadie?" Luke interrupts. "I think I've got a visual. Keep your eyes open, but I think he'll be coming to my position—"

"No he won't," I reply. "He's coming to me."

"You don't know that," comes Luke's response.

I have a feeling.

He continues, "Oh, and Sadie . . . Phil's getting antsy."

I adjust the earpiece and bark back, "Got it," and train my eyes on a rusty steel door twenty feet away.

"You're supposed to say 'Roger,' " comes the voice in my head.

"I'm not saying 'Roger.' "

A shrill, exasperated whine crackles through the connection. "Why do you always have to be such a buzzkill?"

Oh, boy. Fine. "Roger," I say dryly.

"No, now you should be saying 'Over and out.' " Luke is one of those guys whose dream of becoming 007 was hampered by the fact that part of him stopped maturing at 005.

"As much as I'd love to play your Ursula Andress, Mr. Bond, I'm grossly underqualified." The brutal truth is that, even at the age of seventy, I'm pretty sure Ursula has less cellulite and a higher cool factor than I do.

"Say it," prods Luke.

"No," I laugh.

"Saaay iiiit, Sadie. You know you want to," he goads.

"Luke—" I cut myself off as the steel door begins to rattle. I drop my nachos and shuffle backward, pinning myself in a little nook created by the convergence of a brick-lined building facade and the back bumper of the Con Ed truck.

I peer through the truck's grimy windows and spot the thing I've been waiting the last two hours for—a shock of caramel blond hair and the chiseled, classically British features of a very handsome man.

"Got him," I whisper to Luke.

"Damn, you're good."

Thank you, thank you very much.

Luke continues, "Get him, Killer. Over and out."

I wish to God people would stop calling me that.

I raise my camera to eye level and wait.

A bead of sweat forms on my forehead and threatens to dribble down into my eyes. Though the temperature is pushing 80 degrees, I'm positive it's not the heat that's making me sweat. It's only when I'm forcing myself to be perfectly still and quiet that the nerves get me. It's anticipation, fear of the unknown, my body steeling itself for the coming rush of adrenaline. I prepare to be shouted at, insulted, shoved, ignored.

I wait—wait for *Jude Law* to pass a Con Ed truck in the dank alley behind a posh Manhattan hotel.

As my tension peaks, and that little bead of sweat trickles along the top of my eyebrow and down my cheek, Jude Law enters my frame. I've got a bona fide movie star in perfect profile. I depress the shutter button, and the rapid-fire *click-click-click* of the camera's motor whirs to a crescendo. Jude's head turns and his famously blue eyes lock onto my lens. He is shocked, surprised. His eyes widen, cheeks flush. Then, with the flicker of an eyelash and a reflexive sigh, his expression suddenly shifts to exasperation—and maybe just a touch of real anger.

I scramble out from behind the Con Ed truck and ahead of Jude, walking backward to get a better angle of him striding, at an increasingly rapid pace, toward the sidewalks of Manhattan. I widen the focus of my lens and, to my surprise, catch a glimpse of ruffled golden blond hair at the bottom of my viewfinder.

He has the kids with him. My face goes tingly and undoubtedly as red as Jude's T-shirt.

"You've got him, don't you? Does he have the kids with him?" The voice on the line is not Luke's. It's a deep husky growl, the auditory equivalent of salivation. "Saaadiiie . . ." The voice is getting raspier and out of breath—and infinitely more creepy.

"What the hell was that?" Definitely Luke talking now.

"Luke? Where's Phil?"

"Oh, shit . . . he took off."

The next thing I hear is panting, and the *pitter-patter* of feet on pavement. The mysterious voice, which has to be Phil, says triumphantly between wheezes, "I knew he'd have the kids!"

How is he doing that?

I continue to take shots of Jude—and not the kids.

I move the camera away for a second and make eye contact with Jude Law. "You'd better get a move on. Phil Grambs is headed this way," I say loud enough for the mic to pick it up.

Jude Law gives me a brief furtive grin. It's a lovely smile with all the flash and charisma worthy of a man who once played a robot-o-love for Steven Spielberg. With one simple click, that peculiar, ephemeral, almost illusory flicker—that indefinable *thing* that makes some men irresistible to women—has been captured forever. By me.

You want to know how I can handle people hating me? How I can do a job that in the eyes of most people lumps me into a category with the likes of Phil? That's it, right there. I turn transitory moments—these blurs of fame and style and perfection—into immutable objects. I shape ordered little worlds where everything makes sense. Each photograph is a flawless moment in time, completely under my control. I can leave out anything I want, focus only on what's important, on the thing that tells the story I want to tell. The photographs are always in focus, always stable, always blissfully static. From the moment I picked up a camera and aimed it at a celebrity, I've been in complete control—of the pictures, of my career, of my life.

Phil's voice gripes in my head, "Come on, Sadie! Work with me here. Stall him. Those kids have been in the papers before! When he was boinking his nanny they were in every—"

I yank the earpiece from my ear and, with my brain all to myself, get back to shooting.

Like a streak of splattered ink, a black sedan screeches to a halt at the curb. Three little Jude look-alikes are swiftly plopped and cradled into the backseat by a stern-looking chauffeur.

Jude, making to get in the car, pauses for a moment. "Do you have what you need?" he asks me politely, with his signature timbre.

The question sends an uncomfortable shiver up my spine, a knot forms in my stomach.

Oh, right—he's talking about the pictures.

Marveling at how a voice trained for the Shakespearean stage can make even the simplest question seem fraught with significance, I reply, "Yeah, thanks."

With that, Jude Law is gone. The black sedan has been swallowed up by the bustling avenues of Manhattan—just another black car, just another set of impenetrable tinted windows.

These frenzied encounters with celebrity often leave me, experienced as I am, with the feeling of having seen a ghost. When the adrenaline wanes, a tiny part of me still asks, "Did I just see that? Did that really just happen?" When you think about it, it's nothing but light, really, trickling into my camera. Now that I've gone digital there isn't even a physical object being created. Instead, they're these shifty little wisps, tightly knit groupings of electrons cleverly converted to an incomprehensible string of ones and zeroes. They're no more real than ghosts. That is, until they're put into magazines and newspapers. Until then, though, just like an ancient mystic or Dan Akroyd in *Ghostbusters,* the thrill is in chasing and capturing these elusive things. You have to admit, there is just a little bit of magic in what I do.

Phil, panting and sweating through his Are You Looking at My Shamrocks? T-shirt, screeches to a halt beside me. His skin, normally a grayish off-white sort of color, is a disconcerting shade of blazing, oily pink.

"You didn't even shoot the kids, did you?" he spits, swatting at the damp brown hair sticking to his brow.

I answer *no* by way of yelling, "You broke into my signal?"

"Please, that piece-of-shit cell phone you're using might as well be a baby monitor. I'm surprised you don't pick up FM radio." He adds, "You didn't shoot the kids, did you?"

"No, I didn't. *Paparazzi* and *mercenary* are not always synonymous, *Phil,*" I say, infusing his name with as much venom as possible. Some of us have rules, and this just happens to be one of mine.

"Well, that's good for me. I'll get 'em later," he says, showing his yellow teeth. Phil takes a step toward me, so close I can smell the pastrami on rye that he had for lunch. "I don't get how you can be so ruthless, so goddamn good at the job sometimes, and then pull shit like this. You'll never make it to the top of the game if you don't stop being such a pussy. Just a tip, Price— those little diapers were filled with money."

Um, *gross.*

Though I have the sudden and overwhelming urge to shove

Phil's camera in one of his orifices, I simply shrug my shoulders and flash him a little smile. As intended, this compounds his aggravation. Phil's cheeks become even pinker and more oily, he shakes his head at me and waddles off in a huff.

I admit this business is about chasing money. Like Phil, when I see a celebrity I also see the little dollar signs hovering above their heads. Jude Law alone—two dollar signs. Jude Law with his kids—three dollar signs. Jude Law with his kids and the *nanny*—five dollar signs. The difference between Phil and me, apart from the obvious, is that I weigh those dollar signs against my own standards. I work in a minefield of moral and ethical gray areas, but it's still a business. It's not personal. In my book, kids are personal.

Some of the paparazzi are awful, it's true. They invade people's privacy. They yell obscenities and insults to the people they photograph, chase and intentionally terrorize them. I don't. There is a certain, very solid line I will not cross. I don't buzz helicopters over weddings, I don't dig through trash, I don't trick people into getting angry and violent. I just take pictures. Fluffy, silly, harmless pictures of famous people doing everyday things.

And as for the kids, I think it's important to remember that though the children of famous parents are born gnawing rather enormous silver spoons, they still put their onesies on two legs at a time like the rest of us. I think they deserve the same consideration as the children of nonfamous parents—the ones for whom an unsolicited snapshot will get you a one-way ticket to the clink, and a lifetime of registering your name on a special list. But hey, that's just my opinion.

I plug the earpiece back in my ear and adjust the mic. "Hey there, Super Spy. You ready to get out of here?"

"Yeah," Luke replies.

"You're supposed to say 'Roger.' "

As I disentangle myself from the maze of wires wrapped around my middle, I hear a shrill, exasperating wail from my back pocket.

Stupid Sidekick.

I keep my life on that damn thing. A good portion of the time my life is whining, vibrating, and jingling at me, demanding to be heard. Right now it's screaming, "You're late—*again*."

SURPRISE! YOU'RE SCREWED

Surprises are supposed to be a good thing, but in the world of Hollywood tabloids, s-u-r-p-r-i-s-e could spell "disaster." "Everybody wants a big, shocking, surprise exclusive," says Bethany Stone, senior editor of America's hottest up-and-coming gossip paper, "Celeb." "But only if it comes with at least twenty-four hours' notice," she quips. Competition between tabloids has reached a fever pitch, with each outlet doing its best to outwit and outscoop its rivals. A big last-minute story can mean huge profits. It also sends editors, photographers, and writers scrambling, and thousands of dollars swirling down the drain. "The potential profits are staggering, but so are the risks. Each time someone yells 'Stop the presses!' you're re-creating a magazine—a process that takes weeks in some cases—and doing it in a matter of hours. Accidents and errors can be a problem," says Stone. "In the tabloid business surprises are a blessing . . . and a curse." So, a message to Tom & Katie, Brad & Angelina, Nick & Jessica, Britney & Kevin: Some notice next time, please?

CHAPTER 2

Yes, I have a Sidekick. And I am not ashamed of it. Anymore. Like many, I once pictured the Sidekick as an accessory for Paris Hilton–loving tweens who relied on it as both hobby (lets cover it in glitter!) and a modern-day alternative to the "football paper fold" method of passing notes in class (U R soooo hot! LOL!). However, since I haven't missed an appointment in nine months, you can now consider me a total convert.

You know how people say, "When it rains, it pours"? Well, my little corner of the universe is smack dab in the middle of the cloud. Most of the time I manage to hover around the silver lining, but things around me have a distinct tendency to spiral out of control with very little notice.

A couple of years ago, I was planning a big blowout surprise party for Brooke. Her birthday that year happened to fall right between two big, flashy award shows that were going on in New York. Manhattan was crawling with celebrities, and my day planner was straining at the seams. I spent twelve hours a day on the streets, and the other twelve organizing streamers, guest lists, and mini shrimp cocktails. The kicker was, in the weeks prior to the surprise, Brooke and I began noticing a strange smell in the apartment. It was acrid and kind of gross, but it came and went. I was supposed to call the super.

I forgot to call the super.

The morning of Brooke's party, our building was evacuated. I mean the sirens blaring, hazmat suit, bomb squad kind of evacuated. Oh, and did I mention it was evacuated roughly ten minutes after I'd had twelve pounds of ice delivered to my kitchen? Yeah.

The smell turned out to be a man downstairs who had taken up a new hobby—pipe-bomb construction. Brooke and I were out of the apartment for two weeks while they cleared out what a very nice man in a silver space suit called "the residue." Brooke's big birthday surprise turned out to be sitting on the stoop of the building next door, sipping Red Cross–provided coffee while disappointed friends stopped by, dropped off their presents, and went home. When we were finally allowed back in, Brooke and I had an apartment with first-class water damage and a refrigerator full of putrid shrimp cocktail, which, incidentally, was a hundred times more noxious than any pipe bomb.

Don't ask me to explain how these things happen to me. I have no idea. It just seems like whenever one thing goes wrong it causes a cascade effect whereby everything else in my life must go wrong, too—an isolated drizzle turns into a freak torrential downpour. My Sidekick is like a little umbrella, doing its best to keep me dry in a cloudy world.

*   *   *

I jam my key in the apartment door and jiggle it repeatedly, twisting, pushing, and actually begging the lock to cooperate. Rust, apparently, is our new high-tech security system. I can hear the super now: "If the door is this hard to open *with* a key, imagine how hard it'll be for someone without one." Brooke and I have a rent-controlled apartment in a building desperately trying to go co-op. This means that the super performs only enough maintenance to keep us alive.

The prior tenants of our place were two eccentric spinster sisters whose lease was signed in March of 1962. Each of the two bedrooms has its own bathroom and these dreamy built-in bookshelves that form an arch perfectly sized for a double bed to snuggle under. The ceilings are absurdly high and the floors are the original deep-amber hardwood. The floors are so original, in fact, that deep troughs of wear pit the surface, marking the paths the sisters took from room to room. Someone, apparently, liked to look down onto First Avenue from the living room window, because the northwest corner of the floor has a divot so deep that it's practically a health hazard. But try telling that to the super.

With a loud *clang-pop* the lock finally yields. It's managed to give my key a worrisome (but graceful) curve and taken off what was left of the fingernails on my right hand. Excellent, it's a vicious and aggressive *guard* lock.

"Brooke!" I scream, while thundering through the apartment toward my bedroom. Luke shuffles in behind me, loaded down with my camera equipment. "Help!" I try again. I have a date at seven. It is currently six-thirty. I haven't seen the inside of a shower in twenty-four hours. My hair looks like a blond feather duster and my nails give the distinct impression that I've been clawing my way out of a coffin for the last several hours. I am an *Ambush Makeover* just waiting to happen.

"Brooke? Have you seen my—"

"Ta-da!" Brooke says, scaring the crap out of me.

She's standing in front of the TV, pointing and waving her arms around an enormous brown box. Brooke, having been blessed with the ship-launching, traffic-stopping type of facial structure—high cheekbones, perfectly symmetrical *everything*, and bright green eyes—looks like she's in the middle of a challenge for *America's Next Top Model*. I half expect Tyra Banks to saunter in from the bedroom.

"What the hell is *that*?" I ask, eyeing the slender six-foot by four-foot, craft-paper-wrapped monolith.

"It's a plasma TV!" shouts Luke excitedly.

"No," Brooke says, idly tidying her chestnut hair under the triangular scarf thingy she wears when doing household chores. In it she looks like a cross between Lucy Ricardo and Betty Crocker. For some reason, this gives her no end of enjoyment. She continues, "Well, it could be, I guess. But I don't know. You'll have to ask Sadie."

"Me?"

"Well, it's got your name on it. What is it?" she asks, rubbing her palms together greedily.

"I have absolutely no idea," I say, truly shocked. How could I order something that enormous and forget about it?

"This is so exciting!" Brooke flaps, while tearing open a corner of the brown paper.

"Wait!" I recognize that zip code. "It's from *Paige*."

Brooke stops dead in her tracks, and slowly backs away from the package like she's just found out it contains a cache of anthrax.

I cautiously take a seat on the sofa, doing my best not to anger the box. Brooke sits down on one side of me, Luke quietly takes a place on the other. We sit in silence, staring at the monstrosity while muffled, canned laughter from the TV struggles out from behind it.

The box reminds me of Paige, actually. It gives the impression of being larger than life, while also being oddly too thin to support its weight. The box's slim three inches of depth seem grossly inadequate to underpin its volume. Part of me wants to go over there and keep it from toppling over and burying us all.

"What do you think it is?" asks Brooke quietly, her eyes never leaving the package.

If I had to guess . . . "A life-size portrait of herself?"

Biologically speaking, Paige is my mother. But in all the ways that count, she's more like a complete stranger who just happens to have my icy blue eyes, overly long torso, and wavy hair.

Paige abandoned us, my father and me, in 1988. I was ten. She was a vivacious thirty-two then, and looking to improve her life and lifestyle by finding someone who could provide more than the basics of subsistence. My dad, the insolvent manager of a local seafood place, had big dreams of owning his own restaurant. They were plans that, it seems, weren't progressing quite as rapidly as Paige had anticipated. She moved out under the cover of darkness one cold October night, and two months later married Dr. Hank Farmer, DDS. The gust of wind caused by her sprint to the altar actually dried the ink on the divorce papers.

Disgustingly enough, she kept my father's last name. I suspect this was only because Paige Price-Farmer sounds much more like a well-bred country club wife than the alternative, which sounds more like a person who harvests loose-leaf.

The predivorce Paige I remember was glamorous and fun, if a bit absentminded and careless with my safety—and my father's limited funds. She had a costume jewelry chest six layers deep that I spent hours digging through, and she took me to the movies three times a week. She was tall and slender with gracefully curving hips. Her fingers were long and tapered down to tasteful French-manicured nails. She wore cigarette pants and halter tops, and never looked me in the eye.

The postdivorce Paige didn't call me for three years. She was too busy helping Dr. Hank build a successful cosmetic dentistry practice and patent the very lucrative Farmer Bleaching Tray. In the days before Crest White Strips and GoSMILE, Dr. Hank gave thousands of perfectly attractive people obnoxiously white teeth. He now specializes in porcelain veneers—doing his part to homogenize the human race by giving people with already lovely smiles the too-symmetrical, blinding white teeth of a Ken doll. The American obsession with fake teeth affords my mother the lifestyle she loves. This life includes five new Chanel suits per year, a Mercedes the same golden champagne color of her hair, and three Pekingese puppies named Oodles, Munchkin, and Donks.

The last thing I need right now is any of her drama. Come to think of it, there's *never* really a good time for Paige's drama. "I'm not going to open it," I say finally.

Brooke and Luke each look at me with a curious mix of frustration and understanding.

Brooke says, "Of course. Sure. Absolutely."

Luke chimes in, "Good plan," and then nods his head to emphasize his simulated certainty.

This is followed by several awkward moments of silence, during which I glare at the gigantic box in front of the TV and my two best friends shrug their shoulders at each other and mime a conversation about what to do next.

It's just a box.

For some reason I feel the need to keep telling myself that. It's just a box.

But, it's just a box from *Paige*.

I'd really like to chuck it out the window and erase it from my memory. With my luck I'd probably flatten somebody on the street and become the lead story on the evening news. The bomb squad would then blow it up—as a precaution. Hmmmm. Maybe I should just call the bomb squad directly and cut out the middleman. Somewhere in my bedroom I have the card of that very nice man in the silver space suit.

"Uh . . . Brooke," pipes Luke tremulously, "a friend of mine is thinking about buying an apartment. He's looking on the Upper East Side." Luke sounds like he's reading from a script.

"Oh, that's nice. Is he in need of a broker?" Brooke not only sounds like she's reading from a script, she sounds like she's doing it badly.

"I believe he is. I recommended you."

"Thank you, Luke."

"You're welcome," Luke replies in an overly cheery falsetto.

The apartment once again falls into an eerie quiet—save for the garbled, box-filtered opening notes of the *Jeopardy!* theme song.

"So, Sadie," Brooke begins, "hot date tonight, huh?"

"Holy shit! I totally forgot!" Damn Paige. I jump up from my seat. "Help!" I plead. "I have precisely zero minutes to get ready for this date. Brooke, could you just throw an outfit together for me while I'm in the shower?"

Brooke lets out a squeal of delight that I will assume is a *yes*. The fervor of the squeal worries me a little, but I don't really have a backup plan.

"You're a saint, thank you," I blubber while peeling my clothes off. "Nothing crazy, okay? I have some things from the dry cleaner somewhere—"

"Come on!" exclaims Luke, out of nowhere. He slaps his hands to his eyes. "When will you people realize that I don't have a vagina?"

Oh, I'm down to my bra.

Luke struggles with the fact that his two best friends are women who, for all intents and purposes, consider him one of the girls. While he, a completely heterosexual man, does his best to consider his two best female friends just a couple of the guys. He's fallen headlong into one of the great paradoxes of modern life.

I cover myself for Luke's benefit.

"Oh, Sadie?" Brooke says, stopping my rush to the bathroom.

"Yeah?"

"You might want to comb your hair first." She points at my

head. "You've either had a moment of hygienic challenge or discovered a new way of saving leftovers."

I reach up and poke at my hair. The right side of my head is
a thick mass of knots and . . . hmmm, lovely—a bit of nacho
cheese. See, these are the kinds of things Brooke notices. Of
course, had it been her nacho hair debacle she'd have noticed
before coming face-to-face with Jude Law. If she were to find
herself in this situation—ridiculously late for a date and running
around in a frenzy . . . actually no, impossible. Brooke doesn't
do frenzy.

Before heading into my room I turn briefly back to Luke.
"Hey, Luke . . ." I drop my arms and flash him my bra.

"Aw!" he groans, before turning a glorious shade of pink. I
do so love to torture him.

After hastily shampooing the cheese out of my hair, and not
waiting the recommended three minutes for the conditioner to
do its thing, I sprint out of the bathroom, towels draped hap-
hazardly over my head and body.

Finding no outfit neatly laid on my bed, I race through the
apartment and blast through Brooke's bedroom door. "What
have you got for me, O beloved stylist?"

Walking into Brooke's room is like stepping into a layout in
the Williams-Sonoma Home catalog. She has an organizational
system for absolutely every need and occasion, beautiful linen
covered boxes for every wayward bit of clutter. Even her chaos is
organized. Behind a reproduction Georgian folding screen is a
receptacle for dirty laundry, another for garbage, and a third for
things that she hasn't decided how to classify yet. Brooke's

mother sent all of her old high school yearbooks a few months back; they've been in the "unclassified" receptacle ever since. Brooke can't decide whether they should be placed with books or with photographs. This is a decided contrast to my half of the apartment. My half *appears* organized, but is actually a cleverly concealed nightmare. I am routinely attacked by things that rebel and explode out of drawers, closets, and the apartment's many crannies.

"I came up with something fabulous," Brooke says, turning from her wardrobe. She holds up a dress, a very *small* dress, dripping in bright colors—tangerine, lemon, celery.

"Brooke, that isn't a dress. It's a salad. Come on, seriously. Where's the stuff I brought back from the dry cleaner the other day?" I press.

"You mean that boring old black number with the confusing fabric corsage thingy on the lapel?"

"Yes," I reply.

"I hid it."

"Brooke!" I plead.

"*Sadie,*" she mocks. "Step out of your comfort zone."

"I *have* one of those?"

"Yes, it's called 'the black death.' "

I really should have seen this coming. Brooke, like male birds, beguiles the opposite sex with vivid blazes of color—and feathers. I, on the other hand, prefer to let my personality do the enticing. *That* is why I wear a lot of black.

Oh, all right . . . I wear a lot of black because it's allegedly slimming and has unrivaled stain-hiding properties. But really, is that such a crime?

I glance at the clock and watch it tick from 7:09 to 7:10.

Ugh!

I give Brooke a very stern glare and reluctantly reach my hand out to receive the dress.

"You won't regret it," Brooke says, glowing with pride.

Yeah, right.

HOLLYWOOD'S
MOST ELIGIBLE

It doesn't matter who they're dating (or married to), they won't be for long.

- Orlando Bloom, Date-ability Quotient = 5 (Minus 5 for manscaping and general girly-ness)

- Colin Farrell, Date-ability Quotient = 4 (Minus 6 because F*%#-ability Quotient = 10)

- Ethan Wyatt, Date-ability Quotient = 8 (Minus 6 for being a dawg, but +4 for being super hot)

- Tom Cruise, Date-ability Quotient = -2 (Minus 8 for being older than my mom, and Minus 4 for jumping on Oprah's couch)

- Jake Gyllenhaal, Date-ability Quotient = 6 (Minus 4 for making "The Day After Tomorrow")

- Ben Affleck, Date-ability Quotient = 7 (Minus 3 for high turnover rate)

—List by: Staci Ellen Garth,
Grosvenor, OH

CHAPTER 3

I said I haven't *missed* an appointment in nine months, I didn't say I haven't been late.

Blatantly disregarding the cautionary placards on the escalator, I race up two steps at a time without holding the rubber handrail. I need one of my hands to keep the dress from riding up, and the other to apply lip gloss and finger-comb the wet, stringy blonde mass on top of my head into something that approximates a hairstyle.

Ten more minutes. If I'd had ten more minutes I wouldn't look like a drowned rat right now. Man, Paige has a real gift for complicating my life.

At my high school graduation, she spilled, "I don't know that I ever really loved your father," as casually as a normal person might say, "I've never been fond of mayonnaise." Just the thing I needed to help me through the already building turmoil over leaving my father all alone when I went off to college.

At my father's funeral, Paige let it slip that I was the result of that onerous 1 percent gap in the birth control pill's 99 percent effectiveness rating. She went on to describe in detail how unprepared for motherhood she was and how relieved she'd been when I turned out all right. I assumed that *all right* was her term for responsible enough to take on the mountain of outstanding debt racked up by building the restaurant my dad didn't even live to see open.

When we read my father's will, it turned out that he had left Paige his most prized possession, a fully restored 1979 Camaro. It was the only thing of value he owned. *Ever.* My mother's response to this surprising and deeply heartfelt gesture was to say, "I never liked that car. Too noisy and small. It should be yours, Sadie." This came, of course, just as I was preparing to move to a city where a spot in a parking garage costs about four hundred bucks a month.

And now, there's this gigantic brown . . . *thing* in my living room. Whatever it is, it's sure to disrupt the relatively smooth, nearly complication-free existence I've been basking in for a while now.

Gasping for breath, I reach the lobby bar and spot Todd.

"I'm sorry," I wheeze. "I got caught up with Jude Law and—"

"If I had a dime for every time I've heard *that* excuse . . ." quips Todd with the twinkle of at least two glasses of wine in his eyes. "Don't worry, I lied to you. The reservation is for eight."

"You *lied* to me?" I mutter, completely caught off guard.

He nods yes as a frisky, superior sort of grin spreads across his face.

I don't know what bothers me more, that he tricked me or that he knows me well enough to know—without a shadow of a doubt—that I would be an hour late.

Todd chooses to ignore the look of scorn and bafflement currently contorting my facial muscles, and hails a swarthy maître d', who swoops in like a vulture and guides us to our table.

"Have anything you like," says Todd, grinning over his glass of merlot. "It's my treat."

Todd peruses the menu like it's *War and Peace,* squinting his eyes thoughtfully. This makes the two well-manicured black caterpillars clinging to his brow bone (he calls them eyebrows) curl a bit to form a sort of fuzzy smile.

I'm pondering the oddity of this display when he speaks to me again. "Sadie?"

"Uh . . . what did you say?" I ask dumbly, pretending I've just looked up from the menu.

"Have anything you like."

"Oh, sure. Okay. Thanks," I stammer.

Todd has the meaty physical presence of an old-school enforcer for an illegal OTB. He's thirty-five, stocky, dark, and attractive in the way that mobsters are. His face is pleasing enough, but most women are drawn to him as a protector. Todd, physically and otherwise, heavily favors his father's side of the family tree.

The elder Adler used the family's kosher deli as a front for his numbers-running and bookmaking operation in Queens. Todd, like his father, has a distinct tendency toward the unscrupulous. Unlike his father, Todd lacks the fearlessness required for flagrantly breaking the law. In other words, Todd's fear of poverty is superseded only by his fear of incarceration. Which is, I think, the only reason he became a photographer and not a stockbroker.

Todd and I have been at this—the dating—for about three months, and I've known him for nearly five years. Yet, with all that, this is the first time I've ever seen him in a tie. It's a bit odd, really. He almost doesn't look like himself. He's almost . . . dashing.

Maybe it's this place.

The music, a slow and sultry Lena Horne album from a bygone and much more elegant era, is creating the kind of auditory ambience that makes all the little hairs on the back of my neck stand up. Lavish gold and amber tree limbs rise from the many circular banquettes around the room, creating a graceful, glittering woodland canopy. It's like we're nestled in a magic forest. A magic forest where light doesn't slam into your skin and highlight every imperfection, but bounces off the gilded foliage and skims over you like a breeze, erasing every flaw. It's really a spectacular setting. And, to be honest, it's making me a little nervous. There's something ugly in the air, something heavy and sinister, and I don't just mean the near toxic levels of Chanel No. 5 that are wafting off the lady sitting behind me.

"Starters?" Todd asks.

"I hear the polenta here is really good," I say, trying not to stare at either his tie or his caterpillars.

"Yeah, I've heard the same thing," he replies. "We should try it."

"Okay, polenta it is." Why does this feel so strange? I'm in a great restaurant. I'm going to eat. I love eating. And . . . Todd is in a *tie*. Maybe that's what's giving me the willies.

I stare at the menu. I try to focus, but the double-digit prices for things like peas and spinach are making my eyes water a bit. Twelve dollars for a bowl of corn?

Oh, wait, it's all coming together. This place is modeled on the magic forest where they raise the eighty-five-dollar-a-plate Kobe beef they're serving.

Come on, eighty-five dollars for a *steak*? Forget Japan, if I'm going to pay that much for a piece of meat, that cow better be shipped direct from freaking Middle Earth. She better be doing her free-range grazing side by side with unicorns and lapping her water from the hands of enchanted wood nymphs. Otherwise, it really wouldn't seem worth it.

"I'm going to have the Kobe beef, and we'll be sharing the polenta," Todd chirps to the waiter who just appeared out of nowhere.

He's getting the eighty-five-dollar steak? What on earth could he be—

Oh, no. Expensive meal, candlelight, the whole romantic magic-foresty thing we've got going on here . . .

Oh, come on!

"Sadie?" Todd prompts, caressing my hand. "What are you having?"

"Chicken," I reply bluntly, while surveying the room for emergency exits.

The waiter strides off toward the kitchen, and I'm left alone with Todd . . . and his caterpillars . . . staring at me—all three of them grinning.

"Sadie," Todd starts, "I've been thinking. . . ."

Oh, crap. I hate it when they do that.

He continues, "You've been spending a lot of time at my place lately. So, I thought, well . . ."

He reaches in the pocket of his sport coat and whips out a toothbrush—with a bow on it.

The sight of it makes me jump. My knees bang against the tabletop, sending cutlery and crystal careening into fine bone china. The clatter it makes can be heard from space; I'm pretty sure I've just disrupted satellite communications.

Every head in the restaurant turns toward our table. What feels like a thousand beady little LASIK-ed eyeballs peer at me over the golden foliage and velvet booths.

I can't stand being the center of attention. Even when it's something positive, like a birthday, I'd much rather be just to the left of attention's center. Or possibly in another room. With the door shut. Hiding under a blanket.

I give an overly dramatic chuckle and throw my head back for the sake of the onlookers. I sigh, "Oops!" Clumsy me. Nothing to see here, everybody.

I look back to Todd, who's still holding the toothbrush up, waving it slightly from side to side. The big white bow flops this way and that, like a flag of surrender.

What is going on here? Todd is not this kind of guy.

Ah, but he does love a good prank. He once had me completely convinced that Jerry Garcia was his uncle. He had supporting documentation, childhood photographs, a mean impersonation. This has got to be a joke.

"I, uh . . ." I smile nervously. "Do I have something in my teeth?"

"No," he laughs. "It's yours. To keep at my place. You know"—don't say it, Todd, don't say it—"taking it to the next level." He said it. With a heap of sincerity. Oh, God, it's not a joke.

Okay, right. Let's apply some logic here. A toothbrush is the next level? If this were the 1700s and I were a dentist, then yes, that would be the next level. In a relationship, I don't think so. A toothbrush is a quarter of a level at best. Oh, and by the way, I don't want the next level. I *detest* the next level. The next level is unbelievably messy and complicated—or so I'm told. It's filled with emotional outbursts, and compromises, and, oh . . . I don't know . . . antiquing.

Damn it, I thought commitment phobia was supposed to be this pandemic crisis in New York City. Every other day I hear a horror story about the selfish urban male, how he's just too happy with bachelorhood to settle down. Men all over Manhattan are apparently running for their lives, cowering in fear as women share their apartment keys and point out lovely engagement rings. Guys are fleeing this way and that like rats from a sinking ship. And yet, somehow, I remain ratless. I must not be going to the right bars, or something.

"Uh . . ." I begin, without any clear way to finish.

Todd's eyes squint again, this time the strange behavior of his eyebrows clearly stems from confusion.

"Uh . . ." I stall.

I desperately want to tell Todd that I only got involved with him because I thought he was the kind of guy who didn't like to be tied down. I thought he didn't like making commitments of any kind, even those involving dental hygiene.

I also would like to explain to him that I'm just a regular, plain old, garden-variety girl, and that men aren't supposed to want to get all emotionally entangled with me. They're supposed to string me along, spend too much time with "the boys," and dump me unceremoniously. Men are not, under any circumstances, supposed to introduce me to siblings, invite me on extended vacations, or—God forbid—"take things to the next level."

But I don't know precisely how to phrase all of this without hurting his feelings, or explaining in detail why my slightly too-chunky thighs, persistently bloodshot eyes, and rapidly forming crow's-feet should be a turnoff.

Why won't this man just play by the rules?

Todd looks at me, concerned. "Sadie?"

"Um, Todd . . ." All right, think of something, Sadie. "I . . . you know . . ."

"No, I don't," he says defensively.

My heart is throbbing against my chest. My palms are going moist and my upper lip is beginning to quiver. I have to get out of this. I can feel the weight, the pounding pressure of panic, setting in.

"Maybe this isn't the best time to say this," I continue, ". . . but I don't think we should see each other anymore." Completely unbidden, a sigh of relief escapes my lips.

Todd chuckles loudly but uncomfortably, obviously waiting for me to join in the laughter and confirm that I'm joking.

There's nothing I can do but stare, and hope that he doesn't explode—or take flight like the characters in *Mary Poppins*.

After several awkward moments of feigned giddiness, Todd stops cold and grunts, "You're kidding."

"No," I reply in a gentle yet unmistakably firm tone.

"Oh, shit," he says, stunned.

"Sorry," I whimper.

"Why?"

"Things are just moving too fast. You know?"

"This is because of the toothbrush, isn't it?"

"Well . . ." Um, *yeah*.

He stares at me a moment, then looks away—out to the gorgeous and irrepressibly luminous New York City skyline. He heaves a frustrated "Huh" and looks down at his cutlery. "I thought girls loved this shit."

"Todd, come on. Have I ever been that kind of girl?"

He rolls his eyes, but I can tell this is something that never occurred to him.

I try to think of something—anything—to soften the blow. "It's a great toothbrush, though, thank you. Oral B! Nine out of ten dentists—"

Todd lets out a noise, half grunt, half laugh, that shuts me up. He shakes his head. "You are something else, Sadie Price."

Given the hint of a smile twitching at the corners of his mouth, I'm almost convinced that was a compliment. Given the context, however, I'm not so sure.

"Todd—"

"No, Sadie"—he waves his hands at me—"I think it would be best if we just let this go. . . ."

"Okay—"

"And never speak of it again."

"Right," I reply nervously.

"Ever."

I nod and make the international symbol for zipped lips.

An actual smile creeps across Todd's face. He begins, "The good news is"—he looks at his watch—"you've dumped me in just enough time to get to the airport."

"You're going to the airport?" I ask, surprised.

"No, *you* are, Killer. Donny Osmond is coming into Newark at midnight. If you get in the car now, you'll get there just in the nick of time."

"You're serious?" I ask, dumbstruck. Donny Osmond?

He looks at me, his dark brown eyes two little lumps of Christmas coal, and gibes, "Oh, yeah."

Ah, so *this* is why they tell you not to get involved with your boss.

HOT CELEB NEWS

Yet another hot young thing is trading L.A. for the Great White Way. Superstar Ethan Wyatt ("Felony Charge," "Out of Harm") is just the latest celeb to choose the Big Apple over Orange County in search of a lower public profile and increase in career cachet. In recent interviews the hunky celeb suggests that he's looking to "challenge" himself in "meatier" roles. Perhaps to finally erase our collective memory of that shining turn as Fletcher the sex-obsessed lifeguard in "Motion of the Ocean".

Word on the street, however, suggests the twenty-eight-year-old stunner is frustrated with the paparazzi's unquenchable thirst for dish about him. Wyatt *is* a tabloid fave, but how could he not be? Ethan has a well-known fondness for hard partying and navel-bearing starlets. Speaking of which, no one knows if Maya Dunn, Ethan's costar in the upcoming "Charming Samantha," will be joining him on the East Coast. Rumor has it the two have been "charming" each other regularly since principal photography wrapped in February. We'll have to see if bad boy Ethan can shake his Hollywood demons and wiggle his way into the New York acting elite.

CHAPTER 4

Donny Osmond?

Todd is only making me do this because I broke up with him. This is punishment. I mean, no offense to Donny (I loved his work in *Mulan*), but he's so far down the priority list he has to look up to see that kid who played Urkel. I could be eating steak right now, or better yet—having a rare evening where the only thing scheduled is a bubble bath. Instead, I'm standing in the lobby of a major international airport dressed like Barbie, waiting to get photographs that won't make enough to pay for my parking. God, I hate being a pawn in someone else's game. One of the reasons I love this job is that, with or without Todd, I can do whatever I want—when I want. I caved under the weight of toothbrush guilt. I should have told Todd and his caterpillars to shove Donny Osmond to where the sun don't shine.

And another thing, do you know how difficult it is to feel professional when wearing a dress that's slightly too small and intended to be worn by a person four inches shorter than you? If it weren't for the rather impressive-looking camera in my hands, I'm sure I'd have already been ejected from the airport on the grounds that I look like a hooker.

Whatever. No matter what I look like, I'm here to do a job. I will prove to Todd how indifferent I am to the "punishment" by getting pictures of Donny Osmond without a single complaint. I will get great pictures of Donny Osmond. Shockingly *beautiful* pictures of Donny Osmond. Okay, that may be stretching it. What I'll do is photograph Donny Osmond walking to the baggage claim, walking to a car, getting into a car, and driving away. This so an editor can have the five shots of Donny Osmond *walking* that she desperately needs for a groundbreaking exposé of former child stars who handle their own luggage. I probably should have thought through the whole Todd breakup thing before actually going through with it.

Come to think of it, I could have spent a little more time thinking before I got involved with him at all. It was just one of those things. He was there, I was there. I was single, he was single. And I thought he was the kind of person who, like me, doesn't like to take things to the next level. You can't blame me for thinking that, either. Todd normally dates women who make a large percentage of their income in one-dollar bills, which they have to retrieve from their own underpants. These women are typically named after colors or seasons—including, but not limited to, Amber, Spring, and Winter. (Please, we all know that Winter is the easiest season to get into bed.) But you want to know the clincher? He owns a "crystal silver metallic" Porsche Cayenne.

Granted, a lot of paparazzi buy expensive cars so that they don't stick out when driving around the high-class neighborhoods preferred by celebrities, and yes, the Porsche SUV is good cover when parking near hip restaurants and nightclubs; but Todd only bought the thing because he thinks it's a chick magnet. And I'm sure it is. Women who enjoy being called "chicks" are probably drawn to it by some primal urge; it's a big humming vortex of superficiality.

Don't get me wrong, Todd's a nice guy. He's smart, wickedly funny, and doesn't skimp on the compliments, but I'm honestly floored by the toothbrush thing. How could I have misread him so completely after knowing him for *five years*?

Ugh. Well, that settles it; I am officially no good at relationships. Actually no, I have no idea if I'm good at relationships. I don't *have* relationships. I have *situations*.

I once dated this guy named Greg. He was a Ph.D. student who told me I "built up walls." So would any woman in her right mind when faced with a man who learned how to play tonsil hockey by watching the NHL. Every time he hugged me I felt like I was being checked. Our entire time together felt like training camp.

Then there was the "Lars Situation." Lars barely spoke English—which, by the way, is not as great as you would think. He pestered me about "my feed-lings." (It took me three weeks to figure out he meant *feelings*.) I had to resort to sign language to break up with him. It was a horrible scene. The only thing missing was a chorus of twelve-year-olds behind me doing choreographed hand motions and singing "This Land Is Your Land."

Despite the fact that I can watch cheesy romantic movies and secretly long for the kind of powerful, irrefutable, true love they all advertise, I can never seem to get things right in real life. I enjoy the companionship, and the dinners, and the kissing and all that, but I just don't get the other stuff. I don't understand the need to answer to someone else, or be all soft and helpless with them. For me, relationships are like foreign countries—fascinating and fun for the most part, but I never enter one without a clear escape route.

As I stride through Terminal A, I notice that the "Delayed" message next to Donny's flight number has switched over to a blinking "Arrived."

I sprint to the nearest escalator and descend to the underbelly of the airport.

The claustrophobically low ceilings and glaring fluorescence of the baggage claim area instantly perform their intended function, making me want to do what I came there to do and then leave as soon as humanly possible. The brilliant thing is, the industrial airport lighting, in its glorious shades of bright and brighter, blur the lines of race and color by turning absolutely everyone and everything the chalky gray of a day-old cocktail olive. I have a feeling I don't look half as slutty or ridiculous in olive drab as I do in salad.

Travelers who've lost their luggage, and people waiting to greet their loved ones, meander here and there amid the skycaps and security personnel. Nearby, a cluster of limo drivers waits patiently for fares, their white cards and signs declaring who they'll be driving. I spot a brawny bear of a man, his black jacket straining to stay buttoned, whose white card reads "Mr. D. Osmond." Bingo.

I move around the crowd of drivers, find a spot with a clear line of sight to the escalator, and back myself against the nearest baggage carousel. If the crowd gets too thick, I can stand up on it and get a better angle. As a bonus, I might just make some tips from the group of pimply teenage boys nearby. If I stand on this thing, they'll get a very nice view of my panties.

I prep my camera and keep my eye on Donny's driver. That is, until I spot something interesting just off to the driver's left—a petite woman in a neatly pressed green uniform. A button on the woman's lapel declares her affiliation with a car rental company. Interesting . . . VIP Concierge Service—*very* VIP. Despite the fact that nearly 99 percent of said VIPs are able-bodied adults, the rental company will help them bypass the lines, pull the car directly to the arrivals area, and hand over the keys without question. They'll even carry the bags. I don't know about you, but the last time I rented a car I got a lecture about not smoking and signed a fifty-page contract that I believe entitles them to my firstborn child.

I train my eyes on the concierge as she moves her sign to between her knees and opens a compact to fix her makeup. She applies a fresh coat of lipstick and swipes on a layer of blush. The blush, I might add, is that most coveted of colors—NARS Orgasm. Though you won't find Orgasm in a box of Crayolas, the name is a perfect description for the shade. It is afterglow in powder form, with just the faintest hint of shimmer. This attention to detail strikes me as just slightly out of the ordinary.

She's at work. How often is shimmery blush required at the office?

The rumble of people struggling with their bags on the escalator shakes the assembled masses to attention. The petite concierge claps her compact shut and shoves it into her pocket. She pulls her sign up and stands at the ready. I cautiously move forward and lean over to get a better view of her sign.

It reads Vlad von Trapp. Classic.

Very VIP *indeed*.

Suddenly, the crowd around the escalator begins to grow. Scores of weary travelers rub their bloodshot eyes, yawn, and stagger around the pack of limo drivers and off to their assigned baggage conveyers. Squeals of happy reunions and tear-choked greetings pepper the air.

The eyes of Donny's brawny driver light up. He makes a gesture of hello to someone coming down.

Okay, I have two options here. I could follow Donny Osmond and get the shots Todd wants me to get, thus appeasing his bruised ego. Or, I could forget about Donny and stick with the petite concierge whose von Trapp could be a much bigger fish. If my instincts are correct, Vlad von Trapp is not the distant Hungarian relative of an Austrian family choral group that the sign would suggest. Of course, if I'm wrong, I've got nothing—no shots and a wasted evening dressed like one of Charo's backup singers.

Donny Osmond steps off an escalator looking as bright-eyed and freshly scrubbed as if he'd just walked out of a spa instead of a 747. He signs a quick autograph before being ushered to the baggage carousel by his driver.

Okay, come on, Vlad. Where are you?

As the escalators continue to dump travelers into the baggage claim area, I turn my attention back to the concierge. She's gone all flush and is swaying ever so slightly from side to side.

This has got to be it.

I ready the camera and move in.

The concierge pushes her shoulders back, causing her jacket to part slightly and reveal a low-cut pink blouse. Her face lights up and a sexy grin spreads from cheek to cheek. A few seconds pass before I see the cause of her preening and primping, not to mention the joyous flush that is spreading rapidly across her face:

Ethan Wyatt.

Unsurprisingly, the level of chatter in the room rises from a low murmur to an excited buzz.

There is a star among us.

I put the camera to my eye and aim it at Ethan Wyatt.

Oh, my God. He's beautiful. No, it's beyond that; something about him is making my hands go all sweaty and my heart beat a little faster. Standing on the escalator, with a strangely subdued and dignified look about him, he looks like some sort of ancient god descending from the heavens.

Ethan Wyatt is tall, well over six feet. He has that not-too-lean, not-too-bulky thing happening—rock solid but in a lithe way, like an Olympic swimmer who does thousands of sit-ups everyday. His hair is dark and thick, cut short, modern and care-frcc. His eyes are a deep, almost cobalt, blue. They're so ridiculously blue that they give the slight impression of incandescence. He's so . . . *pretty*. There's really no better word for it. He's pretty, yet still undeniably masculine. I guess that's what gives his face its timeless quality. On first glance he seems boyish and innocent, but his eyes have this special something, a sort of world-weary brooding that hints at some deep vulnerability or profound personal pain lurking just below the surface. It's the sort of quality that makes women instinctively want to comfort and protect him. I imagine this is why he keeps getting cast as the lonely reluctant hero in World War II and Vietnam dramas. No need to bother about plot, setup, and characterization—when he gets blown to bits, women will weep.

I lay my finger gently on the shutter button, my brain sends the little message telling my finger to push it. But . . . I can't get a shot off—I can't make my finger hit the damn button.

I flip the camera around and hit the button again. A bright burst of light stings my eyes.

Ouch.

I point the camera back at Ethan Wyatt, frame his scruffy black hair and gleaming blue eyes in my viewfinder.

Oh, my.

In person, most celebrities look like watered-down versions of themselves. I mean, even in person it's clear that they've won the genetic lottery, but they still seem ordinary somehow. More than anything, the casual encounter with a celebrity gives you a new appreciation for the talent of the professional hair and makeup artists who sculpt and paint them into something *extra*ordinary. This is, in general. Ethan Wyatt's offscreen appearance transcends anything that can be captured on film. It's really quite . . . alarming.

Okay, Ethan Wyatt is alarming. Big deal.

"Oooh" accidentally escapes my lips as he passes.

Shit. What is wrong with me? I could have had a perfect close-up.

Wyatt looks good on the big screen, appears charming and handsome on *Oprah,* and I recall a *Vanity Fair* spread last year that was particularly mouthwatering. At the time, I thought its effect on me had more to do with Annie Leibovitz than him. I was wrong. So, so wrong.

Across the room, Ethan Wyatt thoughtlessly rubs at his dark and already artfully disheveled hair while talking to the concierge. She's gone all doe-eyed and moony—very unprofessional. Speaking of which, maybe I should stop staring at his butt as he sprints out of the airport and, instead, get up off this stupid baggage thingy and shoot some pictures!

Ethan darts outside and out of view.

Damn.

I lift my jaw off the floor and quickly sidestep through the flock of bored and bleary-eyed travelers waiting for their Samsonite—that is, the ones who didn't catch a glimpse of Ethan as he sped past them.

Racing through the glass doors, I scan across the street, then left and right down the sidewalks. He's gone. Did he get into a car or something? Maybe he spotted me and ran back into the building through another door? Man, he's fast. Better get back in there and track the concierge. She's waiting for his luggage, he has to meet up with her eventually—

I hear myself bellow, "Oh, good God!" as I stagger back from shock.

Holy shit! Not ten feet away, just outside the doorway, Ethan

Wyatt is lighting a cigarette. He catches my exclamation and smiles innocently at me as if to say, "Yeah, it's me."

I impulsively return his warm, easy smile.

As his eyes flicker up to meet mine, I suddenly want to know more about him and have him smile at me all the time. I wish I were wearing blush with just the faintest hint of shimmer. I desperately wish I wasn't dressed in fruit. And is that . . . the Musak version of "My Heart Will Go On" being piped throughout the terminal?

Suddenly, Wyatt's frame goes rigid, almost defiant. His gorgeous, dreamy smile fades and is replaced by a bitter, hateful scowl.

Oh, he's noticed the camera. Hi . . . Sadie Price. People hate me.

He takes a long, slow drag of his cigarette while glaring at me—warning me not to shoot. It's incredible. Even with a really angry sort of frown, his eyes almost sparkle with tenderness.

The stiff collar of his motorcycle jacket perfectly frames his face; it's a sooty black, the color of his hair, and casually cool enough to be worthy of Steve McQueen. I wonder . . . was it plucked from the racks of an out-of-the-way vintage shop by some enterprising stylist, or are each of those scratches and worn spots a memory? What would that sooty black hair look like tangled up with mine on a rumpled white pillowcase?

I lift the camera to my eye and, through the viewfinder, see him sullenly shake his head and turn away from my lens.

"Do you have to do that?" he asks me with an air of defeat rather than anger.

"Sorry, it's my job," I reply matter-of-factly, unable to marshall any weapons from my arsenal of defensive quips and phrases. Okay, back to basics. "Give me the shot, and I'll get out of here," I try.

I wish he would just turn his head a little so I could get the shot. This one-on-one with him bothers me for some reason. There are no fans or bystanders. No witnesses, no chatter to validate my flash bursting on, over and over again. This happens often enough, but for some reason there's no surge of adrenaline to take the edge off the weird, irritating—yet somehow pleasant—fluttering that is gripping my entire body.

Wyatt doesn't turn around, but rather makes an incredulous huff and says, "Doesn't it bother you that your job is to invade people's personal space? To suck the enjoyment out of every little, simple moment of their lives?"

"Uh, no," I blurt dumbly to the back of his head. I wanted to say "Doesn't it bother you that your job is to prance around in front of a movie camera while playing dress-up?" but it got stuck in my throat.

In one swift motion Ethan Wyatt turns around and shoots me a sharp glare. Sharp like razors. His expression is so menacing, so filled with contempt and revulsion, that it bursts into my camera, cuts straight through my eyes, and rattles around in the back of my brain. It finally settles with a thud, somewhere near the pit of my stomach.

"It *should* bother you," he demands. "What you do is disgusting."

Ethan Wyatt is not a ghostly collection of ones and zeroes, but a living, breathing human being who, it appears, would like me to drop dead. Immediately.

I am forced to swallow hard and regain composure. I move the camera from my face and try to look at something, anything else. Anything but that tender face now warped and twisted with a look of . . . repugnance. Directed squarely at *me*.

I suddenly feel slightly ashamed to be holding this camera, and hyper-aware of the weight of it dangling from my neck. Gazing down at my feet, I inhale deeply and try to steady my nerves.

This is not a big deal, Sadie. It's a picture. A silly, stupid picture. You've done it a thousand times. You've been admonished for your profession even more times, in much crueler and more biting words. You have to get a shot of his face.

Oh, shit. I didn't get a shot of his face!

As I turn back toward Ethan Wyatt, I see nothing but a dying wisp of smoke rising from the ashtray.

The automatic doors slide open and he stomps back into the airport.

I force my feet to follow him, but when I get within camera range, my knees go a little funny. They're jittery, weak.

Across the room, Ethan Wyatt helps the concierge girl load several large suitcases onto a cart.

It takes will and *courage* to get three or four shots off. Three crisp shots of the back of his head.

I should sprint out in front of him and get his face. I should. But, I can't. He would look at me again, and for some reason that terrifies me.

I've retreated back to the glass enclosure between inside and out. My nervous foot shuffling makes the automatic doors whir open and closed. I watch as Ethan Wyatt pushes his luggage cart toward an exit.

I have never frozen up like this. Never. Never ever. I've been spit at, cursed out, flipped off, and pushed around by more celebrities and celebrity handlers than I care to remember, but every time I got the shot. Once, a twenty-million-dollar-a-picture star, in a particularly steamy relationship, "accidentally" elbowed me in the stomach and knocked me to the ground. Still, I got up off my ass and got the freaking shot! That's what I'm known for, damnit. I get the shots that nobody else can get. They call me Killer, for Christ's sake. Stars don't get to me. I'm not attracted to them. I don't care what they think. I'm not one of those women with quixotic celebrity fascinations. Well, there was a brief period in the late eighties when Ralph Macchio had a very special place in my heart—and my bedroom walls—but I outgrew him. I mean that literally; the guy is, like, five feet tall.

So why did I have the sudden urge to flip my hair and giggle when Ethan first smiled at me? What was with that bout of nausea at his insults? Oh, and who is Ethan Wyatt to tell me what I should and shouldn't be ashamed of? This is a guy who has always done everything he can to grab his bit of the spotlight, or at the very least, show how little he cares about having his mug shot stamped across the front page. Yet he looks at me like it's my fault. Like I put him in the papers. I absolutely cannot let some random . . . *reaction* to some random . . . really hot *guy* throw me off my game. I mean, this is what I do. It's what I am! And for crying out loud, the guy got his start dropping trou on Calvin Klein billboards. Does that really sound like the act of a man who closely guards his privacy?

I have to get hold of myself. I need to regroup, take a deep breath . . . and then get him.

MAYA DUNN IN LOVE?

Sources close to last year's Golden Globe nominee Maya Dunn ("The Truth Whispers") are saying that she has fallen head over heels for Ethan Wyatt, her costar in the new chick flick "Charming Samantha". Though the pair has tried to keep their budding relationship on the D.L., they have been spotted in intimate tête-à-têtes at some of Hollywood's hottest nightspots (see this month's "Who's Where"). It would seem that these two fine young things are on their way to becoming one of Tinseltown's cutest celeb couples. Or are they?

Wyatt's reps vehemently deny that the two are an item, while word from inside the Dunn camp suggests Maya's friends are worried about her crush on the famed lothario, Ethan. Maya is said to have "real feelings" for Wyatt, while his feelings for her are described as "sketchy." "He's notorious around L.A. for being a player," says one friend. "His life is just an accident waiting to happen, and none of us wants to see Maya get hurt." In an attempt to cool Maya's affection, her pals have planned a monthlong summer jaunt to Hawaii. Guess they hope absence will make Maya's heart go yonder.

CHAPTER 5

Out of the corner of my eye, I spot Ethan Wyatt being helped into the driver's seat of his rental—a brand-new Mustang convertible.

The sight of him sliding into the plush leather seat sparks a cascade of palpable frustration through my entire body. No, this is more than frustration; it's making my hands shake and my eyes water.

I can't let him get away like this.

Clutching my camera to my overly exposed chest, I take off through the airport doors and sprint toward the parking garage.

I make a beeline for my car, the rigid soles of my heels clicking out a strident rhythm through the cavernous parking area.

This isn't a chase.

I am not chasing him, because I don't do that.

No, this is just me nonchalantly trying to get the shot that I missed before.

Oh, shit, he's taking off.

I jump into my Camaro and, with the camera still around my neck, peel out. The screech of rubber on pavement echoes across the deserted building, which gives me the strange sensation that I'm in a chase.

But this is absolutely not a chase. It isn't even a follow. I'm just exiting an airport three cars behind a celebrity.

Make that four cars behind a celebrity . . . stupid cabs! I'm too far behind.

I yank the steering wheel and make a questionably legal move to the right, scooting past the slow-moving cars ahead of me. I squeeze between two cabs, just before the exit ramp narrows from two lanes to one.

An angry honk cuts through the darkness.

Up ahead I see the Mustang move onto the shoulder, out of the line of traffic, then abruptly swerve back.

With a resounding screech, my field of view is flooded with bright red light.

The unmistakable sound of crunching metal and shattering glass fills my ears.

The song on the radio stops, my engine howls like a wounded animal, then sputters slowly to silence.

Oh, my God. I think I've just been in a car accident.

A man's voice breaks through the clanging of metal and hissing of car engines. "Are you all right?" he asks calmly.

I look down at myself, take a quick survey . . . arms, legs, fingers, and toes. No blood to speak of. Luckily, my camera is still in one piece, though I think it got jammed between my chest and the steering wheel on impact.

"Yeah, yeah, I'm fine," I say. "But my car!"

By the light of a flickering streetlamp, I watch as silvery fumes billow from the front grill. The hood, normally marked by a stout but aerodynamic slope, is now shaped like a W. Its peaks point skyward, blocking the view through the windshield. The dashboard is slightly off kilter, now pitching down toward the passenger seat.

A great wave of sadness rushes over me, a quiet sob grips my throat as tears begin streaming down my face.

This is my father's car.

"Miss, I think you should get out if you can. I can't tell if that's smoke or steam coming from up there," the man says, pointing to what used to be the hood of my car.

I unhook my seat belt and, with the aid of the stranger, try to open the door. It won't budge. I lay my shoulder into it, but all I manage to do is slam my camera into the immovable door.

After taking the camera off and placing it gently on the passenger seat, I tip my head through the open window and use my arms to push myself out of the car, like Daisy Duke exiting the General Lee. The kind stranger lends me his arm to steady myself.

"Thank you," I tell him.

"No problem. You sure you're okay?" he asks, his eyes dancing over my tear-streaked face.

"Yeah."

"I'm going to check on the others then," he says, pointing to the knot of vehicles ahead.

I nod yes, and he jogs away.

It's hard to tell for sure, but it looks like four or five cars have been involved—a chain reaction. Police and fire personnel have already begun to stream in, the one good thing about getting into a car accident a stone's throw from a major international airport, I guess.

There's honking in the distance as impatient drivers eager to merge onto the exit pile up behind us.

As though driven by some primitive instinct, I find myself walking toward the flashing police lights.

After a few fitful strides I see the cause of all this drama—a brand-new, bright red Mustang convertible.

Ethan Wyatt stands deep in conversation with an attentive group of law enforcement. It's a sea of uniforms, ill-fitting suits, and plastic windbreakers with POLICE, FAA, and HOMELAND SECURITY, plastered on them in big block letters. I've inadvertently stepped into a bad Tommy Lee Jones movie—costarring Ethan Wyatt.

I edge up to eavesdrop on the conversation.

"I'm telling you," Ethan says forcefully, "someone was following me and, I don't know, I took my eyes off the road, thought I saw something, and—" His voice drops off. Ethan's eyes catch mine.

He raises his arm, slips it cleanly between two slender police officers. His finger wags like a dog's tail—pointing directly at me.

"Her!" he shouts. "It was *her*. That's the paparazzi that was chasing me!"

At least six heads and twelve menacing eyes swivel around and appraise me.

The two slender cops begin walking in my direction, one slapping a hand onto his gun.

"Wait a second," I implore. I lock eyes with Ethan. "Listen here! This is New York, Bub." Did I really just say *"Bub"*? "We don't do chases here." I have never been comfortable around cops. I always end up sounding like a character from a 1930s gangster movie.

"You were *following* me!" Ethan blasts indignantly.

"Was not!" I say, moving toward him.

"Was too!" He replies, inching toward me.

"Was *not*!" Or, a Three Stooges movie.

The slim police officer with the very large gun spreads his hands wide as if to keep Ethan and me from jumping on one another. "Okay, okay. Calm down." He looks to me. "Where's your car, miss?"

"Way down there," I say smugly—to Ethan.

"Doesn't matter," Ethan insists. "She was after me. I saw her."

"But you stated before, Mr. Wyatt, that it was your own negligence that led you to stop short. Am I correct?" asks one of the guys in uniform.

"Ha!" I exclaim, pointing at Ethan.

Ethan's features screw up into a scowl. Then, just as quickly, a cocky serenity washes over his face. It's like someone literally wiped the anger right off him. Amazing.

Ethan tips his head to the most stern-looking officer. "Look, I'm just grateful that no one got hurt. And I know what good work you and your men do. I'm sorry to have inconvenienced you all in any way. I did some research for my role in *Out of Harm* with some of your guys. You know Chuck Larsen?"

The stern officer gleams. "I just got back from a fishing trip up at his place on Findley Lake."

Ethan gives a deferential smile to his assembled audience, shakes his head wistfully. "He does have a nice piece of property up there, doesn't he?"

"Sure does," comes the response from the officer.

Oh. My. God. He's charming them. That sneaky, slimy . . .

"Hey!" I snap. "*Hey!*" But no one hears me; Ethan's just made a joke or something and the whole group is chuckling.

I circle around them and try to get the attention of a heavy-set man with a bristle-brush mustache. "*Hello?*"

He takes me by the shoulders and, with one eye still on Ethan, says, "Ma'am, you're going to have to calm down."

Unbelievable.

"Are you *kidding*?" I ask indignantly. "He's *acting,* can't you see that? He's manipulating you—"

Still with one adoring eye on Ethan Wyatt, the policeman takes me by the hand. "Ma'am, please come with me. If you can't remain calm, I'm afraid I'm going to have to ask you to be seated."

Before I know it, the policeman has managed to guide me to a squad car. He opens the back door.

I stare bewildered at the dingy metal mesh closing off the

back of the car, eye the blank space on the door where a handle should be. The interior has a curious smell, a strange blend of pleather, industrial disinfectant, and sweat.

I stutter, "I admit that I may be partly responsible, okay? But Ethan Wyatt is just as—"

The police officer stares me down, his bristle-brush mustache twitching irritably. He tightens his grip on my wrist. "Ma'am, please be seated." I can tell by the way his voice dropped down an octave that, loosely translated from police speak, his friendly "Ma'am, please be seated" actually means *Sit your ass down or I'm going to make you.*

I slowly sit myself down in the back of the police car. The officer puts his hand on my head, shielding it from the door frame—just like they do to the perps on *Cops* . . . and *America's Most Wanted.*

He slams the door shut.

"Wait a second!" I shout through the thick glass. "Am I under arrest?"

Oh, man, I hope I'm not under arrest.

No, I couldn't be. Nobody's told me I have the right to remain silent or anything, right?

Oh, my God, this is so humiliating.

Staring out the window, through the flicker of red flashing lights beaming from the roof above me, I watch as Ethan Wyatt slaps backs—and has his back slapped.

I am helpless as he cavorts, jokes, and signs a few autographs.

The officer with the bristle-brush mustache hands over his handcuffs to Ethan Wyatt. Ethan swings them around on his finger with great flourish. Then, in one swift, rakish motion he stares directly at me, winks slyly, spins the officer around, and places him in the handcuffs.

You have got to be kidding me.

This guy getting the royal treatment from law enforcement is the same guy who was splashed all over the headlines because he got caught frolicking with (and just plain *licking*) a model on a very public Miami beach. The model happened to be topless—and married—at the time.

A year or so later, he proved that the slogan "What Happens in Vegas, Stays in Vegas" is not, in fact, the elusive Eleventh Commandment, but rather a total crock cooked up by delusional advertising executives. A Las Vegas stripper called Cocoa—"with an *a*," as she liked to remind people—claimed (for the bargain price of $5,000) that she'd recently ended a relationship with Ethan. The relationship (read: three nights at The Palms while he was filming *Celebrity Poker Showdown*) had, according to her, decimated her stripping career—she was six months pregnant. Ethan admitted to having slept with "Cocoa with an *a*," but denied that he was the father of her baby. A DNA test confirmed that he wasn't, in fact, the cause of Cocoa's career bump, but the fact that a chunk of his past can be described using the words "Cocoa the stripper" and "DNA" says something about him, don't you think?

Later that same year, the poor *beleaguered* Ethan Wyatt was arrested for drunk and disorderly conduct after starting some sort of brawl at Bar Marmont in L.A. If I recall correctly, he and Duncan Stoke got into it over something and ended up overturning several barstools and a cocktail waitress. There were two weeks of coverage about it before Kelly Ripa had a baby and knocked him off the cover of *Star*.

The officers around Ethan clap and, no doubt, compliment his technique. While he beams at me—gloating. I have the sudden urge to bang my head against the car window and kick my feet against the metal mesh—just like they do on *Cops* . . . and *America's Most Wanted*.

After what feels like several days in the back of the cop car, the officer with the bristle-brush mustache opens the door. I practically leap to freedom, taking a deep gulp of fresh air.

He begins, "I wish there was something I could charge you with. . . ."

As the officer continues to belt out admonitory advice and lament the fact that he can't lock me up, I watch Ethan Wyatt finish up his performance.

He shakes hands as a black limousine pulls up beside his audience. A chauffeur exits the limo and opens the door. With one final, patronizing wink of his frighteningly blue eyes, he shoots me a smug grin, slips into the vehicle, and is whisked away from the airport—headed straight for the soft, welcoming glow of Manhattan in the distance.

". . . do you understand me?" the officer says, craning his neck before me.

"What?" I ask dumbly.

"I don't ever want to see you in my jurisdiction again."

"Yeah, sure." I never liked New Jersey anyway.

*   *   *

I now have the great honor of paying two hundred dollars to spend an hour with a tow truck driver who smells of diesel fuel and decomposing tofu.

On the bright side, I have sixty solid minutes to sob quietly and plot the most effective ways of exacting revenge on Ethan Wyatt.

ETHAN WYATT'S
SEVEN-YEAR ITCH?

In the seven years that Ethan Wyatt has been on Hollywood's radar he's made steady strides toward the top. His paychecks have increased steadily and he's carved out a niche for himself as the go-to guy for gritty, explosive thrillers. It seems, however, that Ethan is taking stock of his past and hoping to change his future. "I've been in this business long enough now to be able to look back and see where I've been," he said in a phone interview last Thursday. "I'm proud of all the work I've done, and the people I've done it with, but there are a couple of choices that I look back on and think, Maybe I should have done something else instead." He refuses to be specific about his least favorite roles, saying, "Everybody makes decisions that they regret later. You can never see the full impact of the consequence until the deed is done. All you can do is hope you don't screw up too badly and make a decision that can't be *un*done." As Ethan Wyatt attempts to broaden his horizons, it's going to be up to the public to decide if this seven-year itch gets scratched—or scrapped.

CHAPTER 6

I woke up to the sweet smell of coffee wafting into my bedroom, but have spent the last ten minutes trying to deny its siren call. Brooke was asleep when I finally made it home last night, so she doesn't know about the whole "movie star wrecking my dad's car" incident, or the less traumatic but still disturbing Todd-wrapping-up-a-toothbrush fiasco, and I really don't feel like discussing either. Brooke, being more detail oriented than Martha Stewart on a knitting bender, will want to break the whole night down into nanoseconds. There are great blocks of nanoseconds I'd prefer not to relive.

I am now carless, nearly jobless (as my work requires a car), on the verge of being broke (as 1979 Camaro parts don't come cheap), and incapable of taking a picture of Ethan Wyatt. All I really want to do is crawl under the covers and forget that last night ever happened.

I pull the comforter over my head and try to push every thought from my mind.

Not working.

My dad loved that car, and it's the only thing of his that made it through the bank auction. He vacuumed and waxed that Camaro every Sunday, an exercise that was more ritual than cleaning, as it always sat under our rickety aluminum carport and Dad never ate in it or casually tossed trash into the backseat like I do. He would have hated that, and he *really* would have hated this. He would be disappointed in me—for having wrecked his car while doing . . . what I was doing. And disappointing my dad was the absolute worst.

The words seem so innocuous: "I'm disappointed in you." But there was something in the way that he said it. His big, tired, almond-shaped eyes would bore into me, they'd blink and appraise. He'd wring his rugged, blistered hands and languidly shuffle his feet. He'd shake his head and scratch at his prematurely gray hair. As the word *disappointed* trickled over his lips he gave the distinct impression of a man who'd had a tiny little piece of his heart ripped out and stomped on.

I can see that look now, as clearly and vividly as if he were still alive and boring his weary eyes through my duvet—guilt from beyond the grave.

And Ethan Wyatt came out of this with nothing more than some tedious insurance paperwork to suffer through, paperwork that I'm sure someone else will fill out for him.

I clutch at my aching chest, rip off the covers, and pad directly into the kitchen—driven by the promise of caffeine.

Slumping against the wall, I watch Brooke prepare cereal made of what appears to be twigs. She always eats right, and actually goes to the gym—daily. I'm a "better slimming through chemistry" girl myself. In other words, I much prefer potions to Pilates. The closest thing to a workout I get is fighting my way from Sephora's anticellulite lotion section to the cash register.

"I knew the coffee would get you out here," Brooke chirps happily.

I groan and shuffle over to pour some coffee. I'm not sure my foul mood can handle her pep.

She turns around, mixes up her twigs with soy milk. "How was your date with the macho man?"

I lift the coffee to my lips, anxiously anticipating its wondrous effect. "Before or after I dumped him and he sent me to track down a member of the Osmond family?"

I gulp some coffee and am about to launch into the whole story when Brooke interrupts me with a shocked gasp. "Jesus! Sadie, what happened?"

"We broke up," I say, confused by the look of absolute horror on her face. "I mean, his ego might be a little deflated but it wasn't that bad."

"I'm talking about *that*!" she says, ogling my chest—her eyes wide with concern.

Looking down, I freeze. My stretched-out old tank top reveals that I am black and blue, pink, green, and yellow. The center of the bruise is about four inches in diameter and located just above my heart. From there it stretches out toward my left shoulder and down over my left breast like a pastel spiderweb. It is gigantic . . . and ugly.

"Oh," I say softly—startled. *"Oh!"*

Brooke's eyes continue to widen and examine the bruise. I

can almost see the thoughts bouncing around in her head. She's wondering whom she's going to have to beat up.

I start, "I'm okay. I think my camera just—"

Brooke is incredulous. "You don't look okay. Who did this to you—Donny or Marie?"

Before I can begin my twisted tale, the door buzzer hums loudly.

"Luke's been out all night. He's stopping by for breakfast before he crashes," Brooke says distractedly. Luke *technically* has his own apartment, but *practically* lives with us. He keeps his own pillow in the hall closet because he sleeps on our couch so much that the cushions were getting, according to Brooke, "that nasty, sleepy *boy* smell."

The same front door that Brooke and I can never seem to unlock swings open with no problem for Luke.

"What day is it?" Luke asks, striding toward the kitchen with a smile.

"Friday," replies Brooke. While I chime in, "Saturday."

Luke looks at us, waiting for a definitive answer. I never know for sure what day it is without consulting the calendar on my cell phone. I defer to Brooke.

"Friday," she says. "I have the day off. Definitely Friday."

"Damn, that means I have to work tomorrow," grumbles Luke. "Oooh, coffee."

He heads for the coffee, but stops short when he sees me. "Sadie, what happened to you?" he whispers.

The concern and compassion in his voice tug at some deep part of me. My eyes fill with unwanted, ridiculous tears. "Ethan Wyatt wrecked the Camaro."

*   *   *

I am lying on the couch with the remote control in hand and a plastic sandwich bag full of ice on my chest. I think it's too late for the ice to do any good, but I let Brooke do it anyway.

I told them everything, from toothbrush to tow truck. At once they turned into doting parental figures, coercing me to lie down, force-feeding me Cocoa Puffs and raisin toast, and agreeing with everything I said. It was kind of nice, but as pity parties go, a little on the lame side. At some point I'm going to need a little less toast and a little more tequila.

"Who'd you get last night, Luke?" I ask, turning my attention from *Good Times*.

"De Niro again, Kate Hudson, Owen Wilson."

"Not bad," I reply, impressed.

"Eh," he says, shrugging his shoulders. "What are you going to do about the car?"

"Stop buying shoes, eat only bread and water, hope that a mysterious benefactor has upped my insurance." Sue Ethan Wyatt for all he's worth. Crush him like a little bug.

Or . . . I could call Paige. She has the money.

I glance over at the corner of the room, and my eyes land on the big brown box.

No, she wouldn't help. She's always thought my job was beneath me—or more to the point, beneath *her*. I think she's intrigued by the fame and fortune aspect of it all, but the fact that I'm on the blue-collar side of the business doesn't appeal to her sense of decorum and good breeding. She tells her friends that I'm a photographer, and then quickly changes the subject. *Paparazzi* isn't part of her lexicon; it certainly isn't part of her vision of the perfect daughter. Not to mention my mother is not exactly the most reliable person to call for help. A real emergency would illicit a response like "Darling, can I call you back? I'm late for the hairdresser, and you know how Franco hates to wait. Thanks. Bye." The follow-up would come two weeks later. . . . "All right, I'm here for you now. I got your message. No, no, darling—you cut the *green* wire, not the red one."

The three "years of silence," as I like to call them, went something like this: 1989 was all about feeling sorry for myself and watching Disney musicals. Then 1990 was a year of alternately hating Paige with a fury and experimenting with the latest exfoliation techniques outlined in *Seventeen*. In 1991 I wanted to be Christy Turlington and wished, more than anything, that my mother had taken me with her. Then, near Thanksgiving of 1991, gifts began trickling in.

At first they were trinkets, small pieces of jewelry, hair accessories that I couldn't use because I'd chopped all my hair off that summer (when Christy did). Then, at Christmas, a makeup kit arrived—a *Chanel* makeup kit. New Year's brought a journal. It was leather and velvet with a lock that looked to have been swiped from a medieval text. By April of 1992 I had amassed quite a collection of things, the value of which I still believe totaled more than the entire contents of my father's tiny house. The period that followed I have generously entitled "Paige's Mother-Daughter Adventure"—she began having me over for weekends.

I had just turned fourteen and was outstandingly awkward and plump. Puberty was very unkind to me. My breasts and hips emerged long before my upward growth spurt, so I resembled a lumpy apple for the first gruesome year of high school. But, as Paige used to remind me, my *hair* was so pretty—smooth, shiny, and sun-bleached to a honeyed platinum blonde.

One day, completely out of the blue, Paige sent me a note instructing me, in no uncertain terms, to proceed directly to her house Friday after school. She said she'd spoken to my dad about it and that he knew not to expect me home until Sunday evening. The kicker? The note came attached to a brand-new cashmere Benetton sweater. If I had had any inkling of what cashmere was, or what it cost, I probably wouldn't have worn it. I would have hidden it under my bed with the rest of her gifts so my father didn't know I was "cheating" on him with my mother. But as it was, when Friday came around I wore the sweater to school. I loved it—so soft and delicate and creamy white, like an eggshell. All day I got compliments on it, and all day I fantasized about what it would be like to hang out in my mother's enormous house surrounded by all the expensive things that I was sure would make me feel just instantaneously happier. The only thing I was nervous about was the bus.

Paige lived, quite literally, on the other side of the tracks. This meant that to go directly to her house I had to take a different bus from school. I had to take the *cool* bus, the bus that all the cheerleaders rode (well, the few not driven to and from school by their much older boyfriends). There were no band geeks or math league members on this bus. It was a bus filled with superlatives—Best Couple, Most Likely to Succeed, Cutest Butt. I was completely petrified. Though not a math league member myself, my best friend at the time (who, incidentally, was infinitely cooler than I) was first chair tuba in the marching band. But when I walked onto the cool bus, I held my head high and tried to look like I belonged. Apparently, my routine didn't quite hit the mark. The hottest, most popular guy in my grade, Marshall Holmes, tapped me on the shoulder as I passed him and said, "Uh, Sadie. I don't think you're on the right bus."

He didn't mean it to be cruel. I honestly think it was well-intentioned concern that prompted him to speak (Marshall grew up to be a very wealthy, very gay doctor and adoptive father of four Cambodian orphans). But, nevertheless, his comment sparked a cacophony of laughter and snickering at my expense. It also caused a face-reddening cringe and the sudden desire to crawl under a seat and assume the fetal position.

Believe it or not, that was the highlight of the weekend.

I very quickly caught on that my mother had not invited me to the home she shared with Dr. Hank, DDS, so that I could be folded into the warm embrace of a happy privileged home. She had invited me as an accessory, a prop.

I was greeted at the front door with two air kisses. The only touch that came by way of greeting was a nudge propelling me inside the foyer. And even that, I think, was done with the dull, flat tips of her acrylic nails.

There were two parties planned that weekend, she informed me. "One tonight with my golf ladies, and one tomorrow with Dr. Hank's business acquaintances." She directed me to follow her up the long, winding staircase to the second floor. "We're just so excited to have you!"

Paige showed me to "my" bedroom. It looked like Holly Hobby had been held prisoner there, tortured, and then blown herself up MacGyver style using only a paper clip, some Pepto-Bismol, and a thousand yards of lace. Two gorgeous brand-new outfits hung neatly in the closet—one for Friday night, one for Saturday. The weekend spiraled ever downward quite nicely from there.

I was the only nonadult at either party. Paige paraded me around like a sideshow oddity, showing off my outfits and forcing me to "tell people how well you're doing, honey." I was like a new sofa she'd acquired for the occasion. Look at it . . . isn't it nice. The upholstery's beautiful, and the frame is so *sturdy*!

Everything about the house was foreign to me. Despite its lavishness compared to my father's place, it felt totally empty. There were no memories there. I didn't know the bikes that hung in the garage, couldn't recall how the ding on the fender came about. There were rules I didn't know to obey—taking your shoes off before entering from the backyard, not touching the screen of the fancy TV ("You'll leave fingerprints!"), not feeding Oodles table scraps because she had a sensitive stomach. On the living room bookshelf was a picture of my mother. She was on the beach in a skimpy white bikini. She held a tiny little fish in her hand. Her skin was golden and smooth, her hair the same sun-kissed platinum as mine. The bikini clung to her sculpted curves so precariously that it seemed to cover her by sheer will alone. I couldn't identify the exotic tropical locale and had no idea why she looked so proud of that silly little fish.

As bizarre as the whole experience turned out to be, I couldn't stop coming back each weekend. The only way I know to describe it is that it's like when you watch one of those shows on the Discovery Channel about babies born with two heads, or people forced to cut off their own limbs to save themselves from certain death. Something about it grosses you out, freaks you out . . . it may even give you nightmares. Still, you *have* to watch. You become mesmerized with curiosity and wonder. That's what it was like growing up with Paige for a mother.

Week after week I was trussed up and polished. I was paraded around and gawked at, prodded and given diet advice by my mother's leather-skinned golf buddies. I was leered at by Dr. Hank's mysterious "associates" and given off-the-cuff orthodontic tips by his "business acquaintances." Looking back on it now, I can see that my mother's increasing *interest* in me, if you can call it that, makes perfect sense. She and Dr. Hank had spent three blissful, romantic years as a couple. They'd had their time together and Paige was ready to start a family. Lucky for my mother she didn't have to get fat and incontinent to do so. I was a ready-made family, the finishing touch for my mother's home—the pitter-patter of little feet that rounded out and perfected the image of domestic bliss she wanted to be envied for. If I hadn't been a wimpy doormat of a self-conscious youth, I probably would have rebelled. If I hadn't felt so completely curious and slightly helpless, I either would have refused to go along with these performances or spoiled them in grand fashion—explosives, poison, dirty body-pierced boyfriends. But as it was, I went along with them for years. Monday through Friday I was myself, Saturday and Sunday I was Paige Price-Farmer's "darling daughter."

That box over there could be anything. A plasma TV, a giant velvet Elvis, a killer python. There's really no telling how good or bad it might be, or what Paige expects in return.

*   *   *

It's time for the evening news. I don't mean the local variety that's so abundant here in New York, or the kind of broadcast by the roughly seven million twenty-four-hour news networks. No, I'm talking about the evening *entertainment* news. It's part of the job for Luke and me, and one of Brooke's most beloved guilty pleasures.

This is a somewhat tedious, but occasionally amusing, job-related diversion. Tonight, however, it's turning my stomach to knots. I know they're going to cover the airport pileup, and I know they're going to make it out to be my fault. Since Lindsay Lohan got her driver's license these stories have become a mainstay of the nightly entertainment news—and it's always the photographer's fault. Always.

"Oh, damn!" whines Brooke as I make my way back from the kitchen with a load of stress-reducing snacks in my arms. Brooke sits, as she always does, perched on the edge of her seat as though ready to pounce.

"What? What is it? What did they say?" I ask breathlessly, dropping the snacks on the coffee table.

"No, no. It's nothing about you. I just missed *E!* 'Behind the Scenes of *Finding Her*.' Damn, I forgot it was on! There's only five minutes left."

Finding Her is the upcoming release starring Brooke's true love fantasy man, Duncan Stoke. Duncan Stoke is an all-American hunk, Brooke's current celebrity obsession, and the one man in Hollywood with a name more improbable than Vin Diesel.

"He has two movies coming out this summer. He's going to be all over the TV," Luke tells her.

"Hallelujah!" She points to the screen. "I mean, look at him. He's gorgeous. I saw him on Leno the other night, Sadie. He's so perfect for me in every way. If I were just a *little* bit crazier, I could totally become a stalker."

Brooke is somewhat of a nascent celebrity freak. The further along she's gotten in her chosen career of real estate, the less she's been inclined to do it the rest of her life. She's got it into her head that she's going to marry into fame, fortune, and a life of leisure. For most people this would be a harmless fantasy. For Brooke, given her complete focus, dogged determination, and proximity to people who track celebrities for a living, this becomes very dangerous. She's a heat-seeking missile.

"I wonder if he's coming to New York to do publicity," she says ominously, while watching Duncan Stoke's chiseled, action-hero features flicker across the screen. Something about his oh-so classically manly form, or his pitch-perfect combination of cockiness and boy-next-door charm, has enraptured her.

Unlike me, Brooke is a dreamer who wholeheartedly believes in true love and happy endings. (Her parents have been married for thirty-five years and have always been blissfully happy.) I believe this is the root of her celebrity obsession and her all-consuming fantasy life that centers on hooking up with one.

It is so much easier to believe that the right guy exists, and that you just haven't met him yet, if that guy's face is known to you. It's much more frightening to think that he's out there and you might not recognize him.

What if you meet him and you don't understand his importance? What if you miss it altogether? What if when he asks you out for coffee you say, "Sorry, gotta feed my cat," not knowing that he's The One? (And not actually owning a cat.)

The feeling of knowing that a perfect someone is out there is comforting, soothing. In lonely times you can console yourself with the knowledge that circumstances out of your control (namely, his bodyguards) are all that's keeping you from romantic tranquillity with the man of your dreams. The sense of hope this creates, no matter how unrealistic the celebrity match, is important to the single girl's sanity. The only thing scarier than the possibility of missing The One is the possibility that he's not out there at all.

In times of disappointment or stress, Brooke can always dive into her quixotic infatuations. They give her hope. For this reason, I find them hard to discourage.

Brooke sighs as the show ends. She stares off into space with a dreamy look in her eye, no doubt mentally picking out a Vera Wang wedding gown, or redecorating Duncan's beach-side cottage in East Hampton.

Brooke's show gives way to the precommercial tease of the night's celebrity news. What do you know, the centerpiece of their coverage tonight will be "the lowdown on steamy rumors of Ethan Wyatt's on-set canoodling, and his harrowing paparazzi-involved car crash."

Yep, I can tell by the condescending way the host said "paparazzi" that they're going to make it out to be my fault. Obviously, I'm not surprised, but for some reason seeing it on national television makes my blood absolutely boil. And I didn't even get a shot of his face.

I blurt, "Ethan Wyatt swerves in and out of traffic, slams on his breaks, destroys my car, and they are going to say that it's *my* fault."

"You admit that it was partly your fault," says Luke.

"I didn't get a ticket, remember?" I say, doing my best to defend myself. "He's the one who swerved off the road and caused the whole pileup."

"Because you were following him." Luke adds, "Bit of a chicken/egg thing there, isn't it?"

"I—"

"Okay, enough of that," Brooke says, cutting me off. She looks at me quizzically and adds, "I still don't get why you couldn't get a shot of him. They could have had *your* pictures to frame you with on the news."

"I have no idea." And to be honest, it completely freaks me out. This job is my life. Trust me, I know it's not supposed to be that way. We're all supposed to "work to live," not "live to work." I get it. I mean, I've read all the same articles as everyone else, seen all the same experts on the *Today* show. But, as stupid, silly, and slightly pathetic as it may sound, I don't know what I would do without it. I finally have my life in some sort of order. I finally feel relatively stable. My job makes me calm, if you can believe that. Last night was the first time I haven't been able to summon that calm at will.

"What if I'm losing my edge?" I ask, while petitioning Brooke with my eyes to tell me it's not possible.

"*You?*" quips Luke.

"Luke, I couldn't take the picture. It was like . . ." I take a deep breath. "It was like I was paralyzed. It felt . . . wrong somehow, or something." Too personal? "When he looked at me

I . . ." completely lost all control and turned into a stuttering, unprofessional heap of jelly. "I just couldn't do it. What happens if I can't do it anymore?"

Luke shakes his head. "You think you could just—*whoosh*—lose the ability to take pictures?"

"Yeah," I reply matter-of-factly. "I read somewhere about this artist who went to bed one night halfway through a masterpiece and woke up the next morning and couldn't paint. Couldn't *finger* paint. Couldn't—"

"Were you reading the *National Enquirer*?"

"I'm serious!" I say, suddenly desperate to get Luke off my back.

"So am I!" he retorts.

"I have an idea," chirps Brooke. "Practice on me. Pretend I'm famous."

Brooke races across the room and back, delivering my camera. She immediately begins posing.

"It's not the same," I say after taking several shots. "It was Ethan Wyatt—"

"You want him?" Luke asks bluntly.

"No! I am not the least bit attracted to him! Why would you assume I want the guy just because—"

"Calm down, Killer," coos Luke. "What I meant was, do you want to get a *shot* of him? Do you want to try and *find* him?"

"Oh," I say, as a sudden and rather overwhelming rush of embarrassment makes my cheeks go warm.

Brooke flips through the channels searching for the other celebrity news outlets.

A voice from the TV peals, ". . . Billy Bush with the latest from the Big Apple. He'll give us the lowdown on Ethan Wyatt's dangerous run-in with an overzealous paparazzi."

The *Access Hollywood* theme song rings through the apartment like a battle cry.

I *can't* let him win. I can't let some cocky, sexy, talented, fairly amazing actor beat me. He's supposed to be afraid of *me*—not the other way around.

"Yes," I say boldly. "I'd like him served up on a platter, if possible."

Luke makes a goofy face at me, then winks conspiratorially at Brooke.

"Right on." Luke whips out his cell phone dramatically. "Give me ten minutes."

In a matter of *five* minutes Luke has discovered Ethan Wyatt's shoe size, his mother's maiden name, and his exact location. Ethan Wyatt is, at this very moment, eating dinner with a "mystery woman" at a new restaurant called blé.

Jackpot.

SEE AND BE SCENE:
NEW YORK

blé, 150 Varick Street, Soho, $$$$$

The latest entry in the "if you have to ask, you can't get in" category of Manhattan eateries is blé, brainchild of restaurateur Charles Picard. With blé, Picard caters to a crowd that doesn't just appreciate luxury, but demands it.

The main dining room is airy and drips in quiet, yet sumptuous, opulence. The design and menu are inspired by the rich wheat fields and refined country manors of France ("blé" is French for "wheat"), and the menu is as decadent and astonishing as the ten enormous Swarovski crystal chandeliers that adorn the space.

blé is sure to lure the hip as well as the haughty. The five private VIP dining nooks (each with its own serving staff) are the perfect place for you to escape the prying eyes of the paparazzi—or your current spouse. Be aware, however, a tryst at blé will cost you. A three-course meal will ring up at two hundred fifty dollars, and the restaurant's champagne-laced signature drink, the Cristini, runs a cool thirty-five dollars.

CHAPTER 7

Oh, I do love field trips," purrs Brooke as we stumble out of the cab.

"Brooke," I say soberly, "you're going to have to work with me here."

"What does that mean?"

"No touching this time."

"I only *grazed* him, Sadie," she says innocently.

"Yeah, right." I remember, quite clearly, Matt Damon being mowed down by a slim brunette lineman in four-inch stilettos. When I broke things up, she was about to begin CPR.

"Look, I have to get this shot." I need it. I can't walk around for the next week with the rancid taste of defeat in my mouth. I have to prove to myself that I can take a picture of Ethan Wyatt. Simple.

Luke and I stare across the street at the unassuming yet luxurious exterior of blé. The warm golden light from inside is diffused by Chantilly lace the color of whipped butter and splashes onto the sidewalk in creamy pools. A brick red awning proclaims the name of the restaurant in golden script so elegant that it practically screams a warning: "Not for the poor or unrefined."

The early summer air has gone unseasonably cold as the clock ticks down from evening to night. Luke tells me it's got something to do with Arctic winds from Canada. Just like Canada to pawn off its bad weather on us. Isn't it enough that we've taken Alan Thicke and Howie Mandel off their hands? Will the madness never end?

"What do you think?" I ask Luke.

"I think your best bet is the side alley. We could wait. I'll watch the front, you cover the alley."

"What will *I* do?" asks Brooke.

"Freak out when Ethan walks out of the restaurant," says Luke wryly.

"Very funny," she quips.

"Are you up for a little recon?" I ask them.

"Oh, yeah," says Brooke, as she takes off across the street—almost skipping.

"You know how I love being a prop," Luke says with a wink.

I quickly shove my camera into the deep kangaroo pocket on the front of his sweatshirt. He drapes his long left arm over my shoulders, and I put my right around his waist. We stroll casually across the street.

Passing the dimly lit alley, I notice that a small tent has been erected around the side entrance. It's the perfect place for a quick getaway. A car could back into the alley and let the customer slide into the backseat without ever being exposed to the elements—or the cameras.

"No-go on the alley," I say to Luke as we slow our pace and do our best to peer through the finespun lace.

"You'll never get in, or get a shot through the curtains," says Luke quietly. "We'll have to wait."

"I don't know. I want to get him with the chick, whoever she is. They'll probably come out separately, especially if someone notices a suspicious almost-giant and known autograph hound lurking outside."

Just clear of blé's picture windows, Luke stops and turns to me. His jaw tightens and he shoves his hands in his pockets.

Brooke says, "Why don't we just try to get in?"

Brooke, with her lethal feminine wiles, could probably get a table. Me, probably not. Me with a camera—definitely not.

After what seems like an hour of watching Luke tighten and loosen his jaw muscles, I blurt, "Okay, plan B. Who's your source?"

"Dave, a waiter I know from when I worked at Pasta Fiore."

"He's working tonight?" I ask.

As if a lightbulb just popped on over his head, Luke's eyes go wide. "Oh, I feel you."

Luke takes out his cell phone with one hand and grabs my hand with the other. In one smooth movement, he drags me past the restaurant while punching numbers into the cell.

At the alley, he makes a sharp lateral move and sprints past the little tent, then scoots through a narrow opening in the chain-link that partitions off the back of the alley. Brooke and I follow as swiftly as we can. Somehow, I manage to curb the all-consuming desire to scream "Watch the camera!" as Luke's kangaroo pouch, and my livelihood inside it, jostle precariously up and down.

We stop, and I catch my breath. I inhale slowly and my whole body is seized by the mouth-watering aroma of roasted garlic, warm cheese, and chicken stock. I think back on the last thing I ate today—measly raisin toast.

blé's kitchen entrance is wide open. Steam rises toward the halogen bulb above the door. The clanging of pots and plates makes my stomach groan with envy.

Luke's eyes dart between the LCD screen on his cell and the open door.

I sputter, "Did you—"

He holds up a finger to shush me. "Wait for it . . ."

In a matter of seconds, a paunchy Kato Kaelin look-alike emerges from the kitchen. His hair is the color of straw and cut in a long shag. Feathery wisps of hair flap ever so slightly from either side of his head. I guess, in fairness to all the decent man-shags out there, this guy's haircut is more of a mullet—with wings. He attempts to simultaneously light a cigarette, walk down the steps, and answer his cell phone.

"Dave!" shouts Luke.

"Dude!" the Kato look-alike replies. He points to his cell phone. "This you?"

"Yeah."

"Niiiice," he says in a raspy surfer drawl before lighting his cigarette. He reminds me of the guys I grew up with—the ones who considered Spicoli from *Fast Times at Ridgemont High* the founder of their lazy, pot-smoking order. Harmless, but slightly pathetic guys, blind to the absurdity of feeling nostalgic for a teen comedy that came out when they were learning their ABCs.

"Ethan Wyatt still in there?" Luke asks.

"Yeah, man. I've got him—one of the VIP rooms."

"Who's the girl with him?" Luke prods.

"Nobody," he says. Clearly Dave, like so many people these days, lumps people in only two categories—the famous and the *un*famous. He adds quickly, "Hot as fuck, though."

"Oh yeah?" Luke asks with a twinkle in his eye.

Dave puckers his face and makes the universal hand motion for "bodacious ta-ta's." That's it. That's the hook. A little thrill courses through my midsection—the promise of a big story. She's not his rumored girlfriend. She's unknown. She has bodacious ta-ta's.

Luke nods his understanding of Dave's juvenile visual aide and then points to me. "Do you think you can get her in?"

I suddenly feel like a desperate groupie pleading with a roadie to take me backstage. I dig my hand in Luke's pocket and retrieve my camera.

"Not with that, I can't," he says, pointing to my camera and exhaling a gray mist into the night air.

Shit.

"How about with this?" I ask, pulling out my picture-taking, call-making, overpriced bit of annoying technology.

"Nah, they make customers check those things at the door."

"Could I give it to you and get in on a last-minute reservation—"

"No way," Dave says, his head wobbling around like that of a bobble-head doll. "The management at this place is like the fucking gestapo."

I decide to translate this into language he can understand. I lighten my voice by an octave. "Shit, I *totally* need that picture." I bite my lip seductively. Though I feel like an ass doing it, it seems to have the desired effect. Dave looks me up and down, calculating his odds. Faking a look of all-American surfer-girl innocence—and trying to be blonder—I add, "You really can't help me?"

Dave takes a long drag of his cigarette and eyes me suspiciously. He exhales through his teeth and winks. "What'll you give me for it?" His eyes dance between Brooke and me. Disgusting, but I can work with that.

I reach into my back pocket and retrieve three crisp one-hundred-dollar bills (that Todd better reimburse me for or I'll have him whacked).

I hand the cash to Dave, who fingers the bills with a faraway look that tells me his dealer is going to be a happy man. Before he has a chance to mull it any further, I pass my camera to Luke and shed my zip-up hoodie, giving it to Brooke. I unbutton Dave's uniform jacket and peel it off him, much to his delight.

I have to look like I belong in there. Dave's jacket will help, but my jeans won't do at all.

"Brooke, I need your pants."

"What?" she yelps. "No. Absolutely not." She locks her eyes onto Dave, who is smiling lasciviously while ogling her legs.

"Come on," I say, dragging her by the hand to a tiny alcove between the chain-link fence and a massive dumpster.

The area smells like rotting vegetables, red wine, and what can only be described as *death*.

"Help me out here? Please?" I beg her.

She sighs and folds her arms over her chest. Finally, unable to resist my very convincing pout, she rolls her eyes and unbuttons her pants. "You owe me, though. Big. *Huge*. It's going to cost you a face-to-face with Duncan Stoke . . . with touching."

What am I, a celebrity pimp? But I nod vehemently. "Sure, whatever you want."

As a cool rush of air makes the backs of my exposed thighs tingle, something suddenly occurs to me: Has anything good ever come from an activity that begins with partial nudity by a dumpster?

In under sixty seconds I have transformed into an androgynous waitress who appears to be suffering the effects of body dysmorphic disorder—pants too tight and short, jacket at least two sizes too big.

I shove my cell phone into my pants and head back to Dave and Luke.

Luke hands over my camera. I almost take it, but then think better of it. "No," I tell Luke. "You hold on to it. I'll use my cell." If, by some horrible chance, I get busted in there, I would really hate to have my lovely, expensive camera smashed into oblivion.

"Okay, let's go," I say to Dave while tramping up the steps to the kitchen door.

He looks up at me nervously.

"Don't worry," I say, flapping my hand at him. "I've done this a million times. It'll be fine. A snap." I try to illustrate the guaranteed success of my plan by actually snapping my fingers. They sort of slip off one another, not making a sound.

Dave caresses the pocket where he stuffed the money, then cautiously climbs the stairs behind me looking a bit like a man headed for the gallows.

"It'll be fine," I say again. But it comes out more like an incantation—a wish—than a real declaration.

It's not like I've never done this before. Okay, I've never done *exactly* this before, but I've done other things that were sort of like this. Just not quite this brazen. Technically speaking this could be slightly illegal. I don't think I'd get arrested, but I may be open to some civil liability—private property, hidden cameras, stalking. But my intent isn't malicious. Is it? No. I just need the shot that I didn't get before. That's all. Simple.

I take a deep breath and let Dave take the lead. He guides me through the less inhabited parts of the kitchen, stopping every once in a while and forcing me to crouch behind stacks of pots and great mountains of dirty dishes.

As I peek through a shelf piled high with boxes and bread baskets while a trio of cooks sprint past us, I remember something my father told me. "Sadie," he said, "never do anything that you can't show your face doing. The most important thing is to be proud of who you are and what you've done to get where you want to be."

I'm only setting a toe over the line. No, not even over the line—just *on* the line. The line I won't cross is still there, and just like tennis, anything on the line is fair. Right?

Right.

Dave pops up and ushers me around a corner and out of the kitchen. After a few steps, we've entered a long softly lit corridor, where the clanging of pots and shouting of orders gives way to the low hum of conversation and the gentle clicking of silver on porcelain. The walls are upholstered in a deep gold silk. To our left is a wall of velvet drapes the color of summer corn. Little beams of light glint through their folds.

Halfway down the corridor, Dave stops me and whispers in my ear, "He's in the third booth from the last. Get in, get what you need, and then get the fuck out of Dodge." He points to a door back at the other end of the long hall. This, he tells me, will open out to the awning that Luke and I noticed earlier in the alley. He instructs me to leave his jacket by the door, hints with his eyes that he'd rather not see me again, and then disappears around the corner.

Okay. I have to get a clean shot with both of them in the picture . . . both of their faces. I'll probably only get one chance at it, so I have to make it a good one.

Shit, I hope it doesn't come out too grainy.

And, I hope everyone is fully clothed. As long as they've got clothes on there shouldn't be any lawsuits . . . I think.

I walk up to the VIP booth Dave pointed out. I spot a sliver of light where the velvet curtains meet a wall panel, creating a cozy little nook. I inch up slowly and squint to see through the slender crack in the drapes.

He's there. He's really in there. With a woman. A woman in a low-cut top and the promised bodacious ta-ta's. Her dark hair, pale skin, and light eyes give the impression that she's a very well-dressed porcelain doll.

Right, this is it. Now or never. No going back.

I grab the phone from my pocket. It feels absurdly heavy in my hands. Like a brick.

I'm nervous. I'm actually nervous about taking a picture. This is ridiculous. I have to be able to do this. I have to.

I take a deep breath and slip my hand through the break in the curtain. I repeat silently to myself, "Aim for the line, Sadie, not over it. You're right on the line."

I close my eyes, cross the fingers on my free hand, and push the button on my phone.

There's a barely audible click, a very audible gasp, and the sudden clanging of plates.

I retract my arm, shove the phone in my pocket, and practically gallop to the exit.

In one swift movement, I whip off the jacket, plop it on the floor, and slip out the VIP door.

A cool rush of air strikes me as I step out from under the awning. The clammy sensation on my skin alerts me to the fact that I've been sweating. I'm suddenly cold, and though apparently safe, my heart rate only seems to be increasing.

I walk swiftly down the alley while bringing up the picture on my cell phone. A little part of me hopes the shot didn't come out and that I never have to admit to anyone that I did that.

Oh, my . . .

My feet plant themselves in the pavement.

The shot is in focus, and as clear as can be expected from a phone. What is *crystal* clear, however, is that there is a beautiful young woman leaning into Ethan Wyatt, her head tilted downward—*way* downward—almost directly over his crotch. Good thing there's a big table in front of him or that whole "fully clothed" thing might have been an issue.

A knot forms in my chest. I rub my queasy belly.

No. I will not feel bad for the guy who trashed my dad's car and somehow made me feel like I couldn't take a damn picture. I just need to send this shot to my email and be done with the whole thing. I'll file Ethan Wyatt under *A* for *asshole* and forget about him.

I take three long strides toward the mouth of the alley while scrolling through my phone's many useless functions.

A noise, coming from somewhere in the vicinity of the exit, startles me. Bad. Very bad.

Just in case this happens to be a manager, or a psycho alley killer, I should pick up the pace a bit.

I hear the clomping of feet behind me—getting more and more rapid. A male voice rings out, "Hey!" Indignant. Very *very* bad.

Must speed up, but not too much. I don't want to alarm this person, whoever he is. Dark Alley in New York City 101: must pretend to be strong and unfazed—or completely insane.

Maybe I'll just pretend I don't hear him.

Once I'm out of the alley I'll yell for Luke, or a cop . . . nope, not a cop . . . maybe I'll just scream "Fire!" That's only illegal in theaters, right?

The stomping behind me gets louder and faster, more emphatic.

The shadowy figure darts out in front of me and stops on a dime, shoving his hands out to keep me from running him over.

Shit, Ethan Wyatt.

He's hot in more ways than one. A little vein on his neck throbs erratically. A veil of pink rises up from under his Armani necktie and disappears behind his five-o'clock shadow.

I wish I'd thought to comb my hair before I left the house.

"Did you just get a shot of me on a camera phone?" He grunts in baleful tones. His eyes widen as he takes a good look at my face. "Wait. I know you. . . ." He aims a finger at me. "The airport . . . last night. That was *you*!"

I try to maneuver around him, edge left, then right. He matches every move, spreading his legs for stability and digging his heels into the ground—like he's prepared to take me on in a shoving match.

"Let me see that phone!" he demands.

I try again to scoot around him, but he won't let me pass. I stretch just far enough to see that Luke and Brooke are nowhere to be found.

"What phone? I don't know what you're talking about . . . crazy man." Crazy man? Oh, yeah, that was smooth.

"The one in your *hand*," he retorts, as a patronizing grin spreads across his face.

Oh, crap.

"No, I won't give you my phone. I'm going to dial 9-1-1. You . . . crazy . . . stranger." I begin scrolling through the many options on the phone's main menu.

"Stranger? Ha! That's cute. Go ahead, call the cops. Save me the trouble! That's private property in there—a goddamn VIP room, for Christ's sake!"

Email, damnit! I just want to email! I've got to get the picture off this phone. The dim light of the alley and my need to bob and weave are making this exceedingly difficult.

The phone whines in short bursts. "La Cucaracha," Beethoven's Fifth, the Partridge Family classic "Come On, Get

Happy." Stupid ringtones! Why do I need more than one? Why won't it just shut up?

I frantically push the buttons—designed for use by infants and leprechauns—but the Partridge Family won't stop: *Hello world here's a song that we're singin' / Come on, get happy . . .*

Okay, screw the ringtone. What I need is email.

Ethan lunges at me, reaching for the phone, but gets air.

I sidestep and pirouette. Rush forward, lean back. He won't give up, and I can't shake him.

"You know what your problem is?" he asks me.

"What, you maniac? What is *my* problem?" I reply acerbically while trying to duck and scurry past him—without success.

"You *people* . . ."—he spits out "people" in a wickedly facetious tone—"you think you can do anything. That you can get away with anything. Because, though it's sick and sad, someone's going to buy that picture. And you'll be the fucking hero of the day. Not giving a shit who gets hurt in the process."

"Aw, are you worried what *Cocoa* might think?"

He glowers at me, astonished.

I continue, "Oh, I'm sorry. You probably know a lot of Cocos. I'm speaking specifically of Cocoa with an *a*. As in D-N-*A*."

"You think you know something about my life because you take pictures of me for a living? Because you read all the dirty gossip on the fucking Internet? Let me tell you something, you don't know *anything* about me."

"And you know so much about *me*?" I bite back. "You guys

call us parasites for doing the work your publicists ask us to do. We keep you *alive*, Ethan Wyatt, you pompous prima donna. I pay your fucking bills, whether you want to admit it or not. And . . . and you wrecked my car!" I don't know, that last bit may have been off topic.

He makes another quick jab at the phone, but I pull it back just in time. I return to punching at the keypad, and he tries again.

This is the most absurd, ridiculous situation I have ever been in. I am in a dark alley playing keep-away with a movie star. Correction: an incredibly attractive, remarkably agile movie star.

He lurches forward, swipes at me again. "Give it!" he shouts over the unstoppable, cloying twitter of the Partridge Family from my cell phone.

I can't help but chuckle. "What are you, ten? Knock it off."

He flashes me a playful smirk, his posture slackens. "Come on, give me the phone," he pleads like a tired teenager.

"No," I giggle back.

"Pleeeease? Do me this one favor?"

"I did you a favor last night. I couldn't get a single decent shot off." I don't know why I just said that.

"Why couldn't you get a shot off?"

"You turned around, remember?" Very weak comeback, *very* lame excuse. "You ran into the airport like a . . . a . . . scared little girl."

"That's never stopped you guys before."

He looks to me for some response, but I can't think of one.

He's right. I have no idea why I didn't chase him down and make him beg for mercy. I'm usually so good at that.

Ethan Wyatt stops his bobbing and weaving, tilts his head, and flashes me his signature pretty-boy, irresistibly flirty smile. He shoves his hands in his pockets and coyly glances at my waist, then my neck, mouth, eyes. Women pay their hard-earned money to see that grin; they drool over it and dream about it.

For a moment, I fall into a trancelike state, measuring his features—sucked into his sweet and sour million-dollar expression.

A honking cab startles me out of the daze. "I'm going to go now. *With* my phone."

"All right," he sighs.

"Good." I resist the urge to say thank you—for the smile. Sick. He's an evil genius. A flirtatious hypnotist. I am but a helpless pawn in his plot for world domination.

I take a step toward the street.

He calls out, "Hey," low and smooth, like a lullaby.

I stop and turn around. "What?"

"What's your name?" he asks, closing the gap between us.

"Sadie," I reply, unable to resist him.

He leans in even closer, so close I can smell him. No cologne, no sharp alcohol-laced hair products, just warm and sexy Ethan Wyatt. There's something reassuring about his scent, like the smell of hot cocoa on a cold day. I drink it in.

He mumbles, just above a whisper, "Thank you, Sadie."

"For what?" I whisper back.

He steps away suddenly. "For the phone." His posture, his entire demeanor falls back into that of aggravation—but this time with a twist of arrogance.

I look down at my hands—empty.

When I raise my eyes, Ethan is strolling back into blé, whistling, "Come On, Get Happy."

I can't believe it. That fucker just stole my phone.

COURTNEY'S WYATT SHRINE

Breaking News

A friend of a friend of my sister (who works in Manhattan) said that she knows for sure that Ethan Wyatt and Maya Dunn are definitely not going to make it! I can't tell you exactly how she knows (Top Secret), but I can tell you her sources are very good. We here at the Ethan Wyatt shrine are very encouraged. Ethan will be back on the market in no time. And, for all my fellow Jersey-based Wyatt lovers, he has definitely moved to New York! More updates as they happen!

—Courtney Jackson (soon-to-be Wyatt)

"Love is like a craving that you can't satisfy."

—Ethan Wyatt as Vince Hager in
"The Hager Saga" (2003)

www.courtneys-Wyatt-shrine.com

CHAPTER 8

I stumble into the kitchen with my ear to the phone.

"The guy's banging his girlfriend's sister?" Todd asks with a chuckle of admiration, eliminating any guilt I may have had about dumping him.

I did manage to send the email last night. I'm not sure how I did it, but when I got home it was there in my inbox. A closer look at the picture revealed that Ethan's dinner date was not just some random wannabe starlet.

"Lori is her name, Lori Dunn. She's Maya Dunn's sister, so, yeah, it would seem that it's something like that." There goes my stomach again, doing a tumbling routine worthy of Mary Lou Retton. "Or not, you know. I don't know."

"Are you all right?"

"Yeah, why wouldn't I be?" Other than the fact that I feel like I may have pole-vaulted over that invisible line separating myself from the stalkerazzi. Oh, and I've lost my freaking Sidekick. I'm like a ship without a sail, a train without an engine,

Mariah Carey without a hairdresser. I'm adrift. Powerless. Dull and lifeless.

"Okay," he says, unconvinced. "You came in just under the wire for *Celeb*'s print deadline, so they have the exclusive. It's gonna go wide after tomorrow. There's nothing out there right now." What he means is that no one has been photographed looking freakishly skinny yet this week, so the papers are hurting for things to report. He continues, "The dailies are drooling over it. The glossies will run it up front next week. *Entertainment Tonight . . . Access Hollywood*. Wide."

"Great." I pour myself a glass of orange juice and settle into the eating nook in the kitchen. It is great, damnit. I got a shot with a big juicy story attached—sex, love, *and* betrayal—the tabloid trifecta. I wanted it, and I got it. I might actually make enough off this shot to pay for my car repairs. But, it was supposed to make me feel *better*.

Right, the feeling of satisfaction hasn't hit me yet, but it will. I'm sure it will. I got a picture of Ethan Wyatt, right? Of course, my eyes were closed at the time. I didn't have to see him sitting there, *hating* me. Whatever. I still got it. I'm not losing my edge.

"Do you know where he's staying?" asks Todd.

"Yeah, Luke found out. But I'm not doing the follow-up."

I hear Todd hit something, like his desk . . . or the cheap acoustic tiles on his office ceiling. "Like hell you're not," he responds firmly.

I don't ever want to see Ethan Wyatt's smug, obnoxious face again. Too bad, really, because *Charming Samantha* looks kind of cute. "Todd, I've already had two close calls with this guy—"

"That's sort of the point."

Under normal circumstances, I'd have no problem waiting for him outside his hotel. But there's something about him that makes me really nervous, unsure of myself—unreasonably girly.

Although, I wouldn't mind the opportunity to have Ethan see me wearing something that fits. No. No, not worth it.

I make excuses. "I am not that girl, all right? I am not going to follow him around and egg him on. That's just not my style. Besides, he already wrecked my car; he could go all Tommy Lee on my ass in a heartbeat. I refuse to risk—"

Todd interrupts, "You did it last night."

I'm rendered speechless. He's right.

"Look," Todd says, obviously trying to keep his temper in check, "I'll put somebody else on him today, but that's all I'm giving you. You hear me? Whatever is going on with you, you need to buck up and get over it, *pronto*."

Pronto? Who even says that anymore?

"Whatever," I reply.

"Sadie"—Todd's tone softens to a moderate grumble—"it was a nice piece of work."

My instinct is to say "Thanks," but when it comes out of my mouth it sounds more like "Ugh." There is something absurd about being congratulated for getting a picture of a man on a date.

"Hey," Todd says, and then pauses for what feels like an hour. "Why didn't you just tell me you were seeing someone else?"

"What?" I chuckle.

"I called your cell first. Some guy answered."

"Excuse me?" I ask, shocked, dropping my breakfast bowl on the table with a crash.

Todd huffs, "A guy. You know what those are, right? Hairy, stronger than you, easier to talk to. One of them answered your phone. I assume you know him?"

He answered? That crazy, arrogant bastard!

Should I explain the situation to Todd? Admit to him that I lost my cool and my focus and allowed a millionaire-slash-thief to coax a phone out of my hands? Of course, if I tell him I'm seeing someone so soon after our breakup, he'll probably think I'm a slut. This raises two important questions: One, do I care? And two, which is more humiliating—sluttiness or stupidity? Hmmm.

I answer finally, "Uh, yeah. I, uh, must have left the phone at his place." Silence. I add hastily, "Nothing happened when we were together." I don't know why I said that. I am so bad at off-the-cuff lying. For me, lying takes preparation—a solid story, hours of practice in the mirror, margaritas.

"Right," Todd replies. "Well, take today off if you want."

"Uh, Todd?"

"Yeah?"

I pose timidly, "What did he say?"

"You mean did he tell me that he's totally hot for you and ask me to pass you a note in study hall? No." Wow, bitter much? "I asked if you were there. He said no. I hung up."

"Oh, okay. Thanks. Bye."

I hang up with Todd and immediately begin pacing between the kitchen and the living room, the cordless phone in my right hand begging to be dialed.

Should I do it? Should I call my own freaking cell phone and see if that idiot answers? What would I say?

Well, "Give me back my phone, you egomaniacal slime" might be a good place to start.

I punch in the area code.

No, the story has already hit the papers. He's probably foaming at the mouth by now—while a team of highly paid spin doctors and ass kissers massage his ego.

Wait a second, *he's* the bad guy here. He's the one who caused the crash and *didn't* have to sit in the back of a cop car. *He's* the one who stole my personal property. I am but an innocent victim of street crime! Right?

Yeah.

I dial the number with both thumbs, have to get it in there before I lose my nerve. I march between the sofa and the bookcases and embolden myself by staring at one of Brooke's fitness books entitled *Be Firm and Confident.*

The phone rings three times, and then silence.

"Hello?" I say, meekly.

"Hello," replies an accented male voice in a wildly superior tone. "Who may I say is calling?" So superior, in fact, that it has to be Ethan himself.

"The woman who owns the device you're holding, you psychotic phone pirate." *Psychotic phone pirate?* Really, Sadie.

"I wondered how long it would take you to call simpering and begging for your phone back," Ethan says, slipping out of the lame accent he opened with.

"I am not going to *beg* you for anything. It's my phone, and I demand its return."

"Not gonna happen. But, I am duty bound to relay your messages," he says in a ridiculously sarcastic tone. "Someone named Todd called looking for you. And I chatted with a very nice woman named Paige for about fifteen minutes this morning. She says hi. Oh, and you'll be happy to know that last night you won a free stay in Kissimmee, Florida. A salesman will be stopping by next week to discuss time shares."

He spoke to my mother? Oh, dear God.

I squeeze the top of an orange juice bottle to release some of the tension that is currently turning my limbs to stone. I have to say something—jab back. "Speaking of duty bound, have you seen the cover of today's *Celeb*?"

My stomach churns the second it's out of my mouth.

"Proud of yourself, are you?"

No. But I am pissed off. "Yes, as a matter of fact, I am."

"Job well done, hey? You've caused the pain and heartbreak of no less than three people in the last twenty-four hours. Mission accomplished."

"*I've* caused it? I'm sorry, but where do *you* fit in to all this?"

"I was living my life, you bottom-feeder." His voice drops to a deep, grating hiss. "None of what they printed was even remotely true. Lori wasn't even doing anything. She was reaching for her purse. And, by the way, Maya and I weren't dating."

"Oh, no?" I bite back. "Then how did I hurt all of you so badly?"

"I will tell you this, not because I feel the need to explain myself to you—because I don't—but because you should know the extent of the stupidity you peddled. Maya had a thing for me. I had a thing for her sister. Bad timing, yes. Cheating? No. Not that it matters to you or the fucking editors. You spread lies. You hurt people, and what's worse, you *know* you're doing it. You are low—lower than low."

I swallow hard to maintain the strength in my voice. "Aw, come on," I say in a sarcastically whiny pitch, "you're gonna hurt my feelings."

"Your *feelings*? You don't have feelings." Like a punch, the words set my ears ringing. He didn't say that like an accusation, or an impassioned insult, but as though it were a fact and he felt pity for me. He continues, "My only consolation is that you'll pay for it."

"Are you threatening me?" I snap.

"No. I'm talking about karma, sweetheart. It packs a bigger punch than I ever could. What goes around comes around."

Did he just call me *sweetheart*?

The line goes silent, but I can still hear his breathing and the distant buzz of a television somewhere behind him.

I should say something, contradict him. Tell him that this situation is the result of *his* karma, not mine. Scream at him. Tell him that I don't usually do this kind of thing. Apologize?

No. There will be no apologizing. Not to a man who thinks Paige is *nice*.

"I think," Ethan-freaking-Wyatt continues smugly, "you're broken. Like sociopaths, and wolves, and . . . I don't know . . . invertebrates—you're missing something . . ." He pauses, and I hear him sort of humming to himself, as if mentally winding up for the next punch. He adds finally, "In the head."

I'm missing something?

Hold on, *am* I missing something?

Wait, why am I giving any credence to what this guy says? How does he know exactly which buttons to push? It's sick.

Snap out of it, Sadie.

I grumble, "You're right. I *am* missing something—"

"I'm right?" he asks, surprised.

"Yes," I say coolly. "I'm missing *my phone*!"

The line again goes silent. An age seems to pass with no sound but the hum of background noise, and the pounding of my heart. Should I just hang up? I don't really want to hang up.

Maybe I should hang—

"I'm curious," Ethan says earnestly. "What is it about your job that makes it worth selling your soul and selling out your fellow man? Is it just the money?"

"Selling out my fellow man? I'm not a war criminal, you whack job, I'm a *photographer*."

"You're not a photographer," Wyatt responds calmly. "Real photographers make a contribution. Their pictures say something, they *mean* something. You take meaningless, vapid snapshots."

"I—" I don't know what to say. "I . . . I contribute!" I stammer. Oh, I probably shouldn't have said that.

"Oh, yeah? *How*?" Ethan asks bluntly. Yep, there it is.

The word—*how*—echoes through my empty skull. I can hear my own restless heavy breathing over the phone line. I feel like an unprepared, hungover college student who's been called on by a professor. I feel like I've been asked by my father to explain something I did wrong. *How.*

I rack my brain for something solid and true to tell him, some meager contribution to the world or tiny sense of meaning I get or give through my work. Then, I rack my brain for something made up.

I get nothing but the irritating swish of blood thumping through my eardrums.

Hang on a second . . .

"Huh!" I say, the only alternative to "Eureka" that immediately springs to mind. "I suppose the same goes for actors, right? That real actors make a contribution, that their movies say something?"

"Of course!" he replies stridently.

"I suppose, then, that you think you're a *real* actor?"

"Absolutely," he says with a little less conviction.

"Ha! Tell me, what is the grand contribution to the human race made by *Motion of the Ocean*? What significant impact has *Execution Style* made to humanity? What new and insightful things do we learn about the human condition by watching that paragon of profundity *Loose Girls*?"

"I've done independent films," he says defensively.

"When you first started out, maybe. But now, Wyatt, you're a big walking, talking action figure."

"I . . ." he says, stumbling over his words. "I'm . . ." he tries again, without success. "You're not a real photographer!"

"I want my phone back!" I reply.

"Well, tough luck, lady. You're not getting it." His words make my heart pound heavily against my chest.

I hang up the phone and collapse onto the couch, shaking.

I can't let this guy get to me. He can't be getting to me. What the hell do I care what he thinks? He's just angry at me because he got caught.

Ha! Do I do it for the money? Of course I do it for the money. It's my *job*. That's what jobs are for. And he said it as only a man with an American Express Black Card can: "Is it *just* the money?" *Just* money? No, jackass, it's the stuff you can buy with the money—like food. I'm no good at being poor. I've done it. It sucks. And even now, if you were to ask me my net worth, I'd have to count all the money in my wallet to give you an accurate assessment. I make just enough cash to keep myself from feeling that I'm drowning. Because that is how being poor feels—like drowning.

And contributing? I'm not a *real* photographer? I *am* a real photographer. I have a degree in it! Granted, I've been really busy with the paparazzi stuff lately and haven't been doing the proper art photography as much as I should. But it's not like I've never done it; and it's not like I won't do it ever again. I'm just busy, that's all. I even have a website to promote my work. It's probably gathering little digital cobwebs given the infrequency with which I update it, but it's there contributing, twenty-four hours a day. Why I couldn't think of that when I was talking to Ethan, I'll never know.

Brooke walks out of her bedroom and leans over the back of the sofa. "Who were you talking to? You sounded pissed."

"Todd," I lie, trying desperately to seem bored and nonchalant.

"Come on, get dressed. I know just the thing to make you feel better," she coos, patting me on the head like a dog.

"Oh, God. Not another package from my mother."

"No," she says, lowering her voice to a whisper. A naughty little twinkle glimmers in her eye. *"Shopping."*

ETHAN TAKES
A GUILT TRIP . . .
TO THE MALL

The morning his all-in-the-family-hanky-panky scandal hit the newsstands, Ethan Wyatt was spotted dropping thousands at stores around New York. Could it be he's trying to win back the good graces of his now former flame, Maya Dunn? Are they apology gifts for his new and, word has it, humiliated paramour Lori Dunn? That I can't tell you.

What I can tell you is that Wyatt picked up several expensive toys at the Soho Apple Store—an iPod nano and state-of-the-art Mac among them. He was then spotted further downtown at J&R Music and Computer World, where he went nuts for their low, low-priced goods.

Maya, honey, don't take him back. He's shopping discount—hold out for the diamonds.

Fresh Gossip—
Your Internet Celebrity News Source

CHAPTER 9

Saturday is a holy day. For Brooke this means her weekly visit to the promised land—Madison Avenue. There, she worships, she prays, she pleads forgiveness for coveting thy neighbor's Chloé. She communes with her gurus of choice, their holiness the Dalai's Dolce & Gabbana. She is such a devoted follower of this religion that she limits herself to shopping *only* on weekends. She fears that the extended operating hours of Monday through Friday would lead her too far into temptation.

To tell you the truth, I'd much rather spend my day off sitting in front of the TV, thinking of more comebacks to Ethan Wyatt's insults, while shoving Chocolate Fudge Frosted Pop-Tarts down my throat. You've got to love any dessert that can disguise itself as a breakfast food and get away with it. And I do *so* love to lie around. I hardly ever have time for it and it's good for the soul. Much better than that Chicken Soup crap they keep trying to pawn off on us—*Chicken Soup for the Woman's Soul, Chicken Soup for the Teenage Soul, Chicken Soup for the Vegetarian Soul.* I say, give me *Chocolate Fudge Frosted Pop-Tarts for the Judge Mathis Lover's Soul.* Seriously, I've considered alerting the AMA; in my experience, small-claims court programs and talk shows involving paternity test results have exactly the same effect as Prozac.

Brooke and I have wandered into La Perla, international purveyors of all things soft and girly. As I weave my way in and out of the many wispy bits of silk and satin, I start to feel as delicate and feminine as they are. La Perla is a veritable temple of femininity, the place women come to remind themselves that they are girls with *feelings* and soft spots that deserve pale blue satin and deep chocolate velvet.

Maybe I'm a weirdo, but I always feel better about myself if I'm wearing pretty panties. Maybe it's just that I feel more put together, or maybe it's that whole "If I get hit by a taxi and a hot young surgeon must cut off my clothes, I want to be wearing nice underoos" mind-set. (I've seen *ER*; I know what those doctors look like.) Whatever the reason, nice undies up my confidence level. I could use a little boost just now, even if it is only superficial. For some reason the crisp, fulfilling rush of satisfaction that I usually have after a really big "get" hasn't hit me. Its absence has left a nagging bit of hollowness in my middle. I can't explain it, I can only try and fill it. With panties.

I gingerly pick up a pair of canary yellow satin panties that are way too tiny and expensive for my consideration. I glance around to make sure I'm not being eyed by a nosey shopgirl before gently grazing the fabric against my cheek.

Too soft and sublime to be legal, frankly. I lift the teensy panties and inspect them; thoroughly examine the graceful stitching and ultrasoft fabric for imperfections. None. No excuse not to buy them. Man, if only I could justify spending ninety-eight dollars on something with dimensions suspiciously similar to those of an eye patch.

I stand before a full-length mirror and hold up the eye patch and companion chemise against my body. My breasts, which used to be perky yet unobtrusive (that's code for small-ish but nice), have suddenly begun to migrate southward. It's a minor shift that no one but myself could appreciate, but I see it as just the beginning of a disturbing trend—I've also noticed tiny little puckers appearing on the backs of my thighs. I wonder, far more often than necessary, whether my ass is *destined* to look like the rind of an orange or if, by some miracle, the wizards at Igea will invent a cellulite-removing machine for two easy payments of $29.95, with a "Yours to keep!" fluffy terry bathrobe included.

I'm curious. Would the monetary value and sheer loveliness of the eye-patch panty set make my butt look less ripply and more perky? Would the sumptuous lace and silk billowing around the chest area of the chemise distract the eye? Maybe that's why all the "ladies who lunch" shop here. I mean, apparently they're always eating—perhaps their rears, like mine, are also careening to earth faster than Britney Spears's career.

As I take one last look at myself in the mirror, I suddenly feel a distinctive tingle on my neck. It's the disturbing prickling sensation of being watched. My looks of unrequited panty-love (and possibly a little drool) must have inadvertently alerted the shopgirl that I'm a suspicious person.

I turn to find the source of the feeling.

Brooke is admiring a beaded bustier near the rear of the store, and the only shopgirl in sight is busy fawning over a middle-aged woman carrying a $12,000 Hermès Birkin bag and an armload of silk lacy underthings. No one is staring at me.

I put the chemise down and scan the store again. Nothing. Even the security guard is staring off in another direction.

An involuntary shiver works its way up my spine. Goose bumps spread from the back of my neck, across my shoulders and down my arms. You know the feeling, right? That strange, warm, jittery sensation on your skin that only occurs when someone's eyes have landed on you and won't let go? It's that palpable sense of being ogled, or appraised. Oftentimes, like in a singles' bar when you're in your hottest outfit, it's a welcome sensation. Other times, like on a nude beach—or, for me, right now—it's a little creepy.

Okay, this is crazy. Clearly I'm imagining things. They probably lace the racks with narcotics to break down your natural defenses. Which is the excuse I will use to soothe myself when I get the credit card bill for my eye patch.

After purchasing a new but sadly empty Sidekick . . .

"Sadie, look!" Brooke exclaims as we traipse further uptown.

She stops dead in her tracks and points at a newsstand clerk who's picking his nose.

I swat her hand down. "It's gross, yes. But don't you think that's a little rude?"

She chuckles at me. "Not him. The paper!"

The newsstand overflows with the daily rags. Four stacks of *Celeb,* severely depleted, are positioned front and center. "Ethan Wyatt Shocker!" it says in bold red letters. The subcaption reads: "They're Dunn!"

I resist a sudden and somewhat bizarre urge to scurry away, and instead walk over and pick up the paper.

"Good job, Sadie," Brooke says over my shoulder. She loves it when my shots make the cover. I can't say that I share her enthusiasm this time.

I quickly flip through and find the layout. My grainy picture of Ethan Wyatt and Lori Dunn covers the whole page. On the facing page is a shot of Wyatt and Maya Dunn together. They're on set, a Southern California back lot dressed to look like Nantucket at Christmastime. Ethan is obviously in costume, as I doubt he'd wear a suit that ill-fitting out in public. And Maya is dressed like a prim librarian—not a navel in sight, with her ginger brown hair pulled back in a dainty chignon. The two of them are hugging. *Just* hugging. It's not a passionate, sexy kind of hug, either—just a regular old hug.

"Is that really the best they could do?" I mumble. If they were really a couple, you'd think they'd have something a bit juicer than an on-set hug. Could Ethan have been telling me the truth this morning about the two of them not really being a couple? But it was reported everywhere. I mean, *everywhere*. I thought for sure—

"That's how it started for Brad and Angelina," Brooke enjoins gravely.

"You really know too much about this stuff."

"Spare me the jaded paparazzi act," she says with a smile. "You know you love it as much as I do." No, I really don't. "Man that guy is hot," Brooke adds as she stares at a close-up of Ethan. "Is he that good-looking in person?"

"*More* good-looking, actually," I reply, trying my best to sound clinical and not like the person who gasped out loud when she first saw him.

"*Really* . . ." Brooke's voice trails off and her eyes glaze over. She's drifted off into fantasy land.

Brooke digs further into the article. Other shots show Maya arm in arm with her sister Lori at VH1 Divas Live, at a movie premiere and—oh, *ouch*—at a fund-raiser called Sisters Helping Sisters.

> New York has a new resident bad boy. La-La Land import Ethan Wyatt was caught getting down and dirty at Manhattan's newest, chic-est dining spot, blé. He and a mysterious (yet oddly familiar-looking) young brunette chowed down, and then . . . ahem . . . went down. The woman in question? Lori Dunn, younger sister of Ethan's current flame, Maya Dunn.
>
> Maya is said to be "livid," tells one *Celeb* insider source. Maya had recently convinced her family and friends that Ethan wasn't as

bad as his press would suggest. Whoops. Her happy ending has now exploded, due to a "happy ending" of another sort altogether. Maya's heart is said to be broken, and her family shattered, by the news that her dear younger sister has been caught red-handed in a steamy rendezvous with her beau.

In a written statement, the Wyatt camp had only this to say: "The increasing intrusiveness of today's print and television media is not only disgusting, but . . . the accusations are lewd and the photo crass." In PR speak, that means Ethan is not only steamy, but *steaming*, about getting nabbed in the act.

This reporter has a little advice for Mr. Ethan Wyatt: You play with fire, you get burned. You play with fire in public, you get shot.

Maya and Lori Dunn. Huh. I hadn't really considered them as part of the equation last night. I was so focused on getting Wyatt. A sudden sinking feeling overwhelms me. Ethan Wyatt's morning rant reverberates through my mind: "You've caused the pain and heartbreak of no less than three people. . . ."

No, I'm sure Ethan was just putting me on about the "You spread lies" thing. He just wanted to make me feel bad, pawn his guilt off on me. I'm sure Maya and Lori knew what they were getting into. And even if he wasn't really getting a "happy ending" from Lori, he was still on a date with her. If he was so worried about Maya's feelings, perhaps he shouldn't have been putting the moves on her sister.

"It's a big one all right," says Brooke, handing over her money to the newsstand clerk and gathering up a thick stack of magazines. She stops to flip through them, admiring her purchases—all Duncan Stoke. His first summer blockbuster hits theaters on Memorial Day, and the media blitz has started with covers on *Entertainment Weekly, Men's Vogue,* and *People.*

"How could you possibly want to get involved with Duncan Stoke knowing what happens?" I ask Brooke, waving *Celeb* in front of her and disrupting her mini-swoonfest.

Brooke stares off into the distance, considering an answer.

"Well, he's hot." She takes a deep breath. "Like fire . . ."

"Sure, but—"

"Like lightening . . ." she continues wistfully.

"But—"

"Like a raging volcano on—"

"Okay," I say, finally loud enough to get her attention. "Good-looking. Got it."

She continues, "And I truly think we have a lot in common."

I roll my eyes at her.

"All right, you want to know what else?"

I nod vehemently.

She takes a breath, then looks over her shoulders as though worried about being spied on. She begins in hushed tones. "Okay, I imagine that there's this feeling when you walk into a room with someone famous. Knowing that all these other women want him, that he is the most desirable, amazing person in the room. The feeling that you're some-how more special, more remarkable than they are—than anyone else—because he chose you." Brooke looks at me like I should really get it now. She smiles proudly, like she's just shared some closely held solution to one of the great mysteries of life.

She takes my arm and guides me down the sidewalk. I press, "That's it?"

"Yep," she replies matter-of-factly.

"Let me get this straight. You're willing to give up your independence for a feeling that may or may not be based on reality? And if it is, may not last more than, who knows, several minutes at a time?" I ask pointedly.

"I would hope there'd be compatibility, affection, and love in there somewhere, too."

"Come on," I implore. Brooke is not the kind of person who disappears in a crowd. When she walks into a room she's generally envied by every woman in her vicinity—and it has nothing to do with the person she's with.

"All right," she says, throwing her hands up in defeat before shoving the magazines in her La Perla bag. "The money would be nice, too. If I were, say, *married* to Duncan Stoke, I might not have to work at all. Or I could just focus on my charity work." Her charity work? Does donating two year's worth of stained Gap tees to the Salvation Army really qualify as "charity work"?

Brooke continues, "There's just so much backstabbing and conniving in New York real estate, you know?"

"And Hollywood's such a picnic."

Brooke shakes her head, her sleek brown hair flopping from side to side. "You just don't get it."

No, I don't. To tell you the truth, it reminds me of my mother and the dentist, and it makes me a little sad for Brooke. "Are you trying to tell me that you're a gold digger?" I pose, as gingerly as the phrase *gold digger* can be posed.

"No!" she defends. "No, it's not like that!" She goes all quiet and contemplative, obviously trying to form some further explanation of her position. She comes back to earth and adds, "I want the compatibility and love, too. I just don't see why it's so totally out of the realm of possibility that my perfect match happen to be a celebrity. You know, when Katie Holmes was a teenager she said that her dream was to marry Tom Cruise. And I read somewhere that Kelly Preston had a *Grease* poster on her wall in high school. Why am I any different?"

"It sounds a little . . . far-fetched." And pretty damn corny, I might add.

Brooke rolls her eyes. "Oh, whatever. I don't know why I'm surprised that you don't get it. You're just not a romantic."

"Am too!" I defend reflexively.

"Sadie, just days ago you dumped a man because he offered you a toothbrush."

"It was more than the toothbrush. It was what the toothbrush symbolized," I reply.

"Oh, really? What did it *symbolize*? Tartar control? Plaque? Gingivitis?"

"Fine. I have . . . problems with men."

"Correction," Brooke warbles, "you have *a* problem with men. *You*."

"You're the devil!" I say, desperately trying to keep a chuckle from escaping my lips.

"Uh-huh, I see that smile on your face. You know it's true," Brooke says gleefully.

"Okay fine, I'm not good at commitment."

She waves her one shopping-bag-free arm around dramatically. "You go out of your way to hook up with guys you think won't want to commit, because you're terrified of lousing up the status quo. I, on the other hand, have no problem with change or giving up a teensy bit of my independence in return for being blissfully happy." Yeah, 'cause that's guaranteed. "Someday, Sadie, you'll meet a guy that you'll be willing to louse things up for—"

"Like Duncan Stoke?"

"Exactly."

"Uh, Brooke, I hate to be the one to break this to you, but you've never met him."

"Ah, but when I do, sparks will fly. I know it."

"Oh, God. You're not planning on strapping yourself down with explosives or something, are you?"

"Very funny," she replies.

"Covering your body in sparklers to catch his eye?"

Brooke's expression suddenly transitions to one of concern. "I'm serious about this, Sadie. You guard yourself so closely against all these things that you perceive to be so dangerous. So what if you can't take pictures anymore? So what if you fall for a guy and you can't maintain the status quo? Sometimes you have to give something to get something better in return."

"Like your *career*?" I ask earnestly.

A look of dreamy exuberance softens her angular features. She replies, "Maybe . . ."

"Hey, I have a funny idea. . . ." I say, with just a hint of sarcasm eking into my voice. "If you hate real estate so much, why don't you just get a new job?"

A touch of pink rises in Brooke's cheeks. "Why aren't you shooting your portraits anymore?"

My mouth falls open. Her question sucks all the air out of my lungs—all the fight out of my voice. That completely came out of nowhere. We don't talk about that. *She* doesn't ask me about that. My portraits are in a dark little corner of my closet, and carefully concealed by dust bunnies under my bed.

I suddenly feel a bit naked and raw.

"Where did that come from?" I ask, shocked by her leap into conversational no-man's-land.

"Answer," she replies curtly.

"The website is still up! I just paid the bill on Tuesday," I say, for lack of anything better.

"Why aren't you shooting the portraits, Sadie?" she replies, not giving an inch.

"What does this have to do with real estate and Duncan Stoke?" I jab back.

"Why. No. *Portraits*?" She's being just a little too blunt for her own good. I would tell her so if she didn't have a devastatingly hard-boiled, determined look in her eye. She's not going to let this go. She'll bite and claw her way to an answer if she has to.

The phrases "Yes, it's for the money" and "I'm still a real photographer" dance precariously close to the tip of my tongue. "I don't know," I say lamely.

"Ha!" she squawks. "You don't take your portraits anymore because by the time you'd finished college and paid off your father's debts, you'd been *struggling* your whole life and you were fed up with struggling. Not to mention that if you were a starving artist, you couldn't afford the five pairs of Jimmy Choo's you own and wouldn't be buying hundred-dollar panties."

"They were *ninety-eight* dollars!" Before tax.

She ignores me, and continues, "Well, I'm tired of struggling, too. Okay? If I had even the faintest notion how to focus that damn camera of yours, I'd be shooting Ethan Wyatt, too. But, I can't. Instead I have a rather all-consuming—but not uncommon—fantasy that someone with a few films to his credit and whose lap happens to be ever so slightly on this side of luxury will fold me into his fabulous life . . . and arms. Is that a crime?"

"I wasn't accusing you of anything, Brooke."

"Please, I know how you feel about all this," she says, pointing to her stash of magazines. "You think I'm loony."

"They're *real* people. Real photographs get taken of them. Fantasy is one thing, but the reality is . . . different. And, believe it or not, I think you have a good chance at succeeding. You're gorgeous and funny and smart. You have the instincts of a shark and the scrappy tenacity of a prisoner trying to escape from Alcatraz. You could do it. I'm just wondering if maybe there were some easier solution to your problem, or a solution that didn't involve being plastered all over the papers."

She smiles, and then gives way to some other emotion. Her

big green eyes squint down to nothing. "Wait, you want to protect me from the likes of *you*?"

I . . . well. I hadn't really thought about it like that. "No, not me. *Them*," I say, pointing to *Celeb*.

"Sadie, that *is* you."

Oh, right.

WYATT SPEAKS OUT

In an exclusive one-on-one interview, Ethan Wyatt speaks out about the "rabid press" and his own uneasy relationship with fame. . . . "I understand people wanting to know about us [celebrities]. I had a thing for Steve McQueen when I first started out. I read everything I could get my hands on, loved seeing those old Galella shots of him and Ali MacGraw—they defined cool. But nowadays the shots are either mind-numbingly superficial, or they're sick and twisted and taken by low-light cameras, or lenses that can see up to a mile away. Back in the day, they may have hated Ron Galella, but at least McQueen and MacGraw knew he was there. You can't imagine how violated and humiliated you feel when you see a picture of yourself in a magazine doing something you thought was done in private. These people stop at nothing to get what they want. They're chasing you in cars, stalking you at restaurants, waiting for you at the end of your driveway. I know, it sounds like whining. Believe me, I know how lucky I am to do what I do. But at the same time, fame can sometimes feel like a prison, which is exactly where I'd like to put a lot of the paparazzi."

CHAPTER 10

Waking up to an ominous six-foot-long box is not the best way to start the day. Unless, of course, you're a vampire.

I have tried stuffing it under my bed, cramming it into my bedroom closet, and shoving it behind the living room bookshelves—whence it spawned. The only solution with even a tiny hope of success was the hall closet. Unfortunately, Brooke complained that it was creasing her many jackets and coats. The fact that the coats in question won't be in use for five months was not enough to sway her. So, I just have to live with it. Sitting here. Taunting me. It's a monolith. A big brown monument to my cowardice—and Paige. Pretty soon schoolchildren will be made to file past it and ponder its significance. Luke will set up a gift shop in the kitchen and sell little Brown Box magnets and key chains. Brooke will host telethons and direct-mail campaigns to fund Brown Box maintenance projects.

I should probably just open it and get it over with.

Reaching over the edge of the bed, I tug at the bit of paper that Brooke loosened days ago. Pressing my eye to the tiny slash of an opening, I try to catch a glimpse of the contents.

No use. It's a black hole.

The thing is, I know that if I open this box, it'll be a monument of another kind—a gigantic memorial to a vapid mother-daughter relationship.

Our gifts to each other are, and always have been, completely hollow. They never mean anything. They're just *things*. Sometimes they're nice things, but there's never any feeling or thought behind them. They're tchotchkes picked up out of obligation, like company-mandated Secret Santa presents or those generalized charity gift-giving programs. Gifts from my mother always look like they were prompted by a three-by-five card that said, "Needed. Gift for: female. Age: 28 years. Likes: piña coladas, getting caught in the rain."

I'm no better, I guess. I rely on this fascinating category of Hallmark cards called Simply Stated. These cards bypass all the mushy, heartfelt stuff and get right to the point. A Mother's Day card, for example, will have a very tasteful nondescript flower arrangement on the front and an inside greeting that reads "Happy Mother's Day, Mom" and nothing more. The vast expanse of empty white space that surrounds the greeting speaks volumes of its own—something like, "You're technically my mother. It's Mother's Day. As a self-respecting American consumer, I am contractually obligated to participate in this holiday. Here's a card." My mother's fiftieth birthday was a few months ago. That's a major milestone, the kind of occasion that in a normal mother-daughter relationship would elicit some sort of deeply meaningful gift. I swear to you, I tried. I stayed up nights window shopping on the Internet. I dug through every major department store in Manhattan, scoured countless little boutiques. You know what I came up with? A doormat. I bought my mother a *doormat* for her fiftieth birthday. I was completely incapable of finding a gift that meant something.

I'm sure this box has something expensive and age appropriate inside. Just one more reminder of how little Paige knows me. No, I'm not going to open it. I'm going to do something much more productive—I'm just going to lie back down on the bed and stare at it.

Or, maybe I should just peek at the card.

I lie down flat on my stomach and stretch toward the box. Very gently, I peel the small plastic pouch away from the paper—careful not to tear it and reveal too much.

It's my mother's signature paper, expensive correspondence cards from Smythson of Bond. They're monogrammed with her first name only, as though anyone receiving the note should already know who the one and only *Paige* is, in the same way they know which Madonna, Cher, or Elton.

"Dearest Sadie," it reads. "A gift for you. Sometimes the things we run away from should be given a chance to catch up. A reminder of things past—and perhaps future. Your loving mother, Paige."

Things we run away from? A reminder of things past? And future? Who am I, Ebenezer Scrooge? It's just like her to give me a riddle. It's like she knew I wouldn't want to open it. Damn.

You know what bothers me most about this box—besides the fact that it exists? It's got me all twisted up about Brooke's little rant. I know, for a fact, that Dr. Hank was my mom's Duncan Stoke. I know it. She wanted him; she went after him; she landed him. Like a fisherman after a marlin. He swallowed her bait—hook, line, and sinker.

The thing that keeps swirling around and around in my brain is that whatever Paige got from being Mrs. Price-Farmer was worth more to her than me. Just like the money and fame are worth more to Brooke than her independence, for my mother the fur coats were worth more than me. The five-thousand-square-foot house was worth more than me. The stupid nattering, ankle-biting Oodles and Donks were worth more than me. Meanwhile, my dad worked his ass off—always with the caveat of it being "for us." "I'm not doing it for me, Sadie," he'd say. "I'm doing it for you. For us." The only problem was, his dream of owning his own restaurant was the very thing that destroyed the "us" he was trying to provide for. First, "us" lost my mother to the dentist, then me to college and a life that didn't involve worrying whether or not the electricity would be cut off because we couldn't pay the bill. Or, trading my lunch money for gas money so that I could actually get to school in the first place. So, finally, the only bit of "us" that my father had left was himself. And he even managed to lose that. He had a heart attack three days before the grand opening. The result of all his sweat, struggle, and loss? My father's dream is now the cosmetics and feminine hygiene section of a Super Wal-Mart.

I don't think Brooke understands the kind of Pandora's box she's opening. I really don't. She's not thinking about the big picture.

*   *   *

Fighting the urge to delve back under the covers, I slip on the La Perla undies I so lovingly hand-washed the other night and throw on the cleanest clothes I can find.

"Good morning, Sunshine," says Luke, as he groggily straightens out the couch cushions.

"Hey. Breakfast?" One of the best things about long friendships—you don't have to bother with all the tiring connective tissue of normal conversation.

"You making?" he responds.

"Cereal," I say, while padding into the kitchen.

"Sure."

I return from the kitchen bearing two enormous bowls. Snuggling into the sofa with my breakfast companion, His Royal Highness the Count of Chocula, I switch on the television.

"Hey, Luke?" I ask, then turn to him.

"Oh, no!" he says, backing further into his corner of the couch.

"What?"

"I know that look in your eyes. You're going to make me talk about girl things."

"I am not!" Well, only a little. "I just wanted your opinion."

"My opinion on, like, underwear? Hair color? Anything with wax, gloss, or . . ."—his nose scrunches up and his shoulders tense as he wrestles with some insanely objectionable word—"lubrication?"

"No, I want your opinion on Brooke." I laugh. "But you just said *lubrication*."

"Yes, thank you for reminding me. Did you say you had a question?"

"Fine. Do you ever worry about Brooke hating her job so much and this crazy celebrity fantasy she's got going on?"

He takes a deep breath. "She's a little obsessed, yeah. But here's my take on it: even though she has all those damn boxes in her room, and seems all practical and adult or whatever, she pretty much just follows her heart. Her heart said "real estate" first. Now it says "Marry a famous guy." Whatever makes her happy is my basic position. You know?"

Why is it that people think of the heart as this infallible GPS device? Isn't it just as possible that your heart gives bad directions? I mean, if it were really that accurate, wouldn't we all be consulting our hearts instead of MapQuest? Like, "Hmmm, we need to get downtown. Hold on, let me consult my heart for the most direct route."

I guess Luke doesn't know my mother well enough to share my understandable concern for Brooke's welfare. Granted, Brooke doesn't have any kids to be swallowed up in the wake of her fantasy, but I worry that she could be slowly giving up little parts of herself for some ideal image that she's concocted in her head.

"You're really not worried about her at all?" I ask again. I can tell by the look on his face and the cereal milk dribbling down his chin that he thought this conversation was over.

"No, I'm not," he says, wiping his chin with his shirtsleeve.

"Okay," I reply weakly.

"Hey, I've got to get going. Have to see a man about a horse."

"What?"

"It's a little indie film, *A Man About a Horse*. Dakota Fanning is supposed to be there. I think she can sign her own name now. Very exciting." Luke gets up and deposits his cereal bowl noisily in the sink before strapping on his enormous Teva sandals.

"Hey, Luke? One more thing."

"Hit me," he says over the thwacking of Velcro.

"Are you in the market for a six-foot-long unopened box?"

"Sorry, Killer," he says with a smile as he makes his way out the front door, "I'm not in the albatross business anymore."

Damn.

Brooke has received her weekly shipment of glossy tabloids; they cover nearly every square inch of our tiny coffee table. I attempt to gently push them out of the way, and they react by slipping and sliding scattershot over the table and onto the floor. Wily little suckers.

I pick up the two that I can reach and make a mental note to organize them properly before Brooke gets home—I'd like to avoid a lecture.

The Ethan Wyatt Scandal, as it's universally described, still dominates the headlines. In a matter of days, the story has exploded. It's huge. Not O.J. huge (no Bronco chase), but definitely approaching Ben and J.Lo huge (lacks the collaborative music video angle). I'd say it's about on a par with a Britney Spears wedding. Which, as I'm sure you know, is just slightly smaller than a Britney Spears divorce or, say, Gwyneth Paltrow giving birth. In any event, it's big. And though the Maya Dunn/Lori Dunn/Ethan Wyatt love triangle has squashed the

"Ethan Wyatt as victim of paparazzi car crash" *story*, it hasn't solved the actual car crash problem.

The estimates are in. A very hairy Hungarian gentleman (I use the term loosely) who happens to be the only Camaro restoration expert in the Triborough area said, and I quote, "Two month."

"Two months?" I asked incredulously.

His response to that was, "Three month?" Which was followed quickly by, "It cost you ten."

Begging and praying that our little language barrier was the reason this number sounded so scary, I asked, "Ten . . . hundred?"

He laughed a deep, guttural, manly laugh. "Tow-zand."

It is going to cost ten thousand dollars to restore the car to original condition. Ten large. Ten grand. *Ten*. That's twenty-five pairs of Christian Louboutin shoes, or eleven Marc Jacobs handbags. It's five Zac Posen party dresses. It's two weeks at a spa in Maui, or ten nights at the Waldorf-Astoria. It's one first-class, round-trip ticket to Paris. *Paris!*

I've been consoling myself the only way I know how, by reading the continuing gossip surrounding the Ethan Wyatt scandal and getting a petty little thrill at having gotten something positive out of this mess. The feeling of satisfaction I was waiting for finally arrived—at about the same time the hairy Hungarian said "Tow-zand." The check resulting from that grainy image of Ethan Wyatt at blé will make a nice little dent in my car repair bill.

The initial flux of gory details about Ethan and his "two

loves" is dissipating, and giving way to the aftermath stories—career fallout, image overhauls, quizzes entitled "Is Your Mate Sleeping with Your Sister?"

Today, the cover of *Celeb* includes a picture of Lori and Maya Dunn holding hands in a loving, sisterly way. A jagged line splits the image in two, and the headline reads "Sibling Rivalry." I flip through the magazine to find the article.

Huh. That's interesting . . .

A tiny blurb on page thirty-nine reads, "Duncan Stoke's New Mystery Gal Pal?" I love that they end that statement in a question mark. That one bit of punctuation says, "We can't exactly confirm it, but we really *really* think it's true." But that's not the interesting part. What intrigues me is that she looks incredibly familiar. I know her from somewhere.

Who is she?

I could have an exclusive sitting right in my lap, if I could just put the pieces together.

She's blonde, with fair skin. It's a horrible picture, slightly out of focus and awkwardly composed. Her face is partially obscured by a giant blob of what looks to be burrito dribbling from her half-open mouth and onto her shirtsleeve. Cute shirt, though. I have one just like it. Too bad I can't wear it anymore, the other day I got a stain on the . . .

Holy shit!

Those eyes . . . that hair . . . that *blob* . . .

A sudden burst of adrenaline makes me queasy, and I try not to choke on my cereal. My chest tightens as a surge of anger, curiously mingled with fear, cascades through my body.

It's me! That's a picture of *me*!

Wait a second. It can't be real. It just can't. It has to be a prank. That's the only logical explanation.

So why is my heart still beating a mile a minute?

A flash of memory momentarily shakes me—that feeling in La Perla. A deep pang of panic-induced nausea wells up from my belly.

No. This has to be a joke.

It has to be Todd. Todd is a lot of things, and crazy is one of them. He has to be behind this. For his brother's wedding, Todd had the ugliest, most embarrassing of his brother's high school photos turned into a billboard—on the busy exit ramp near the site of the ceremony. Obviously he's still pissed about our breakup or something and he's decided to put me in a tabloid. Very funny.

He went out of his way on this one; he had someone get a whole new photo of me. He could have used any number of ghastly shots from drunken weekend outings with Luke and Brooke. He must be really hot under the collar about this.

Oh, God, he thinks I'm dating someone. Is this some juvenile jealousy thing?

I'll have to ask Brooke. She had to be in on it. He must have had her slip the doctored magazine into the stack on the coffee table.

I inspect the magazine for signs of tampering (erroneous staple holes on the spine, suspiciously wrinkled pages, subtle differences in paper quality and ink color, etc.).

Wow, it's really clean. It almost looks . . . real.

My stomach lurches.

No, it's a fake. It has to be.

I quickly retrieve the telephone and dial Brooke's number at work.

The office secretary tells me in her thick Russian accent, "She eez vit kly-eent." That means her cell phone is off. Damn.

I'm going to have to weasel it out of Todd.

Unfortunately, Todd is a very good liar on the phone. In person—not so much. I'm going to have to confront him face to face and wait for the caterpillars to spell out the truth.

I slip on the nearest pair of shoes and race out of the apartment.

I march out of the apartment building and stride south toward the Lower East Side. I am on a mission. I will not deviate from my path. I won't even stop to window-shop, though I am in desperate need of a new pair of strappy black heels and the boutique on the corner has a gorgeous pair of sumptuous, satiny, bow-laced shoes just begging to be tried on.

I avert my eyes and weave in and out of the midday pedestrian traffic with the speed and agility of a dancer.

I can't let Todd know that this ticked me off—not at first. Todd senses weakness like a shark senses blood in the water. If he gets even the slightest hint that he's winning, he'll grab on and thrash around until I'm thoroughly maimed. I need to cool off, release the tension in my muscles, and put on my poker face.

Is this the kind of thing that ex-boyfriends do? I mean, I've seen various acts of romantic retaliation on *Judge Joe Brown* but I really didn't think it was that common in real life. (For people who don't take their ex-lovers to court over hundred-dollar bail loans, that is.) Truth be told, I don't know a lot about how to maintain a relationship with an ex. My old flames usually just disappear, slip back into the nameless, faceless population of New York—never to be seen or heard from again. I've been spoiled, I guess.

If this isn't just a normal prank, if Todd's motivation does have something to do with the breakup, how long exactly should I expect this sort of behavior to last? A week? Two? I'm really going to have to get Brooke's advice on this. She's been dumped loads of times. Oh, I'm sorry—correction—she prefers to call it being "laid off."

The little hand comes up on the crosswalk sign at Third Street. I pause at the corner and shake the circulation back to my hands and feet, like you see joggers do.

Between the groaning car engines and cab horns I hear a familiar sound over my left shoulder. It's faint, but distinctive. It's the sound of college, of photography class, of the days when I used real film instead of memory cards—the crisp, brisk, *snap-snap* of a camera shutter.

I scan the faces of those around me, survey each approaching person, then the several people waiting near me for the light to change. No cameras. No familiar faces. No stupid Todd.

Okay, maybe it was someone clapping a purse closed . . . or dropping something. Clicking plastic castanets? Oh, good God, I'm losing it.

I need to calm down. This is just a prank by a bitter ex-boyfriend. No one is taking pictures of me.

The sign finally switches over to read WALK and I resume my

stampede toward Adler Images, Ltd. As fellow pedestrians zoom by me, the strange sensation from the other day—the feeling that I'm being watched—crawls its way back up my spine and makes all the little hairs on the back of my neck stand at attention.

I stop and look behind me.

The characteristic double snap of a shutter rings out again.

I glance around, my eyes jumping frantically from face to face, window to window. I see nothing but the occasional embittered glare from a stranger whose face I'm inspecting.

This is silly.

Turning back downtown to resume my march, a sharp flicker of light suddenly catches my attention—not ten feet away—near a garbage can. It's the glare of reflected sunlight . . . off a camera lens!

A scruffy, incredibly creepy man holds a camera at an odd angle, resting its long lens against the top of the garbage can. He has a scraggly beard, a dirty red baseball cap, and an enormous camera bag. A pair of sunglasses hang crookedly from one of his ears, obscuring his nose and mouth. With his one visible eye he catches me staring at him and quickly rises. He does an awkward pirouette and stumbles into the alcove entrance of an all-you-can-eat Mongolian barbecue.

An instantaneous and violent shift has occurred. My eyes fill with thousands of little white dots. A bitter, coppery taste fills my mouth. My heart is thumping like the bass line of a 50 Cent song.

Someone is following me. With a camera.

I should run after the guy, root him out, get him to talk the way they do in the movies—with a sledgehammer or needle-nose pliers. As fun and satisfying as that sounds, I can't reconcile it with the apprehension and anxiety now spreading through my body. That guy is strange. There's something not quite right about him. My fight-or-flight instinct is screaming "Run, you idiot! Run!"

But I will not run—running is for wimps.

I will, however, walk briskly.

I start back down First Avenue as quickly as I can. I break into a jog only when I need to cross the street before the light changes to my disadvantage.

The creepy guy follows me for three blocks. He keeps up—matching my speed—but stays several paces behind. He conceals himself, by darting into shop fronts, each time I look over my shoulder to check his position.

I want to scream. I want to flag down the police and blab my story—but my pride won't let me. How demeaning would it be for me, *me* of all people, to beg for assistance because I'm being followed? Besides, I know who's doing it. It's Todd—or, rather, one of his cronies. He probably roped some friend of his into putting on a fake beard and doing this. If Todd gets wind that I am truly frightened, I'll never live it down.

I just have to get this guy off my tail, then I can find Todd and rip him a new one. This stalking thing is taking the prank a little too far.

I glance over my shoulder and spot the creepy guy behind me.

Approaching the next crosswalk, I see the sign begin to blink, warning that the light is about to change. A U-Haul box truck sits poised, ready to cut across.

Okay, this is my chance to make a break for it.

I stop, turn around, and with hands on hips, glare menacingly at my pursuer. He freezes, stunned. In a remarkably clumsy lateral move, he trips into an Everything-a-Dollar store—nearly taking out a homeless man, his dirty Shitzu, and his cart of cans.

The second the guy with the camera is out of sight I dart back toward the intersection. Ignoring the big hand telling me to stop, I race across the street—just as the U-Haul's engine kicks into first gear and lurches forward.

Safely on the other side, I sidestep a group of tourists and a priest. A tiny Chinese woman, carrying a handbag bigger than my apartment, sees me sprinting in her direction and twists slightly to avoid a collision. Her massive handbag reels up from her side and clips my left kneecap with incredible force. A piercing, searing pain shoots up my leg.

My God, what does she keep in there? Bricks?

Clutching my leg, I stumble into the nearest building—a grocery store.

The rush of cool refrigerated air is refreshing. I inhale and exhale slowly to calm my breathing and, hopefully, acquire the appearance of a typical afternoon grocery shopper.

I survey the surroundings slowly, looking for a place to hide. Bury myself under a pile of radicchio? Eat my way through the creamy poufs at the pastry counter and hide behind the giant oven? Wait, what am I, a rat?

To my right is a long bank of plate-glass windows facing the street. The checkout lines spill out in front of the windows and deposit paid customers at a door near the one I just entered.

I grab a box of macaroni and cheese from a cardboard display unit and limp into the longest line, all the while keeping my eyes trained on the windows and the sidewalk beyond.

A few moments pass, and then I see him. The creepy guy walks slowly past the windows. I raise the little blue box to my face and try to look fascinated by a recipe for franks 'n' noodles.

Outside, the creepy guy looks left, then right uptown, then downtown. He shakes his head and moves on, further downtown and out of view.

I let out the breath I didn't realize I was holding. My shoulders give a quick shudder, then relax.

"This is insane," I mumble to myself without thinking.

The man behind me smiles, a warm and open smile that makes me feel better. That is, it *almost* makes me feel better, until my eye lands on the magazine display to his left—front and center is *Celeb*.

I slowly reach across the aisle.

My heart beats faster with every inch.

This is silly; it's not going to be in there.

I grab the top copy of the magazine and flip through the corners to find page thirty-nine. Before looking at the page itself, I take a deep breath and attempt to laugh at my own foolishness.

Of course it's not going to be in there.

I open the magazine and scan the page from top to bottom. Oh, God. It's in here.

I drop the magazine on the floor and pick up the next copy on the rack . . .

. . . and the next . . .

. . . and the next . . .

I'm in all of them! ALL. OF. THEM.

The man who smiled at me now steps away—alarmed.

Actually, everyone is backing away—the lady in front of me, the cashier. The only person not backing up is a husky security guard; he's headed straight for me, fondling a nightstick.

Instinctively, I drop the box of macaroni, hop over the puddle of magazines at my feet, and race out of the store.

Okay, now it's time to run.

HOLLYWOOD'S HOT
NEW RELATIONSHIP TREND

The hip new Hollywood romance trend is the Secret Relationship. Nubile young thesps seeking to cash in on the fashion keep their paramours locked up and their lips sealed. No flitting hand in hand down the red carpet or breathless jaunts to the Ivy for them. Industry experts like über-publicist Marty Fergusson suggest it's the paparazzi who are responsible for the trend. "A lot of actors would like their relationships to progress the way regular people's do—without the pressure of being offered up for public consumption." Sex therapist Connie Cowen cites another theory. "It's about control and titillation. Many people find secrecy to be an aphrodisiac. Clandestine affairs can often be exhilarating and enjoyable, if not long lived."

Whatever the reason, Hollywood is all aflutter with rumor and conjecture. Matt Damon always prefers to keep his private life on the Q.T. Ethan Wyatt's secret rendezvous with his girlfriend's sister was exposed recently in notorious fashion. Longtime loves Beyoncé and Jay-Z still won't acknowledge they know each other. And the newest whispers indicate that Duncan Stoke has found himself a Big Apple beauty who is rumored to be (gasp!) a nonceleb. Hollywood loves nothing more than a trend.

CHAPTER 11

I stomp up the steps to Adler Images, Ltd., feeling like my skin is on fire. I want to scream, or cry, or . . . something, but I can't. I have to be calm, cool, and collected. I am an ice princess, a warrior, one of those steely-eyed she-beasts from Japanese video games.

I grasp the door handle and catch a glimpse of myself in the absurdly shiny front door.

Oh, crap. I look like a crazy person.

My hair is frizzed out at a dozen odd angles, my mascara has streaked out to my hairline from the right eye, and matted into a blob on the left. She-beast is right. No. No, actually, I bear a striking resemblance to Phyllis Diller.

I search the pocket of my jeans for any bit of tissue or napkin. Nothing. There's only one option: I must resort to the palm-and-spit method favored by cowlick-oppressing grannies. As I finger-comb my knotted hair with one hand, and wipe away the streaking mascara with the other, the door flies open.

"I'm flattered, but you don't have to try so hard, Sadie. I have, after all, already seen you naked." Todd grins at me with a facile smugness that makes me want to drop-kick him with my remaining good leg.

"Is that really how you want to start this?" I say, pushing past him and limping into the office.

"Start what?"

"Oh, you know *what*. You smug, arrogant—"

"Whoa, whoa, whoa!" Todd growls defensively. He lets the door fall closed and approaches me with his palms up, like a criminal miming that he's unarmed.

"You can't *whoa* me!" I bark, circling him as best I can while trying to avoid aggravating the knifelike pain shooting through my kneecap. "I suppose you thought it would be funny, right? Ha-ha! Sadie's in a tabloid. Hilarious."

"What are you talking about? Are you limping?"

"Don't try and change the subject—"

"I don't even *know* the subject!" he gripes, spinning around to make eye contact. "You're limping. Why are you limping? What happened?"

The genuine concern in his tone takes me momentarily off my guard. I stop—too quickly—and lose my balance. My left knee finally gives in to the pain.

Todd catches me under the arm and guides me to one of the garish white vinyl and chrome chairs in the lobby. "What is it?" He asks, while gently touching my ankle . . . calf . . . knee. Good God, that hurts. He winces in sympathy as I groan, and asks, "Your knee?"

I feel the annoying welling-up of tears in my eyes. I try to suppress the sobs rumbling inside me, causing a painful knot to form in my throat.

"Sit tight, Killer," Todd says as he leaps to his feet. "I'll be one minute."

I feel the tears trickle down my cheek, and the stiff knot in my throat relax, as a sob escapes my lips. Oh, God. I'm going to sit here and cry, tattered and broken, like Lucy Ricardo after one of her misguided romps. I am now a ne'er-do-well sitcom character.

Todd emerges from the office kitchenette with a Ziploc bag full of crushed party ice. He looks at me and tips his head in examination. "You're crying," he says empirically, as though he's just discovered some new and unexplained phenomenon.

"Yes, I am." Todd kneels down at my feet and presses the bag to my injured knee. "Why did you do this to me?" I continue, through a wave of cascading tears.

"Me? *I* did this?" he asks, while tenderly caressing my right hand.

Regaining my composure, I snarl, "Oh, come off it, Todd. You put the picture in *Celeb,* you had someone follow me today. You are responsible for what will undoubtedly be very expensive knee replacement surgery—"

"What picture in *Celeb,* Sadie?" Todd asks, in a really impressive display of feigned innocence.

"Page thirty-nine, Todd. Me, eating a burrito. Duncan Stoke's mystery girl."

"Sadie, I have absolutely no clue, on God's green earth, what the *fuck* you are talking about."

I stare at him—eye to eye. He doesn't flinch, doesn't allow

even a hint of cockiness to taint his expression. His thick black eyebrows arch over his black-brown eyes—squinting slightly, as though out of concern.

Oh, no. Oh, no!

No. No. No.

No!

I think he's telling the truth.

"Are you . . . serious?" I ask, swallowing hard. Please, please let him burst into laughter and run around the office in triumph. Please, let that be his next move. . . .

"I'm serious. And you're starting to worry me."

"Oh, shit. You're telling the truth."

"Yes, I am. Now, can you fill me in?"

"Do you have the new *Celeb*?" I ask frantically.

"No. The mail hasn't come yet—" I stand up and hobble toward the door. He continues, "Sadie, I don't think that's such a good idea."

"Get up, let's go."

I stagger past Fung Lau's Chinese Palace and the bustling Fed Ex store, dragging Todd behind me by the hand. The farther I go the more woozy I feel. I don't know if it's my knee or my brain that's the cause.

What the hell is going on? It has to be some kind of mistake, some horrible clerical error. A picture of me was mistakenly plopped into some editor's inbox. Wires got crossed. Something!

I burst into Harry Moisha's Deli and press my way past a delivery guy and three people waiting for Lotto tickets. I screech to a halt at the small stand of newspapers and magazines near the register.

I grab the top copy of *Celeb* and shove it into Todd's hands.

He tears into the magazine, finds the page, and says calmly, "Yep, that's you all right."

"Yeah. It's me."

Todd inspects the picture closely, folds the pages back to look in the crook of the spine. "There's no photo credit."

"Yeah, I know. I thought it was you. Someone was following me, too. The other day when I was out shopping, and then today—"

"You thought I had you followed?"

"I thought . . . I don't know what I thought, okay? Help me out here. I've been slandered . . . and maimed."

"Getting called the secret girlfriend of a movie star doesn't qualify as slander."

"Oh, really?" I bite.

Todd, ignoring my hostility, goes back to inspecting the photo. "I don't recognize the work. Do you?"

I shake my head no.

"It almost looks amateur." He takes a deep breath, appraises *Celeb* some more. "Maybe it's just some kid trying to make a buck. It happens—"

"When does that happen, Todd? I've never heard of that happening."

"It *could* happen," he replies weakly.

I throw my hands up and roll my eyes. "If it's a prank, that's one thing. But this was only taken a few days ago," I say, pointing to the photo in *Celeb*. "How did it get in the paper so fast?

How did it make it through fact-checking? No one's even given me a chance to deny it." Mistakes happen in tabloid news—all the time. But something about this is just too . . . *strange* to have been an accident.

"Look, calm down. I know a couple of guys at the magazine. Let me make a few calls and get back to you. Meantime, you go home and relax. Call your *boyfriend . . .* or whatever," he adds while conspicuously rolling his eyes.

That would be a great idea—if I actually had a boyfriend to call. He would come over with Pop-Tarts and rub my shoulders and help me forget this horrible day. That's the sort of thing real boyfriends do. As opposed to imaginary ones, who just lie there doing nothing—or appear in major national publications.

I limp toward the front door of the deli. Over the melodic *chug chug chug* of Lotto tickets being printed I hear Todd call out, "Sadie?"

I turn to him.

Todd smiles in that easy, confident way he does. "We'll get this sorted out in no time. All right? Not a big deal."

I give him a smile, trying to reciprocate his steady certainty. My head keeps telling me he's right, that this is just a foolish, harmless error. Unfortunately, my gut doesn't seem to agree.

I have a bad feeling about this.

DUNCAN STOKED ABOUT
BURRITO BABE

Cha-cha-cha! A certain mystery blonde, pictured here snarfing down one of those addictive-like-crack Chipotle Grill burritos, is said to be Duncan Stoke's new secret love. Guess *he's* not on a low-fat diet. (Wink, wink.)

—Staff

www.stokecentral.com

CHAPTER 12

"What are you two doing here?" I ask, shocked to find Luke and Brooke sitting in the living room on a workday. "I thought you had a premiere, Luke."

I stumble into the apartment, dragging my injured leg behind me. In one swift motion, Brooke mutes the television and shoots up out of her seat. Startled, Luke mimics Brooke, then moves swiftly to her side. His pale green eyes are grave, troubled. He nervously shoves his hands in the pockets of his jeans.

"Sadie," Brooke croons, "we have something to tell you."

"Oh, God! Someone died."

"No, no one's dead. But you may want to sit down for this," she says calmly.

Brooke elbows Luke sharply in the ribs. He responds by shuffling to my side, taking my arm, and guiding me to the nearest chair.

"What is it?" I ask, becoming increasingly concerned at the anxiety on Brooke's face, and the dense fog of tension and apprehension that seems to be permeating every square inch of our apartment.

"Apparently, well . . ." Brooke begins. "Um . . ." Brooke turns to Luke for help.

He starts, "Brooke saw something today. And then she called me and we did a little digging and . . . well, somebody . . . I mean, it seems a large number of somebodys think that you're dating Duncan Stoke."

I breathe a sigh of relief. "I know. *Celeb,* right? I just came from seeing Todd. I thought it might have been one of his pranks. But—"

"It's not just *Celeb,* Sadie," interrupts Brooke. "I saw it on-line—"

"Online?" I yelp.

"And . . ." Brooke's voice trails off. She grabs a stack of newspaper and sheaves of printer paper. As if in slow motion I watch as Brooke lays each of the publications in a fan shape on the coffee table.

The room slowly, subtly begins to spin around me. I turn my head away from the coffee table and watch the closed captioning on the muted TV spell out CNN's latest on the world's natural disasters—earthquakes, floods, Tom Cruise's love life. I half expect to see "Sadie Price framed as Duncan Stoke's girlfriend . . ." tick across the screen.

The heavy thumping in my chest begins to slow, and the panic I've felt for the last several hours shifts smoothly, quietly into a sort of numbness.

I have now entered an alternate reality.

*   *   *

Each of the magazines features a picture of me. I'm in *all* the papers. Assorted shots of me walking, chattering on my new cell phone, and rubbing expensive silk panties against my cheek are in no fewer than three New York dailies, one national daily, two glossies, and on countless websites.

I. Am. Famous.

I am famous for being the burrito-loving, panty-sniffing secret girlfriend of a celebrity whose name sounds remarkably like that of a porn star. In other words, my life is now the stuff of farce. In two days I've gone from relatively ordinary, skipped straight past slightly odd, rocketed over fairly bizarre, and landed right in unbelievably weird territory.

Oh, but on the bright side, I've finally managed to wrangle myself a boyfriend who is both inattentive and emotionally unavailable. Well done, me.

"One paper could be an accident . . . a mistake. But this . . ." I say, pointing to the massive collection of photos and stories. "This is something . . . *different*." I've never seen anything like it. Ever.

"And all the papers on the same day," adds Luke. "It's not even like *Celeb* had it and the bad information spread to the other papers. That would take weeks, not hours—"

"We're talking in circles," says Brooke.

"Do you have any enemies? Anyone who might want to harm you in any way?" Luke asks. He obviously got all his investigative skills from watching prime-time cop dramas. He sounds exactly like a character from *Law & Order*.

"Do you think if I knew who took these I'd be *here*? No, I'd be out beating him or her to a bloody pulp."

"Are you dating him?" asks Brooke with just the slightest hint of jealousy in her voice.

"No. Are you kidding? No!"

Brooke's shoulders slump down a little, her whole demeanor switches from empathy to relief. "Right. Of course."

I can do nothing but shake my head at her. She actually thought I stole her fantasy man. This is so bizarre.

I reach across the coffee table and pick up the phone receiver to dial Todd's number; I need to see if he's found anything out.

Great, there's no freaking dial tone.

"What's wrong with the phone?" I ask indignantly.

"We had to unplug it," replies Luke.

"It's been ringing off the hook since we got here," adds Brooke.

"Could you please plug it in for me?" I ask Luke. "I have to call Todd."

Luke plods across the room and pushes the cord back into the wall socket. The second he does, the phone's shrill ring floods the apartment.

I click the ON button. "Hello?"

"Sadie, it's you! I've been trying to get you all morning."

I instantly feel all the blood drain from my face, and my hands become cold and jittery.

"Mother," I say—the closest thing to a greeting I can manage just now.

"How are you, darling?" she asks between my deep calming breaths.

"Fine," I say. I really don't want to get into all this with her. This is one of those times when a real mother would come in handy. Unfortunately I don't have a real mother. I have a *Paige*.

"Oh, Sadie. We're all just so excited for you. You're just the talk of the town. The ladies at my golf outing this morning were going on and on about it. They all want to be invited to the wedding," she says cheerily.

"The *wedding*?" I scream.

"Duncan Stoke, of course, honey. You know, it's the funniest thing. . . . Dr. Hank and I rented *Empire of Glory* just last week. I didn't particularly care for it, but Hank positively adored it. Duncan is quite—"

"Mother," I interrupt.

". . . handsome, though. I always hoped that something good would come of this . . . well . . . this *career* thing you've been trying. I had a feeling you would run into one of these celebrities—"

"Mother!" I try again.

". . . and get along. You're so *creative,* after all, darling—"

"*Mother!*" I blast at the top of my lungs. Brooke covers her ears, while Luke sinks down into the sofa, pretending not to listen.

Sweet blissful silence finally prevails. I start, "I am not dating Duncan Stoke. This a huge mistake. I don't even know him. I've never even *photographed* him."

"Oh," she says, disappointed. She adds, "Well, that is a shock." I guiltily imagine her standing on the seventh tee, in her plaid capri pants and pink sun visor, leaning on her golf bag— the same red as her nails—while breaking the "upsetting" news to her golf ladies. Then, of course, she'll have to explain what I do for a living to clarify how the "misunderstanding" might have come about. I have to admit, I do get the tiniest bit of satisfaction from the fact that my job runs counter to my mother's sensibilities.

"I'm actually contemplating legal action," I lie. "I'm going to get it straightened out."

"I'm so sorry." She doesn't say it like she's sorry that I'm in this predicament, or with some empathy for my obvious emotional turmoil. She says it like I should be disappointed in myself for not having landed a movie star.

Brooke, cupping her hands around her mouth, shouts, "Sadie, I need some help!"

"I have to go," I say to my mother. I mouth "Thank you" to Brooke.

"All right, dear. Just one more thing. I sent a package to you—"

Damn, the Brown Box. "I, uh . . . haven't had a chance . . . I mean, I got it. But I really have to go. I'll call you . . ." When? When do I want to call her? Tomorrow? Next week? Next month? Christmas? ". . . soon."

I hastily say good-bye and hang up the phone.

"Okay, I've got to get this under control," I say to no one in particular. "My mother's golf buddies are *proud* of me. This is ridiculous."

Right on cue, the phone begins ringing again. Two seconds later, it's joined by the buzzing of the lobby intercom button.

Brooke sprints to the intercom box, and Todd's voice echoes through the apartment, "Is she there?"

I gingerly get out of the chair, hobble to the phone jack, and yank the cord from the wall.

*   *   *

In no time, Todd is standing in the entryway, panting. He's the only person I know who can get winded from taking the elevator.

Todd bounds toward us with a stack of papers in his hands. He lays the pile on our little dining table and says, "I don't want you to get upset—"

"I've seen them, Todd."

"Oh." His countenance shifts. He casually rests his hand on the pile of papers and looks at me with a devilish and strangely come-hither smirk. "You're dating him, aren't you? Come on, you can tell me. That sob story in my office was just to throw me off, right? Come on, Sadie, your secret's safe with me."

I can't help but let out a chuckle.

"What?" he continues. "He's the guy who answered the cell phone, yeah? That was Stoke. I thought he sounded like an actor—"

But it's the word *actor* that makes my stomach lurch. Change the subject now, Sadie! "So what did you find out about the photographer?"

"I couldn't get any info on him."

I groan in disbelief as Todd expounds. "I'm not kidding, Sadie, no one's talking. All I could find out is that the pictures are coming from a very anonymous source, and the source carries some pretty heavy clout."

"What the hell? Heavy clout?" Someone with clout wants to screw me over? Okay, well, technically lots of people with clout want to screw me over. But who would actually do it?

And, the story shouldn't be this big. Okay, granted, it's just a few blurbs here and there, but they're in *all* the papers. "Well connected" doesn't even begin to describe whoever did this to me. To be able to convince all these news outlets of a complete fallacy is huge. Even when a tabloid story is made up, there's usually a grain of truth in there somewhere—or at least the appearance of a grain. *This* doesn't make any sense. Who would be psycho enough to stalk me, take pictures of me, and then publish those pictures in grand style all over the country?

Only one name springs to mind: Ethan Wyatt.

Ethan Wyatt might just be crazy enough to do it. He blames me for the car crash. For the Lori Dunn story. He said what goes around comes around.

No. It couldn't be. This is way too deranged, even for him. If nothing else, it's far too dangerous. If he got caught the story would be twenty times juicier than the one about him cheating with his alleged girlfriend's sister. No. Impossible.

"We're talking *heavy* clout," Todd emphasizes for effect. "So trusted they wouldn't doubt it . . . reliable . . . *credible—*"

"Where are you going with this, Todd?" I ask.

"Like, Duncan Stoke's manager, maybe?" he suggests, wide-eyed—accusing me.

Dear God, I'm surrounded by the mentally ill.

"Todd, I want you to listen carefully. I am not dating Duncan Stoke. It's a lie. Got me?"

"Fine," he says with a huff.

"No, not fine. *Lie.*"

"Got it," Todd replies with a roll of his eyes.

I know he's not convinced, but at this point I don't really care.

The whole group meanders to the living room as Todd regales us with more details of his investigation. He tells me his friends only knew that the source of my burrito picture was someone who could pull strings, but they couldn't say who.

"Couldn't say who because they were protecting a source? Or couldn't say who because they didn't know?" Luke asks.

"Arnie, the editor over there that I play poker with, he tried to play it off like he didn't want me to poach his source, but my gut tells me *he* doesn't even know who the guy is. He just knows that this guy gives solid information. That's why they printed it."

"Did you tell him it was completely untrue?" I try.

Todd nods his head yes, then adds sullenly, "He didn't believe me."

"Unbelievable," I gripe. "Did you give him the description of the weird guy with the beard who was following me?" I ask, grasping at straws.

"Yeah, but that's just it, Sadie. Nobody's even laid eyes on the guy. He's a ghost," Todd replies. Why do I suddenly get the feeling that Todd fancies himself the hero in a Dan Brown novel? "Oh, and there's something else, Sadie," Todd adds gravely.

"Great!" I snap sarcastically. "Go ahead, hit me."

"*Celeb*, *Star*, and *Us Weekly* all have plans to run more photos next week."

I rub my bloodshot eyes with the palms of my hands. I can't believe this is happening. It's just so completely absurd.

I hear my new cell phone tolling its factory-issued ring in the bedroom.

"You want me to get that? Shut it off?" Brooke asks thoughtfully.

"No, thanks," I say, slowly limping my way toward the bedroom. "Maybe it's Diane Sawyer and I can get this whole thing sorted out in a matter of minutes."

If only.

I release the phone from its charger. The face of the phone blinks a number I don't recognize. Maybe it's someone with some information . . . or maybe Paige went out and bought one of those anonymous disposable cell phones that criminals use. . . .

I'll just have to take my chances. "Hello?"

"I see you got another cell phone," comes a distinctive, irritatingly familiar male voice. A veritable swarm of butterflies begins flapping somewhere between my stomach and my chest. "I guess that explains why my calls to Thailand didn't go through."

"You better mean Thai *food,* Wyatt. If there is a single charge to Thailand on my bill, my lawyers will eat you alive." I think I said that pretty convincingly for a person without so much as a paralegal. (Well, I do know a guy, who is friends with a guy who played a lawyer once on *Monk.* That count?)

"Please do, I'll have them discuss that little incident at blé with *my* lawyers."

Oh, right—*that.* The butterflies threaten to burst free through my belly button.

"Is that it, Wyatt? Is that all you called for?" I ask sternly.

"No, actually. I picked up a copy of *Celeb* today—to catch up on what I've been doing lately—and who should I see there . . ."

It is everything I can do not to scream bloody murder and throw my brand-new phone against the wall.

Ethan continues, "I never would have pegged you as the beefcake, glossy, metrosexual type. I mean, Duncan's so *shiny*. How can you stand it?"

How dare he insult my fake boyfriend! "Oh, you're one to talk. Maya Dunn glows so much she's practically radioactive." I promise, in my head that sounded a lot more like an insult.

"It's amazing how you guys can so completely convince yourselves these things are the truth. You don't actually think I was dating her. Do you? She's totally not my type." Oh, God. They *weren't* dating. "Lori was all right," he says in a low voice, as though talking to himself. "But she was a little shiny, too, honestly. This powdery, glittery stuff, fucking *everywhere*. All over my clothes—" He stops suddenly and raises his voice, as though he's just remembered who he's talking to. "Anyway . . ."

"Is there a point coming anytime soon? Or should I clear my schedule for the next several hours?"

"Oh, let's see," he says, with a touch of real glee in his voice. "I have your schedule right here." He goes silent for several moments. "No, looks like you're clear. But I should remind you that you have a bikini wax on Friday at noon."

Ugh! "I want that phone back!" I shout. My life is on that phone. Every little private thing I do is on that phone. And he has access to all of it!

"And ruin my fun?" he replies smugly.

"Look, it may mean nothing to you, but some of us don't have minions to go around buying cell phones for us every day."

"You think I have minions? Come on!" he says, aghast. "Do you know how expensive minions are these days?"

"All right, that's enough. Good-bye, Wyatt."

"See you around, Sadie." The tone of his voice sends a little shiver up my back. That was one supercharged "See you around."

Could Ethan Wyatt really be the one behind this? I mean, if I were in his place and I'd just had my life split open and exposed for all the world to see, would I do something like this? Wait a second, I *have*. And I don't really care about exposing whoever did this to me . . . I'd rather just disembowel them.

But what if it is Ethan Wyatt? What if he's stalking me and trying to make my life miserable because I got that picture of him at blé? Because I may have gone a tiny—a *teensy* tiny—bit over the line?

No, that's insane, even for a phone-stealing maniac. It's too crazy.

I limp to the kitchen, fix myself a cup of coffee, and dig out as many chocolate-flavored food items as I can find.

"Hey, Sadie," pipes Todd from the next room, "you got any idea where Wyatt is?"

"What?" I say, shocked, fearing, if only for a moment, that Todd can read my mind. I clear my throat. "You mean, Ethan Wyatt?"

"Yeah, *Ethan* Wyatt."

"No. Why do you ask?"

"Nobody's seen him since the blé story broke. He's been finding a way out of the hotel—looking at apartments or something—but nobody knows how."

"Sorry, can't help you," I say as calmly as I can while my heart begins to tap out the bongo drum line from "Copacabana."

"Right," Todd replies glumly.

In a matter of nanoseconds Todd, Luke, and Brooke are back into loquacious nattering, swapping theories about my pursuer and his motives. Brooke and Luke pour through the fresh batch of papers Todd brought while Todd examines Brooke's printouts of the many Internet notices.

From across the room I hear Brooke call out, "Sadie!"

"Yeah," I reply, before cramming a half-dozen donut holes in my mouth.

She holds up a daily newspaper—oh great, a new picture of me—buying tampons. In it, my eyes are sleepy and puffy, and my hair is a matted clump of strawberry blonde. That's just perfect. Great. It's embarrassing on so many levels—new, as yet undiscovered levels of humiliation. Love that.

"I thought you were PMS-ing a couple of weeks ago?" Brooke asks matter-of-factly.

"No." I return her leisurely tone, despite the utter humiliation resulting from the question. "Turns out I was just *bitchy*."

"You don't have to be nasty. I'm just trying to figure this out," she replies.

Todd pipes up, "She's always a little, you know, *off* when it's that time of the month."

Luke and Brooke groan and nod their agreement.

"I'm right here!" I exclaim, but they take no notice. They're too engrossed in Todd's latest theory—that I am the dopple-ganger of Duncan Stoke's actual secret girlfriend and the papers have gotten me mixed up with her.

I turn back and ransack the cupboards for more sweets.

"Uh . . . Sadie?" I hear Luke say, tremulously.

"What?" I reply, immediately turning to him with concern for the peculiar tone in his voice.

His eyes are raised toward the television screen; his index finger points in the same direction.

I follow his gaze—*Entertainment Tonight*.

My lungs empty of air, every muscle turns to jelly.

My face is on *Entertainment Tonight*.

Still shots of me—a little slide show—eating a burrito, drinking coffee, walking to the grocery store.

Holy shit—I've gone omnimedia.

Because the television is on mute, my only clue to the meaning of this horrible new development is the unbelievably unreliable closed-captioning running across the bottom of the screen.

It reads: "Dunkaan Stooke has girlfriend. Sheeis a photo grapher in New York City. Couple sadi to be havin long distinnnce relation ship for &7 seven weeks or moore . . ."

My mind is cloudy, nothing makes sense. None of this makes sense. I can't process it all. I have never experienced this particular level of chaos. It's beyond raining and pouring now. It might be time to start thinking about an ark.

Todd, Luke, and Brooke stare at me—waiting.

"Okay, help me out here," I say with an uncontrollable quivering. "Was I just on TV?" Please, tell me I'm hallucinating.

The three of them nod their heads up and down.

"Yeah, I was afraid of that." I take a breath and clench my fists to keep my hands from shaking. "All right," I state imperiously. "That's it. This has got to stop. *Now*."

DUNCAN STOKING YOUNG
HOLLYWOOD'S FIRE

In a recent interview Duncan Stoke, star of the upcoming "Finding Her" and "The Speed of Light," spoke at length about his fame, the effect of it on his personal life, and what he calls "some women's inexplicable fascination with my buttocks." Nothing new for the twenty-eight-year-old hottie, but something else Duncan revealed is causing a stir. It seems the interviewer asked Duncan how he's managed to stay out of trouble, unlike other hot young Hollywood hunks like Ethan Wyatt. Duncan responded by saying, "Guys like Ethan are clinging to a juvenile and dangerous idea of what it means to be young in Hollywood. They don't take their work seriously and party too hard without giving a single thought to what might happen to them or their careers. I've managed to stay out of trouble in the press by not doing stupid things in public. I keep my private life private. Guys like Ethan will never get that." Duncan is stoking a long-burning fire. A long-standing friendship between the two came to an abrupt end after their notorious brawl at Bar Marmont in 2001, which ended with Wyatt in handcuffs. The two have been sparring ever since. The interview, which took place before Ethan Wyatt's most recent tabloid troubles, will be published in its entirety in July's "Maxim."

—Donna Herschel for HPB NewsWire

CHAPTER 13

We're now beginning stage three of Operation Condor. Luke chose the name—claimed something about it being a God-given right afforded him by the presence of testosterone in his bloodstream. Brooke wanted to call it Shock and Moi, which, I have to agree with Luke and Todd on this one, does sound more like a Barneys sample sale than a serious covert operation. I thought a simple Find Duncan Stoke would suffice, but I lost that little fracas.

See, while I was watching the second night of *Entertainment Tonight* coverage (that is, after my life stopped flashing before my eyes), it occurred to me that *I* may not be the target of this tabloid assault. I don't know why I didn't think of it before, but it's perfectly obvious—Duncan Stoke is the target. He's the one who has the most to lose in this whole thing, right? I mean, it's his precious image they're tarnishing. Maybe I'm just collateral damage, an innocent bystander. I could have been chosen at random, or . . . something. In any event, Duncan Stoke will probably know who's behind this.

So far the highlight of Operation Condor is Brooke finding an online poll about me. Apparently, nine out of ten Stoke fans—or I should say, nine out of ten fans that frequent the Duncan Stoke Hottie McHotHot website—believe that I'm not good enough for him. Oh, and that my head is too big for my body. But in a bit of good news, the other 1 percent of fans think that I am, and I quote, "not too terrible." Things are looking up already.

I know Duncan is in town this week, doing press for the Memorial Day opening of *The Speed of Light*. And we know that he taped Letterman this afternoon. I've tried getting more information from my sources, but I'm not getting anything concrete. The conversations have all degenerated into lame, acrimonious remarks like "What? *You* don't know where he is?" and "It's not *my* problem you can't keep track of your boyfriend."

Suddenly Luke's voice rings through the apartment at high volume. "Really?" he says excitedly into his cell phone. Instinctively, Todd, Brooke, and I rise from our seats.

Luke begins waving his arm around like he's found something. He continues into the phone, "Every time? . . . Okay . . . all right . . . great, man. . . . Yeah, thanks."

Luke snaps his phone shut dramatically. "Got him."

"When? What? How?" I stutter.

"Stoke apparently worked at a bar on the Upper West Side when he was first starting out—"

"The Lodge," Brooke says matter-of-factly, as though everyone on the planet knows that random bit of Duncan Stoke trivia.

Luke is a little weirded out, but continues, "Yeah. And, it seems he always—and my source says *always*—goes there when he comes into town."

"They let him drink for free," I suggest. The dirty little secret of celebrity millionaires: half the reason they're so rich is that they never have to pay for anything.

"Exactly," says Luke. "But here's the thing, my guy also says Stoke goes to another place farther up on Ninety-sixth called . . ."

Luke, Todd, and I all look to Brooke for the answer.

She stares back at us blankly and asks, "What?"

Luke continues, "The Dive Bar."

"So, he could be at either," I state.

"Right," says Luke. "More likely the Lodge, but it might be better to be safe than sorry."

"Okay," I say, while wandering around the apartment, following the well-tread path of the crazy old sisters who lived here before us. "Okay, the point is to talk to him, not get his picture. So I'm going to need a plan."

"*We*," says Brooke sharply. "*We* are going to need a plan."

The Lodge, as it's so aptly named, is clad in grungy knotty pine and features a rather large, rickety chandelier made entirely of antlers. The tables and booths are heavily carved, not with any decorative motif, but rather with choice hand-hewn phrases like "Tim-bo wuz here" and "Rock On, White Snake."

Brooke and I couldn't be more conspicuous if we were buck-naked, singing show tunes. Our femaleness is somehow exaggerated by the surroundings and the clientele. It's as if we're wearing neon signs that say "Look here—boobies!"

Adding to our high profile at The Lodge, we've been here far longer than any sane single women would be on any ordinary night. The youngest and most eligible man in the bar is a surly leather-clad biker in his mid- to late-fifties.

I've been trying to act naturally, and have attempted to engage Brooke in casual conversation, but it's not going well. Brooke is beside herself with anticipation. She checks her lipstick—or asks *me* to—every time she takes a sip of beer. She's also been repeatedly smoothing down her hair like someone with obsessive-compulsive disorder. Brooke has never been a particularly patient person (she's the girl who always gets next-day shipping, regardless of price), but the added excitement of being so very close to her celebrity dream—Duncan Stoke, in the flesh and possibly inebriated—is making her practically vibrate with excitement. I've had to pretend to be engrossed in the copy of *Celeb* I brought along as evidence, so that at least one of us doesn't seem like a jittering, mumbling weirdo.

I feel Brooke's leg flapping away under the table—and then a sharp pain in my shin.

"You need to calm down," I whisper across the booth.

"I *am* calm. Perfectly, totally calm," she says, before letting out an eerie, nervous giggle.

"Whoa."

"No, I'm fine. Really, I'll be fine."

My phone rings. Brooke jumps—nearly over the table.

"Seriously, breathe or something," I tell her.

I answer the phone.

Luke's voice rings out. "Just heard from a guy I know at The Palm. He said that Stoke and his entourage—"

"Shit, he has an *entourage*?" I don't know why I'm surprised.

"Three guys, maybe four. Anyway, my guy says they finished eating a few minutes ago, and he heard them say they were heading to The Lodge."

"Okay, thanks."

"We'll stay here for a bit, just in case. Then head over."

"Perfect," I reply.

I hear some faint crackling and Todd's voice trickles into my ear. "Hey, Sadie?"

"Yeah?"

"Good luck."

"Thanks." I'm going to need it.

I barely have time to hang up before Brooke starts in. "What? Is he coming?"

"Yes, Duncan's coming."

"Great. Fine. All right," she says, as though mentally ticking items off a checklist. "I'm just going to head to the ladies' for a minute. Be right back."

She slides out of the booth and saunters to the restroom with aplomb—practicing for Duncan, no doubt.

Brooke returns from the bathroom in remarkable time. She enters the room a new woman; she is radiant. Her hair flutters behind her like chocolate-colored silk, and as she ambles back to the table her hips sway seductively, as though knocking out the rhythm to David Bowie's "Rebel Rebel." It's definitely not the fresh coat of lip stain and renewed matte (yet, somehow mysteriously dewy) finish of her skin, but a complete change in her countenance. She is calm, confident. Reaching our booth, she drapes herself on the seat like a silver screen seductress. She is Rita Hayworth, Ava Gardner, and Greta Garbo combined.

"What did you do in there?" I ask, genuinely perplexed.

"Just freshened up."

"With *what*?" I find it hard to believe that something that magical is bottled, sold in stores, and I haven't found it yet. "Does it work on cellulite?" I add.

"Really, Sadie."

Yeah, *really*.

A loud noise at the entrance to the bar jostles me out of my cosmetic inquiry—one boisterous, solid-gold movie star, complete with entourage.

I feel around the booth for my camera. Oh, my God, I'm like Pavlov's freaking dog.

Duncan Stoke bounds into the bar to a hail of hellos and handshakes from the bartenders and some rough-and-tumble types that must be regulars.

He's a little shorter than I thought he'd be, about my height, with dark chiseled features. There's a hint of the exotic about him. It's just enough to give his face a touch of mystery and allure, but not enough to escape the moniker All-American Babe. Duncan Stoke is the captain of the football team, the Homecoming King, the slightly naughty boy next door. He just looks . . . fresh or . . . oh, my God, Ethan was right—Duncan Stoke is *shiny*. It's like he's been scrubbed and polished to a high sheen. He's so cleverly fine-tuned that if you flicked him I bet

he'd ding like leaded crystal. Man, this guy was *born* to be photographed.

I only recognize one of the guys in Duncan's entourage—
Tony Servedio. He's a great, classically trained actor who's gotten
typecast as a mobster. He's cute and, I hear, very sweet, but has a
real talent for playing shifty and complicated. The other two
don't look familiar, but they're not slick enough to be agents or
managers. They must be friends from the old days—there's an
awful lot of nostalgic backslapping going on. That's good—an
agent or manager could have spelled doom for my plan to speak
to him.

Duncan and his minions take four seats at the bar. Almost
instantly, overflowing pints of beer and shot glasses filled with a
brown liquid are plopped in front of them.

Well, no time like the present . . .

I push myself away from the table and attempt to stand.
Brooke quickly slaps a hand on mine. "Let's just observe for a
while, shall we?" she says earnestly.

What she means is, let's just sit here and watch him like he's
a zoo animal. Although, judging by the look of absolute concen-
tration in Brooke's eyes, I think Duncan may be a little more
like prey.

"Sorry," I say to Brooke, before rising from the table. I don't
have time to let her formulate a plan for conquest. I need answers—now.

I grab my copy of *Celeb* and march to the bar.

Standing over his left shoulder, I wait for Duncan Stoke to
look up at me.

Duncan, smack in the middle of his three friends, won't even

glance in my direction. I can literally *feel* him avoiding eye contact. One of his nonfamous friends sneers at me and says, "He's
not giving autographs tonight, sweetheart." Ah, a tried-and-true
intimidation technique—patronizing the "little" woman.

It won't work on me, though, especially since there's no way
this guy's a bodyguard. The sneerer in question weighs about
a 130 pounds—soaking wet—and there's no way he's packing
anything more dangerous than halitosis.

I ignore the overenthusiastic hanger-on and speak directly to
Duncan. "We need to talk."

This sends his three friends, and the bartender, into fits of
laughter.

Duncan tries to laugh it off as well, but is visibly unnerved
by me. "I'm sorry, do I *know* you?" he asks, with just a dash of
arrogance, and more than a smidgen of paranoia.

"Haven't you heard?" I ask tersely. I slap *Celeb* down on the
bar. "We're dating."

Duncan's private peanut gallery goes silent. For his part,
Duncan examines me—for signs of homicidal tendencies, I'm
sure.

He spins around on his chair, grabs my wrist with one hand
and the magazine with the other.

Duncan commands, "Come with me."

Duncan drags me by the hand through a dingy hallway. Three
flickering, grime-covered bulbs swing from the low ceiling; it's
barely enough light to see the back of Duncan's inhumanly
shiny hair. My feet clop and splash in pools of who knows what
sort of bar filth.

After a few moments, we pass through a grim, thickly cluttered storage room. With three agile strides, Duncan leads me through a path in the jumble of old bar stools, discarded tabletops, and damaged stemware. He stops when we reach a thick steel door. Duncan flicks a large metal lever and pushes on the door.

I hear the pitter-patter of footsteps behind me. If I'm not mistaken, it sounds like size seven high heels. Hallelujah.

Duncan finally lets go of my wrist as I stumble out of the building and into a grisly, deserted back alley. It's lit by several halogen floodlights, which hang over three unmarked steel doors. Across the alley is a wide truck delivery bay. We are completely alone, save for probably a million huge, disease-ridden rats lurking just outside the random pools of light. I think I can hear them gnashing their pointy little teeth.

"What do you want?" Duncan asks me, a small vein popping out of his neck.

"I want *that* to stop," I say, pointing at the magazine in his hand.

"How do I know you're not the one doing it in the first place?" he asks sharply.

Oh, crap. Could he really be as clueless as I am? "You mean *you* don't know who's doing it?"

He stares at me—appraising, judging.

Okay, Sadie, this is your big chance to be a normal, articulate, rational human being. I speak. "Look, I could be a crazy stalker realizing her dream of kidnapping you and grinding you into dog food. . . ." Right, that didn't come out as planned. "But," I continue, "I'm not." Wow, smooth.

Duncan chuckles. "That's what they all say."

"You really, seriously don't know what all this is about?"

"No," he replies with regret. "You?"

"No."

A loud clattering catches our attention. The door we just came from swings open and Brooke peeks her head around.

"Oh, there you are," she says breezily.

"Who's this?" asks Duncan, stepping away. "Your accomplice?"

"My—"

She interrupts. "I'm Sadie's best friend, Brooke Nolan." She gracefully extends her hand. "Nice to meet you."

As he shakes her hand, I see Brooke's face color. Lucky for her, it's dark out here.

Brooke continues, "I apologize. I interrupted you. Please, go on."

"Hmmm, let's see, where were we?" I say, my voice cracking and getting louder of its own accord. "Oh, that's right—nobody knows *anything*!"

I pace back and forth between Duncan and Brooke—who can't take her eyes off him. It looks a bit like she wants to eat him, though, not date him.

I stop in front of Duncan. "Listen to me, you have to think. Is there anyone who might want to play a trick on you? Have you beaten up any photographers lately? Um . . . knocked up any girls with burly, photographically inclined boyfriends? Refused some starlet who wanted to fu—"

Brooke approaches from behind and slings her arm through mine—half petting my arm, half slapping it. "Sadie, calm down.

There's no need to insult the man." Why does she sound more and more like her mother as this night progresses?

"I have a *ton* of enemies, dude." My fake boyfriend uses the word *dude*. "But I don't know of any who would make up shit like this. It's got to be someone at the tabloid looking for a story."

"I don't think so. I *really* don't think so. This isn't the *Weekly-freaking-World*, okay? We're not talking about babies born with horns and the world's fattest mailman. It was on *Entertainment Tonight*!"

"Wow, this really bothers you. Am I that bad?" he asks, trying to lighten the mood.

"No," Brooke blurts unexpectedly.

He looks at Brooke quizzically, then continues to me, "If there's one thing I've learned over the last few years, it's that these things always go away eventually. Some big story will break and the vultures will circle over some other carcass. They love fresh meat."

"Are you insulting *me* now?" I ask.

Brooke digs her nails into my forearm and whispers, "Ixnay on the objay." Then smiles coyly at Duncan.

"What do you do?" he asks with keen interest.

Brooke lets go of me and raises her arms in defeat. Oh, yeah—shocking. He speaks pig latin. Who knew?

People hate me. "I'm a . . . photographer." Just now, in my head, "paparazzi" has a ring of sleaziness about it.

"What's wrong with that?"

"Acelebrityphotographer," I mumble.

"You're a *paparazzi*?" he asks, aghast.

"That has nothing to do with this. Do I have a camera on me? This is my life we're talking about here, all right?"

Stoke begins laughing—uproariously. Between cackles, he manages to wheeze, "You're a paparazzi, who's being harassed by the paparazzi?" He wipes away a tear of laughter. "Pretty poetic justice, don't you think?" He says before snorting and digressing again into laughter.

I don't know why, but the sound of his laugh suddenly makes me want to pound him. And did he say *justice*? "I am not a celebrity. I haven't been involved in any scandal. I am not a public figure. This doesn't make any sense!"

I feel the heavy weight of tears threatening to flow, a hollow pit forming in my stomach. I cover my eyes, pressing my palms against them, in hopes that it will stem the tide.

"Sadie? Is that your name?" Duncan asks in a low, silky smooth voice. I nod my head. He continues, "Sadie, I'm sorry. I didn't mean to insult you."

I take my hands from my eyes. Duncan puts a hand on each of my shoulders.

He adds, "I swear, it'll all go away. It'll stop. Everything is going to be fine—"

Without warning a bright flashing light breaks through the darkness of the alley. A distinctive *snap-snap-snap* echoes around us.

Instinctively, I turn toward it. Duncan turns away from the noise, backs off.

"Shit!" I hear Brooke exclaim.

Snap-snap-snap rings out again—autowind . . . film . . . camera.

No. This is not happening.

This. Is. Not. Happening!

The flash goes off again, right in my eyes. But I think I catch a glimpse of a red baseball cap, a beard.

I scream, "You *asshole*!" and take off running in the direction of the photographer.

Behind me, Duncan screams, "Stop!"

I don't know if he's talking to me or the guy taking the pictures. Doesn't matter, really. Neither of us is going to listen.

The creepy guy with the camera stops his picture taking and sprints away from me—out of the alley and east on Eighty-first Street.

I fly past pedestrians, zigzag through a maze of flower stands and outdoor displays.

I beg my legs to go as fast as they can, but after about a block my injured left knee begins to scream for mercy.

In the distance I hear Duncan Stoke's voice ring out in the night. "Let him go! It's not worth it."

Fucking actors. What do they know?

Up ahead, near the entrance to the Museum of Natural History, a man walking his dog looks on with interest.

I yell, "Stop that guy!" just as the creepy photographer passes the man and his tiny poodle.

The dog owner swings his hand out and clips the photographer on the arm.

Damn, it wasn't enough. After a brief stumble the photographer regains his stride. He runs even faster now, across the wide lanes of Central Park West and straight into the vast and dangerous darkness of Central Park.

I can't follow him. I'm a single woman with a limp. I'd be like a really large worm on a hook in there.

Damnit!

I lean over to catch my breath. With my head somewhere between my knees, I see something streak by me.

Lifting my head, I see Luke's two skinny legs—the palest pale—stomping out a well-practiced stride, and Todd's flat feet pounding away in a strained, clumsy jog. They disappear in the deep brush surrounding the park.

"You guys!" I yell, afraid for their safety. "He's gone!"

A few seconds pass before I see Luke and Todd emerge from the thicket, dusting themselves off—no photographer in tow.

Well, I hope that he's attacked by man-sized rats, or better yet, mugged by a band of flesh-eating zombie homeless people. Come on, a girl's gotta dream.

I hobble back toward Columbus and say a quick thank-you to the Good Samaritan dog walker as I pass.

He asks, "Shall I call the police?"

"No," I answer, between gasps of breath. "No use."

I limp down Eighty-first Street, silently cursing myself. I did the stupidest thing—I looked *toward* the camera when I heard the shutter clicking. Whenever you catch a famous person out with their unfamous love interest, it's always the anonymous one who looks at the lens. The famous person, trained in the art of camera avoidance, instinctively turns away from the sound of a shutter—not toward it. I don't know why, but my turning toward that camera bothers me more than having the picture taken at all. I feel like my body betrayed me.

On the corner of Columbus and Eighty-first, I'm met by

Duncan Stoke and Brooke. Given the length of time they've gone unsupervised, I'm a little surprised Duncan is still in full possession of his clothes.

Luke and Todd totter up behind me. Luke has the fresh glow of a man who's just had an easy, recreational trot. Todd could be having a heart attack.

"Are you okay?" I ask Todd.

"Need to. Go to. Gym," he says unsteadily. "Fine."

"Did you see the guy?" asks Luke.

"No," I reply. "You?"

Todd shakes his head.

Luke gives me a disappointed "No, sorry."

"Thanks for trying, you guys," I tell them both.

"It's okay, Sadie. Everything is going to be fine," Brooke says, echoing Duncan's words from moments ago.

"No, it's *not* going to be fine, Brooke. The story has just been confirmed. It was rumor before, now it's a documented fact." I lean against a nearby mailbox for support. "How could I have been so stupid? How could I have let this happen?" I ask no one in particular. "It was so careless. We shouldn't have been talking outside. Don't you know *anything*?" I ask Duncan.

Duncan is rocking from side to side, shuffling his feet—deep in thought.

"Hey, Stoke!" I say loudly, trying to bust him out of the little personal conference he's in.

"Hold on, I'm trying to think," he says brusquely. My fake boyfriend needs absolute silence to *think*.

I watch as Brooke approaches Duncan . . . leans in . . . and sniffs him. Oh, my God, she's possessed.

But that got him. Duncan turns to her. "Did you just *smell* me?"

"Sorry about that," Brooke says, and slinks toward me.

Duncan goes back to thinking, while Luke and Todd begin mumbling to each other.

After a few moments, Duncan halts the swaying and says, "Okay, I think the only thing to do is let my publicist release a statement about us just being friends, but only after—"

"No!" Luke, Todd, and I exclaim at once.

"No! No. Nonononono. No. Absolutely not!" I repeat. "Everybody knows that to the general public 'We're just friends' translates to 'We're sleeping together just all the damn time and about to get engaged.' "

"You might be right," replies Duncan.

"Oh, she's definitely right," adds Luke.

"Yep," Brooke concurs.

"Really?" Duncan asks, astounded. "It's that universal?"

"Oh, yeah," says Brooke, nodding her head for emphasis.

"Totally," replies Todd almost simultaneously.

Duncan lets out a disappointed huff. "I guess then we . . . ignore it?" he tries.

"But, you've got interviews and stuff coming up, don't you?" asks Brooke.

"The junkets are over," Duncan replies thoughtfully. "So, that's all good. But if anyone asks I'll just say I prefer to keep my private life private."

"It's not perfect," I respond. "It'll definitely pique some interest, but what other options are there, really?" I hate this. I hate it!

"Another thing," says Duncan. "I'll be seen out with other people. You do that, too. I don't care who—brothers, uncles, this guy . . ." He points to Todd.

"Do you think that'll work?" I ask.

Duncan Stoke looks at me with his big, mysterious, recriminating eyes and hisses, "You tell me. You're the fucking paparazzi."

HOLLYWOOD'S *NEW* HOT
NEW ROMANCE TREND

The latest thing in offscreen Hollywood romance is big actors dating regular girls. Hot young stars are shunning high-profile couplings in favor of less complicated affairs—they're trading in their divas for ladies without all the celebrity baggage. Guys cashing in on the trend go shopping for girlfriends at the grocery store, little out-of-the-way clubs, and their old hometowns.

Matt Damon and Josh Hartnett are credited with starting Tinseltown's clamor for down-to-earth gals. Toby Macguire and Matthew McConaughey have tried it. Jerry Seinfeld married his regular girl—so did Robin Williams.

Duncan Stoke seems to be the next to climb on the bandwagon. He's been spotted getting cozy with New York photographer Sadie Price. Maybe the next cute blonde on a celeb's arm could be you, girlfriend!

CHAPTER 14

S adie! Wake up!"

"What do you want?" I groan.

"Get up—now!" I hear Brooke roar, through the lovely, fluffy, life-sustaining down pillow I have pressed over my head.

I feel the sleepy warmth of my body evaporate as the covers are ruthlessly ripped off my bare legs. I cling to the pillow over my head with both arms as Brooke tugs at it violently.

"No!" I mumble through the feathery buffer. "Why won't you just let me sleep?"

Five days of watching increasingly unflattering photographs of me appear on the Internet, while waiting for a completely ridiculous picture of me and a movie star to hit the magazines, has, believe it or not, helped me get much-needed beauty rest. When I'm asleep I don't worry about tabloids and movie stars, stalkers and embarrassing photographs.

"Go away!" I try again.

Brooke stops her tugging.

Good, now I can get back to my dream. What was it?

Oh, right . . . me . . . at a five-star spa. . . . I'm swathed in a chocolate and seaweed wrap that's guaranteed to perk me up and smooth my lumps. The chirpy little spa urchin says, "I'd love to detoxify your pores, Miss Price, but first I have to *find* them" . . . Ethan Wyatt is waiting for me in the Zen garden. . . .

Okay, now I'm up. What the hell was that?

Just as I'm about to roll out of bed, an obscenely loud and obnoxiously perky voice rings out from the living room—freaking KC and the Sunshine Band: "That's the way, uh-huh, uh-huh / I like it, uh-huh, uh-huh."

"I'm up!" I scream to Brooke.

KC's girls sing, "Doo doo doo doo doo doo doo doo *doo*!"

"Dear God, make it stop!" I plead.

Silence, and disco-free peace, once again reign.

I take my hands from my ears and stagger into the living room, rubbing my aching eyes with one hand and adjusting my baggy old tank top and giant, yet miraculously wedgie-creating, granny panties with the other.

"Sadie," says a familiar male voice—Luke. "Ah! Pants!" It sounds like a compulsive utterance by a victim of Tourette's syndrome.

"Think of this as a really ill-fitting tankini, all right?" I reply.

"I'm a *man*!" he pleads.

"Oh, fine!" I plod back into the bedroom for some pajama pants.

"And what the hell's a tankini?" I hear Luke shout from the other room.

When I reenter the living room, Brooke and Luke are standing in the little divot by the window, looking down on First Avenue—pointing and whispering.

"What's going on?" I ask.

Luke starts. "I came straight over from work. Got here at about six-thirty. On my way in, I noticed three cars parked across the street, each with people just sitting inside." He pauses, inhales ominously, and adds, "All of them watching the front of the building."

Well, I guess the creep did get a clean shot of me and Duncan—and it's hit the papers. That means I'm onto a whole new level of tabloid fervor. Now that the story's been confirmed, all the outlets have to get their piece of the pie.

I grunt. "They're here for background shots. They'll get some usable stuff of me and then stalk Duncan, wait for the money shot—him and me together again."

A sudden rush of adrenaline begins its quivering, pulse-pounding journey through my veins.

I am such an idiot. Five minutes in a dark alley with a movie star and I'm suddenly a big fish. Did I learn nothing from Divine Brown? I should have seen it coming. I should have known better. Why can't I think clearly anymore?

I step around Brooke and Luke and take a look at the street. "Which ones?" I ask.

"The black Escalade, three cars from the corner," he points. That'd be Phil. "The black Honda SUV, seven cars from the corner—" That's Nate! Of all the stupid ridiculous things! He works for Todd.

I stomp across the room, retrieve the telephone, and dial Todd's number with lightning speed.

He says, "Hel—"

"Todd, please explain to me why Nate is parked outside my apartment building."

"He *is*?"

"Yes, he *is*, and you know it."

"Sadie, I wouldn't do—"

"Oh, yes you would," I spit.

Todd replies quickly, "All right, I would. But I *didn't*. Happy?"

I wander back to the window and stare down at First Avenue. "No, I'm not happy. There are photographers staking out my apartment building."

"You were seen with Duncan," he says matter-of-factly.

"Are you going to call Nate off, or what?"

"I'll give him a call. Adler won't be covering this at all. But, Sadie?" he asks, suddenly getting serious.

"Yeah?"

"This isn't going to just *go away* anymore."

"Oh, yes it is. It's all lies, Todd. It has to stop—"

"It won't."

"Oh, I beg to differ."

"Sadie, this isn't a joke."

I believe in truth, justice, and the American way, damnit! This has to end! I'll call the ACLU or . . . Barbara Walters.

"You just take care of Nate. All right?" I fume, while nonsensically pointing down at First Avenue to emphasize my point. "The guy knows me, for God's sake, and he's down there. . . ." The words escape me—they form and then dematerialize in my foggy head. "Gotta go," I blurt to Todd. "I just thought of . . .

Luke, did any of the guys in the cars down there have on a red baseball cap and look exceptionally creepy?"

At these words, Brooke presses her forehead against the window and peers down at the street. I hang up on Todd and press my own forehead to the glass.

"I was getting to that. He's in the white Taurus." Luke smiles.

"Finally!" And now I kill him.

"Do you need backup?" Brooke asks. She must sense what I'm thinking.

"No!" And ruin my fun?

I stomp to the kitchen and dig through the messy drawers for the largest meat cleaver I can get my hands on. Thanks to Brooke's aspirations to throw the perfect dinner party, we are in possession of world's largest Ginsu knife.

I head for the door.

Brooke screams, "Shoes!" while Luke yells, "*Knife!*"

"Sadie." Luke chuckles, slightly alarmed. "Sadie, put down the knife."

"You expect me to go out there unarmed?"

Luke speaks. "You'd be better off—"

Brooke interrupts him with a wave of her hand. "Sadie, those are your favorite pajamas," she says dryly.

Ah, she has a point. Knives are messy, and it took me six months to break in these pants. Let me see, what is less messy than a knife, but still capable of inflicting serious bodily harm? Hmmm.

Oh, got it.

"Fine," I say finally, plopping the knife onto the coffee table.

"Where do you keep the baseball bat these days, Brooke? You got a box for that somewhere in your room?" I head for her bedroom door. "What's it filed under? Sports equipment? Wood? Man-luring props?"

Brooke goes red and Luke cracks up.

"I don't have a box for man-luring props," she lies.

Oh, I know where it is. She keeps it under the bed now. I don't really understand it. The baseball bat really only works as a burglar intimidation technique if you're, say, Barry Bonds. Now, if you're going to beat an unsuspecting photographer to a quivering mass of black and blue flesh, on the other hand . . .

I fly into her room and retrieve the bat. (Fun fact: not a single dust bunny under her bed. Remarkable.)

I slip on my fuzzy duck slippers and march out of the apartment, with Brooke and Luke close behind. They both chatter incessantly over and on top of each other. Convenient, as I don't have to bother ignoring them—I can't understand a word either is saying.

After lying into the elevator's down button, I pace the floor.

"Don't do anything stupid," Luke warns.

I try to reassure him. "I'm not really going to *hurt* the guy." Much.

Leaving Brooke and Luke at the front door to keep an eye on me, I head to the bowels of my apartment building. I found this a couple of years ago when my mother came for a surprise visit, and I slipped out to freedom so that Brooke could honestly claim, "Sadie's not home."

I wander in the dark with a tiny key-ring flashlight and a nervous stomach. This will take me out to First Avenue about a half block from the front lobby of my building. I unlock the rusty door and ram my shoulder into it.

The sudden blast of light in the gloomy hallway briefly stings my eyes. I stumble down the steps into a filthy alleyway. It's littered with clock radios, crusty dead houseplants, books, and other assorted bits of household ephemera that have apparently been falling out of people's open windows for the last hundred or so years. The alley is wide at the back, where I am now, but narrows to barely a crack at the other end. Hopefully my thighs will be able to squeeze through.

Slowly, carefully, and using the bat to push the really disgusting things (toilet seat) or just plain bizarre things (a four-foot-long rubber penis?) out of my path, I navigate the minefield of junk. I guess this is the swan song for my fuzzy duck slippers—Brooke will never let me in the apartment with them again.

It's a warm, sunny day—not that you'd know it from back here. The chill of hard shadows makes the temperature a good ten degrees cooler than out in the sunshine. A flurry of goose bumps tingle along my bare skin.

Finally at the narrow opening of the alley, I squeeze myself between the towering brick apartment buildings. Shuffling my feet and sucking in my belly like a freaking *Sports Illustrated* swimsuit model, I work my way slowly through the crack. At the narrowest bit, it's a challenge not to scrape my face on the masonry.

Oh, my God. If I get stuck here I will absolutely die. That would definitely make the front page: "Duncan Stoke's Mystery Gal Pal Dies of Embarrassment as FDNY Unit Unable to Rescue—Paralyzed by Fits of Laughter."

I think skinny thoughts (I am a toothpick. I am a pencil. I am Nicole Kidman) and I make the final push to freedom. Excellent, still in one piece.

I dust myself off and survey my surroundings. I'm on First Avenue, a good five car lengths behind the Taurus. Perfect.

Ignoring the strange looks from my fellow New Yorkers, I crouch down and clamber to the trunk of the offending white vehicle.

That's strange, it has a rental car sticker. What self-respecting paparazzi would rent . . . a Ford Taurus? This better be the guy. If I bust in on a bunch of vacationers from Kansas, it would be very disappointing—and bad for tourism.

I pop my head up, peek inside the car, and pop back down. One head, in a red baseball cap. Four doors, unlocked.

Okay. It's now or never. . . .

I leap to my feet, sidestep between the car and the curb, and whip open the passenger's side door.

Quickly plopping myself into the seat, I point the head of the bat at the driver's skull. I hiss, "You should really lock your doors."

Holy shit!

A high-pitched wail of misery fills the tiny car and most of the East Village.

I think that was me.

A dark, handsome face turns toward me. I feel a violent stir of excitement well up from deep within me, the frightening consequence of attraction and revulsion intertwining. There's no scruffy beard, but rather freshly shaven skin—smooth and touchable like flesh-colored silk. Locks of wavy, shiny black hair tumble out from under a worn-out Red Sox cap. Two impossibly blue, unimaginably penetrating eyes stare back at me with astonishment.

"You!" I screech at Ethan Wyatt. "It's *you*!"

Wyatt's lip curls in a little smirk. "So, you found me."

"I mean, I *knew* it! But it was just too unbelievable! *You've* been following me and taking those horrible pictures?"

"Wait a second. I think I've shown remarkable improvement for a novice. I gotta give you credit, it's not as easy as it looks."

He's nuts! "Why are you doing this to me?"

"There's this thing my father always used to say: turnabout is fair play," he replies smoothly.

"What goes around? Karma? *Revenge*?" I ask bitterly.

"*Revenge* makes it sound so evil. I prefer to think of it as atonement," he replies with a sickly superior tone in his voice.

"So you do this to every photographer who catches you cheating on your girlfriend?"

"No, unfortunately, I didn't think of it until recently. You're a test case."

"You *asshole*! How can you be cocky about this? You're sick, you know that? You're a slimy . . . disgusting . . . stalker!"

"I'm a stalker, am I?" he asks, calm and poised.

"Yes!"

"What's the difference between me doing it to you and you doing it to me?"

"I'm not a *celebrity*, you idiot. That's what!"

A twinkle appears in his eye. He shakes a finger at me and says, "Ah, but you're *dating* one."

A deep, guttural groan rolls off my tongue. "You're totally

fucking crazy, you know that? You've sunk so low your publicist is going to need an earthmover to resurrect your career."

"I don't think so."

"Oh, yeah? What's to stop me from taking this public?"

Ethan Wyatt looks at me with rancor. "How do you like it so far? The lack of privacy, the fear, the rumors and suspicion? Have you lost any friends over it yet? Has it affected your career? Do you want to lock yourself in a room and never come out?" He pauses dramatically, then lowers his voice to a deep, menacing whisper and says, "Now, imagine that *Star* magazine finds out you're the subject of celebrity stalking."

A wave of nausea forces me to swallow hard. I can't think of any comeback to that. He's right. He's got me, damnit. I am totally screwed. Shit, what if this *never* ends?

"Don't you have a job or something?" I ask him scornfully, grasping at anything that might make him stop this madness.

"I have a lot of free time—"

"Obviously," I huff.

He arches one eyebrow, giving his face a sly sort of glamour, and continues wistfully, "Three months on, three months off. Actors are kind of like deep-sea fisherman, journeymen—"

"Serial killers guided by the zodiac," I add bitingly.

He replies by conjuring up the sucking noise made famous by Dr. Hannibal Lecter and his fava beans.

I gasp. "Are you bipolar or something? That is the mental illness of the moment, isn't it? Are you feeling *manic*?" I turn to him with as much condescension as I can muster under these conditions and gloat, "Oh, no. I've got it. This has something to do with the messy transition from Scientology to Kabbalah as the Official Religion of Hollywood™, doesn't it? Are you wearing your red string?"

"You are *fascinating*!" Ethan exclaims, while looking at me like something he just scraped out of a petri dish.

"Well, can I fascinate you straight out of my life?" I ask, shooing him with my hands.

Not reacting to me, but as though continuing with his own train of thought, he says, "You're so . . . *clever*." A startlingly open, easy grin arches from ear to ear. "I hadn't expected that."

The sweetness of his tone is annoying, and just the slightest bit appealing. His eyes are really quite beautiful—the perfect shade of blue—sharp and somehow cool at the same time.

"How did you find me?" I ask, as the agony of defeat begins to make my head ache.

He smirks. The muscles in his jaw relax, creating an alluring sort of pout. His eyes sparkle with a cunning charm. He leans across the car and coos, "I wonder if you can help me. A girl I . . . ahem . . . met, left her cell phone at my place. I'm so embarrassed, I don't have a clue where she lives. I'd like to get it to her before I leave tonight for *Paris*."

Holy shit, he's good. He could bewitch Ellen DeGeneres into batting for the other team.

"You're, like, a sociopath, right?" I say to him.

He leans back to his side of the car and smiles. "No. But if I want something bad enough, I'll get it."

"Oh, so you're not a sociopath, just a typical fucking actor." I can't believe this. "So, what'd you do?" I ask. "Charm yourself into the pants of every editor at every major tabloid?"

"I would have. But it turned out to be completely unnecessary. I made a few calls through some publicists I know, got a few editors' numbers. I gave them some solid leads, they trusted me—I fed them *you*."

"Well, stop feeding. You've had your fun. You have your *revenge*. Now. Leave. Me. Alone!"

"I don't know, I'm having a pretty good time. I guess you'll just have to wait and see. Which reminds me, your annual Pap smear is Monday."

Humiliating. Humiliating.

The thought of this nightmare continuing makes my blood boil over. The baseball bat shakes in my hands. "Leave me alone . . . or else!"

I jump out of the car as Ethan Wyatt laughs. "Or else what?" he clucks, as I slam the door.

I march toward my apartment building, trying not to trip and fall in my now sticky slippers.

As I press my hand to the front door, I hear the *click-click-click* of cameras.

Oh, God—I forgot about them.

FROM PAPARAZZI
TO STALKERAZZI

Some say it's a fine line, others say it's a
slippery slope. Any way you cut it, celebrity
photographers are going to greater lengths to
dig up fresh Hollywood gossip. While the
stars themselves universally deride the trend
toward chasing, stalking, and other more
cloak-and-dagger information-gathering techniques, the photographers are telling a different story. Phil Grambs, a photographer
notorious for doing anything it takes to get a
shot, says this: "If they'd just give us what we
want, we wouldn't have to do this crap. But
as long as they keep dodging us, we'll keep
dogging them."

CHAPTER 15

"Close the curtains!" Stomping through the front door, I shout to Brooke. "Close them all!"

I toss the bat on the couch and march over to a window, but my attempts to untie the drapes and pull them closed are futile. My hands are shaking too badly.

"He is pure fucking crazy! Off his damn rocker!" It's difficult to grasp. My mind is reeling at the very idea that Ethan Wyatt—*Ethan Wyatt!*—is behind all of this. I really didn't think he was that crazy. I mean, it is *crazy*.

I continue to fumble with the curtain ties until Brooke delicately moves my hands and takes over.

"Who's crazy, Sadie? Who's doing this?" The curtain swings closed as the tie comes loose. I feel myself being pulled away from the window and ushered to the couch. "Who was in the car, Sadie?" Brooke asks in a frightened whisper.

Looking at her, I feel several tears break free and stream down my face. "Ethan Wyatt. Ethan Wyatt was in the car."

Brooke is stunned. Her mouth hangs open like that of a cartoon character, or a soap opera diva in that bizarre pause just before they cut to the commercial. I would laugh if her face wasn't so perfectly descriptive of the thoughts running through my mind. I sink deeper into the couch and throw a pillow over my face, waiting for Brooke to come back to earth.

After almost a full minute, I hear a tentative, "Ethan Wyatt . . . the *movie* star?"

I nod my head and the pillow in time.

Brooke prods again, "Are you sure?"

Lifting the pillow just enough to be understood, I reply, "Oh yes. I sat in his car and the psychotic, demented, self-absorbed, childish stalker told me so himself—with pride."

"*Ethan* Wyatt? *Suicide Mission, Felony Charge, Hager Saga* Ethan Wyatt? Frequently swooned over on *Fashion Police* Ethan Wyatt? Took his mother to the Academy Awards last year Ethan Wyatt?"

"Yes!"

I rise to close the rest of the curtains, but Brooke pushes me back down. "I'll do it. You shouldn't get near the windows when the vultures are circling." My eyes go wide, and she attempts clarification. "Sorry, I mean . . . you know what I mean."

Unfortunately, I do know what she means. I wonder, Are the feathered variety of vultures also cannibals?

"Where did Luke go?" I ask.

"Provisions. I told him to walk down the candy aisle and grab anything with chocolate," she replies.

"Thank you," I squeak, through a new wave of tears.

Just as Brooke has released and draped the last of the curtains, the door buzzer goes off.

"He must have forgotten his key," she says, heading for the door.

I have to think of something, some way to get out of this. Or get back at him. Force him to stop. I can't live this way for long. I'm positive that mere days from now I will have the overwhelming desire to hire a personal yoga guru, seek the advice of a stylist, and speak frankly and tearfully with Oprah. In other words, to sum up: I can feel myself slowly going insane.

From across the room I hear Brooke's voice speaking in a low, concerned tone, "Oh, boy."

"What is it?" I ask, panicking. "What's wrong?"

"Sadie . . ." she whispers. "Sadie, I . . ."

Brooke tiptoes back into the living room. A little wrinkle has appeared over her brow, and her mouth is straining against itself in a false grin. Her smile looks like it was drawn onto her face by one of the cartoonists at *MAD* Magazine. She speaks. "Uh . . . you might want to . . . uh . . ."

"What is it? Reporters? Dogs? A giant ape?"

A loud, whiny pitch calls out from the other side of the door. Even though it's tainted and muffled by rusty metal, I know that voice. It says, "Sadie, honey, I'm here! Mother's here to help!"

THE BUSINESS OF FAMILY

Casting directors have made Ethan Wyatt the poster boy for privilege and polo. He's been cast as the disheveled, self-consciously hip son of old money more times than he cares to remember. But the truth of Wyatt's upbringing is much different from that of his characters. "I grew up poor," he said in a recent interview with "Good Housekeeping," "really poor. But, I didn't know it until I got to high school. My mom did a great job making something out of nothing, and filling the house with so many good memories that it felt three times the size it was." In honor of his mother, Claire Wyatt, Ethan has set up a charity foundation dedicated to supporting the cause of single mothers. "It's important that we remember what our parents sacrifice for us, and give back when we have the means. Nothing is more important than family."

CHAPTER 16

"Open the curtains!" I yell to Brooke.

"*Why?*" she asks, running for the nearest window and frantically stripping open the curtains.

"Because I'm going to jump."

Brooke lets the curtains fall from her grip as she rolls her eyes at me. "I know you guys have some issues, but—"

"Oh, is that what they're called? Issues? I always thought they were called *nightmares*."

"What are you going to do, just let her stand out there banging on the door all day?"

"No, that won't work. She'd just camp out in the hallway. We'd be stepping over her for weeks." I rack my brain, search the ceiling—then the floor—for some kind of solution.

Brooke lets out a loud gust of air. "I'm going to open the door now."

Oh, God.

Brooke walks slowly to the front door. She puts her hand on the knob and gives one last look at me—as pure, unadulterated dread begins to liquefy the contents of my abdomen.

With one flick of the wrist, the door opens and the tornado slips in.

Paige spews, "Oh, hello, Brooke! So good to see you. How are you? How's she doing?" One of my mother's many talents—having a one-sided conversation with someone and still managing to make them feel like they've been heard. Witchcraft, I tell you.

"Good to see you, too, Mrs. Price-Farmer!" says Brooke as she's enveloped in a minihug and given several air kisses. "She's—"

"How many times have I told you, sweet girl? Call me Paige! Where is she?"

She is going to hide in the little nook by the living room window and hope that the divot in the floor finally gives way and she falls through to the apartment below.

"She's—" Brooke tries again.

"I was worried about her, and I had some free time. We're not going to Barbados this year until July." Oh, thank goodness my stalker chose May. "I felt I had to come give her support. This situation is a bit unusual, don't you think? You know, Dr. Hank says she has legal basis to sue."

"I'm sure she'll be glad you came," Brooke says unsteadily.

I run for the little nook and slide into the armchair by the window. The sound of my mother's heels clicking on the hardwood floor sends a cascade of spasms through my limbs. My injured knee once again begins to throb.

"There you are!" Paige says, opening her arms wide as though I'm meant to leap up and hug her like people do in the movies.

Paige has had her hair cut since the last time I saw her. Crisp blonde waves flutter down in artfully carved layers, just barely grazing her collarbone. Long shaggy bangs are swept off to the side and behind her ear. Her makeup, as usual, is flawless. She looks at least ten years younger than her age. In fact, in the right light she could probably pass for thirty.

She's wearing her travel uniform: impossibly high Manolos, long, skinny black pants that cling to her thighs like white sticks to rice, and a fitted linen shirt with the cuffs casually rolled up to her forearms. The collar of her shirt is flipped up in the back, accentuating her long graceful neck and the gold draped around it. This little collar flip, one of my mother's signature style moves, also communicates just exactly how chic and confident she is.

Paige continues to stand in front of me with her arms spread wide. I can tell by the determined look in her eye that she could stand here as long as it takes for me to give in. This is the sort of thing mothers and daughters do—greet each other with great leaping hugs. She won't be living up to her picture of ideal motherhood if I don't play along.

I rise slowly and, before I totally have my footing, she wraps her arms around my waist and squeezes me like a Greco-Roman wrestler going in for the kill.

"How are you holding up?" she asks into my hair.

"How did you get past the doorman?"

"Who, Carl? I just told him I was your mother. He let me

right up." There goes somebody's Christmas tip. "I see that you're not feeling yourself, darling." She lets me go and begins fiddling with my hair. "Let's have a cup of tea and you can tell me everything."

It's just Brooke, Paige, and I. Luke came home with two sacks full of treats. Hearing about Ethan Wyatt, and seeing my mother, he got the sudden and overwhelming urge to play basketball. Go figure.

"Well, this *is* unprecedented," Paige grumbles into her second steaming cup of tea. She takes a delicate sip, slides her Manolo mules off, and props her feet on the coffee table. "You're being stalked by a celebrity," she adds, not talking to anyone in particular.

"Yep," I reply to the wall. My eyes have long since glazed over, and numbness has replaced the frenzied bewilderment of earlier.

"He didn't give you any indication what his goal was for this little experiment of his?" Paige asks.

"Excellent question," Brooke exclaims, leaning toward my mother.

"To make me suffer," I answer. That's the problem with this kind of torture—the end point is subjective. Only Ethan knows what it will take to satisfy himself.

"I'm going to say something now, Sadie, that I know you don't want to hear. . . ." Oh, here we go. My mother turns to Brooke and laments, "She hates my motherly concern." Looking back at me with a condescending flutter of her eyelashes, she chatters on. "I think a lot of your problems have to do with this job."

I groan. "We've been over this—"

Without skipping a beat, Paige continues, "Your problem keeping a steady boyfriend . . ." Oh, my God. "And your tendency to be so . . . scattered. Now there's *this*—"

I try again. "Could you please—"

"I just want you to be happy," Paige says, with something that approximates sincerity.

"My job is what makes me happy." It got me away from you, I don't add.

"All right, darling. Whatever you say," replies my mother. She sets her teacup down and elegantly drapes her arms on the sofa back. A shallow sigh escapes her. She delicately pushes a swish of hair from her forehead. "Short of quitting this paparazzi business and moving away . . . I think the best course of action is to ignore him."

"*Ignore* him? Are you *crazy*?" Well, there it is—the first "Are you crazy?" of this little visit.

Paige taps her hand on mine. "Sadie, if you don't know what it'll take to make him stop, you obviously can't do it. If he's hell-bent on making you miserable, having him think you're *not* miserable could be your best offense."

"Oooh, excellent idea, Mrs.—Paige," says Brooke.

But I want to strike back! To make *him* suffer!

Ignore him?

Really?

Ugh. I think she might be right.

I might have a shot at victory if I show Ethan Wyatt that he's wrong about how hard it is to be a celebrity. Moreover, ignoring him might just get him to see the futility of his vengeance and give it up for good. I just have to settle in, then grin and bear it till Ethan Wyatt sees how cool under pressure I really am and his obsession dies—along with his pride.

If Paris Hilton can do it twenty-four hours a day, how hard could it be? We're not talking rocket science here.

But, man, I hate it when my mother is right.

"I can ignore him," I state—in a tone that clearly indicates I would have thought of it on my own eventually.

"Excellent choice," chirps Paige.

"I agree," concurs Brooke.

"Well, good! Glad I was here to get that settled," Paige says, rising to her feet. "You know, darling—what would you think of getting a manicure and pedicure with me tomorrow? And you look like you could use a haircut, too." She runs her fingers through my hair. "Maybe highlights . . ." she adds, as though penning a little mental note for herself.

"How long do you plan on staying?" I pose, trying to sound casual.

"As long as it takes. I'm in this for the long haul." Yeah, what was I saying about how you never know what the goal is, or precisely when it will end?

My mother passes along her hotel information ("The Waldorf—isn't it sad about the Plaza being closed?"), straightens herself back to "presentable" (her clothes absolutely never wrinkle), and departs, leaving behind—as she always does—a hint of rose water in the air and the trenchant impression that you've just been visited by a whirling dervish. The room seems just the slightest bit emptier after she's left than it did before she arrived.

"I think you give her a bad rap," says Brooke while rinsing out our teacups. "She's not that bad, Sadie."

"Yeah," I reply. "It always seems that way at first, but did you catch that last thing?" Mocking Paige's voice, I add, "*You need a haircut and highlights . . . dahhhling.* It never changes."

"What if she just wants you to take a break and be pampered?" Brooke replies.

"Yeah, and what if she wants to mold me into her clone and jointly rule a despotic empire? Honestly, that's just as likely."

"You might think about cutting her some slack. She did help you out. Which reminds me . . . have you opened the box yet?"

"No."

"This might be the time. It may come up in conversation one of these days."

"Yeah, I guess it could. But I—"

"*Ahhhhh!*" Brooke exclaims, frantically dropping a teacup and wiping her wet hands on her frilly apron. "Is that my cell phone?"

A bit bewildered, I strain my ears. "I don't—"

She doesn't wait for me to finish. Instead, Brooke scrambles out of the kitchen and races through the living room. Speeding for her bedroom, she catches a foot on the area rug in front of the sofa and trips. Trying to keep her balance—and maintain her course—she stumbles headlong directly into her door. The thud this makes actually *echoes* through the apartment.

"Oh, my God. Brooke, are you o—" She flops into her bedroom and slams the door behind her. "—kay?"

Interesting. Apparently, I'm not the only person experiencing a psychotic break.

IT'S NOT EASY BEING SEEN

Ethan Wyatt is lashing out at new reports that his sudden absence from the public eye is due to a pornography addiction. He calls the reports "ridiculous at best" and "pathetic." In a phone interview from New York City yesterday, Wyatt denied the charges of sex obsession and gave some insight into life as a Hollywood bad boy. "It's not as great as you would think, being seen as this sex symbol, or whatever. A lot of women are just attracted to the fame—the glitz. You can never tell if someone's after you for your money, or the tabloid attention, or just to be able to say she's been with you—like some kind of conquest." And what about finding the right girl to settle down with? He says, "It's rare to find someone who doesn't care about the celebrity nonsense, so when you do happen to bump into a girl like that, you've got to give it your best shot." Wyatt was mum about whether or not Cupid has been on aim lately where he's concerned, and no word on whether or not Wyatt is currently "giving it a shot."

CHAPTER 17

Two weeks have passed since the photos of Duncan and me "having a steamy midnight canoodling session in a dark alley" (as *Celeb* so eloquently put it) appeared in nearly every major tabloid in the country. Ethan's vendetta doesn't seem to be waning, and what's worse—he's made significant strides in his technique. The pictures are getting bigger and of better quality. That is to say, they're not as grainy. The quality of me *in* the pictures, on the other hand, seems to be on the decline. To be fair, I think that's partly my fault.

The first few times I tried the cool-under-pressure/ignoring technique were a bit touch and go. My first attempt ended around the time I threw a newspaper at Ethan's head. My second effort went awry in the minutes following my gynecologist asking the question "Is that strange bearded fellow in the lobby your husband? He's making the pregnant women nervous." The third resulted in my purchasing the world's largest Elton John-esque sunglasses and a wide-brimmed hat à la Princess Di. I then walked around Manhattan shaking like a leaf and looking like an enterprising drag queen doing a one-person dramatic interpretation of "Candle in the Wind '97."

Not helping things is the fact that Duncan's movie opened last weekend. *The Speed of Light* is a hit. A major hit. It absolutely decimated all previous Memorial Day records. He's the man of the moment. And I am his accidental It Girl. My fake boyfriend is the hottest gossip story of the summer.

His face is featured prominently on *The Speed of Light* posters that are conveniently situated at every bus stop in the five boroughs. There's a full-body shot of him on a massive billboard that takes up seven floors of a major office building in Times Square. There are television commercials for his upcoming film, and a torrent of continuing press about the one that's already in theaters. He's on the cover of three magazines, in the entertainment section of the *New York Times*—above the fold—and Duncan Stoke has even been poked fun at on *The Daily Show* and *The View*. I'm the famous *nobody* allegedly dating the *somebody* that *everybody's* talking about.

Now, I'm not saying that it's hard, okay? I'm not saying that Ethan Wyatt has a point. I'm just saying it's . . . challenging. Challenging at worst.

All right, it might be a *little* hard.

Even the most casual walk down the street is a test of my self-control. I cannot touch, wipe, or scratch anything on my person when outside the safety of my apartment. I cannot yawn, sneeze, or cough. I cannot wander aimlessly into porn shops or X-rated movie theaters. Not that I did a whole lot of that before this nightmare began, but at least then it was an *option*.

The grocery store is a minefield of possibly embarrassing photographs. The tampon aisle notwithstanding, there are also adult diapers, prune juice, and condoms. Department stores are no better—lingerie, hosiery, and china patterns could all be easily misconstrued. Eating out is a problem, too. I have to sit at the back of restaurants and order things that don't require me to open my mouth too wide, or get too sloppy. On the bright side, I think I've discovered how actresses maintain their figures. Salad is pretty much the only thing manageable in small bites.

So, it's kind of hard. But here's the thing—my situation is different. For Ethan, this is all the bad stuff there is. The cameras scoping him out on the street are the *only* downside of his lifestyle. I'm willing to bet that having several million dollars in the bank is a pretty good salve for the minor nuisance of life in a fishbowl. (First off, the fishbowl would be *huge*.) It has to be twenty times easier for him. Right?

I'm just a regular girl. I have a very humble fishbowl . . . and a fake boyfriend who is currently America's number-one grossing movie star. This means that it's gone beyond Ethan and his silly photos; the stories that accompany them keep getting bigger and better. (By better, I mean *frightening*.)

My favorites so far . . .

One: "Stoke Plans Romantic Reunion as Press Tour Returns to New York." This one was illustrated by a picture of me inspecting a bra in La Perla, and had a list of items said to have been purchased by Duncan for our rendezvous. Among them was fruit-flavored massage oil and a CD entitled *Mozart for Lovers*.

Two: "Duncan's Gal Friday—Stoke's Mystery Girlfriend Said

to be a NYC Photographer." This blurb was under a photo of me reading *Cosmopolitan* and shoving a muffin in my mouth. Pretty inoffensive, right? Yeah, except the article I happened to be reading at the time was "65 Ways to Make Him Go Ooooh." I was genuinely curious, but not for the reasons the papers suggested. I honestly have no intention of making Duncan Stoke "Go Ooooh."

Three: "Stoke's Blonde Ambition." This little gem featured a half-dozen people Duncan Stoke has "dated." I was, of course, the grand finale of the layout—with my head cocked awkwardly to the side, one eye closed, and half of my tongue sticking out. The readers of that particular magazine now believe that I am either outrageously homely, mentally challenged, or both.

These layouts are like bad yearbook pictures, or photo albums from a year that you'd rather forget. I see the pictures of me in the papers just the same way other people see them— oddly removed from their context. Like the tabloid-reading public at large, I see that girl on the page and think, there's a girl who eats burritos on the run and ruins her favorite shirt because she doesn't have time to sit down for a meal. I think, There's a girl who buys frilly underwear that in all likelihood no one but she will be able to appreciate. I think, There's a person who, though perhaps pretty and talented on someone's scale, is nonetheless clumsily stumbling through life. The only problem is, these aren't just bad yearbook photos. Yearbooks get shoved in the back of bookshelves, buried under old prom dresses in your childhood bedroom. These pictures are distributed nationwide, new ones appear weekly—daily in some cases—on the newsstand down the block from my apartment. I can't help but look at them. I try my best to think of these things as a minor nuisance, try not to think about how similar my current situation is to the one I put Ethan in. I *try*.

Adding to my streak of unprecedented bad luck, Paige has taken it upon herself to act as my bodyguard. My mother seems to think that because she's taken cardio-boxing classes at the gym, she is an expert in self-defense. This came as a shock to me, as I thought everyone in the Western world had figured out that rhythmic boxing provides only a false sense of security. The boxing-to-the-beat self-defense technique is only effective against bands of frolicsome marauders who commit crimes solely when accompanied by an upbeat techno soundtrack. (One-two-three, and right hook. Step-ball-change and jab, ladies!) I suppose Paige could cripple an attacker with her stilettos. But then, that would require her to convince the attackers to put the heels on and walk around the city for an hour.

To sum up, Ethan Wyatt is winning.

"No, Todd, I can do it. I *swear*!" I plead into the phone. "I need to work. Please?" It keeps me sane. Todd's been reluctant to give me the best assignments—the last-minute and very profitable kind—because my car's in the shop. I think I've almost got him convinced that I can make it to the Upper East Side before Naomi Watts finishes a Madison Avenue shopping spree.

"Todd, I'll give you my firstborn."

"Take that back and you have a deal," he quips.

"Thank you! Thank you! Thank—"

"Okay," he says. "Go!"

I drop the phone on the bed and run through the living

room gathering my camera equipment, purse, and a couple of PowerBars.

Paige languidly looks up from her copy of *Harper's Bazaar*. "Where are you off to?"

"A job . . . Upper East Side . . . Naomi Watts . . . Gotta go!" I stutter breathlessly.

"Oh, I'll just get my shoes!" she replies with a sudden cheery sort of look about her.

"No really. I'll be fine," I say, slamming the front door behind me.

I step out into the city and head for the subway station. It's rush hour, the express train will be much faster than a cab.

"Sadie!" my mother screams behind me. "Hold on! Here I come!"

I look behind me to see Paige wobbling down the street. A man power-walking by her smartly gives my mother a wide berth. I have to say, though, I'm pretty impressed. That's the closest thing to a jog I've ever seen anybody do in a pair of Manolo mules.

"Really, I'll be fine," I tell her as she catches up. "You can go back to the apartment and . . . sit or something."

"No, no. I'm the *muscle,* darling. Remember?"

Paige and I descend the steps into the subway station and, looking behind me, I see Ethan—in his stupid disguise—right behind us. I force my mother, teetering on her heels, to race through the turnstile, and cram us both into the jam-packed train just before the doors close.

Wiggling between suit-clad commuters, I find a spot to stand.

My mother takes a position nearby, but across the aisle. We barely have time to catch our breath before the train lurches to a start.

I glance around, hoping against hope that Ethan didn't make it onto the train.

No such luck.

Looking over my left shoulder, I spot a dirty red baseball cap at the other end of the car—inching its way through the crowd toward me.

"Oh!" I hear myself exclaim, before slapping my hand over my mouth. That was somebody touching my butt.

"What's wrong, darling?" my mother asks, clueless. Okay, so it wasn't her.

Right, whatever. It's a crowded subway car. It was probably just an accident. I inch my way forward the slightest bit—closer to a middle-aged woman in a crisp white maid's uniform who's sitting directly below me on the bench. She seems to be a low risk for groping. I clutch my camera gear and handbag close to my chest.

I slowly turn my head to catch a glimpse of the possible psycho and/or embarrassed commuter who got a piece of my tush.

A tall, unbelievably hot guy is just inches from my face. His rather muscular left arm is raised, hand grasping the top commuter pole. He smiles at me warmly and says, "Sorry."

"No problem," I say, flirting back. Not sure if he's flirting, but I'm willing to take the chance. For some reason this random opportunity to flirt and be girly in front of Ethan sends a surge of adrenaline through my veins.

The stranger smiles some more and says, "You got enough room there?" Totally flirting—and really good-looking.

"Yeah, I'm fine. Thanks."

I could so use a diversion right now. It'd be nice to have a date with a handsome man who, by the looks of the snappy leather messenger bag and casual yet business-appropriate attire, is gainfully employed in something other than the entertainment industry. I'd like to be just a normal girl—who isn't being stalked—going on a date with a cute guy.

The train slows suddenly, making everyone rock forward with a jolt.

There goes his hand again.

"I swear to God, that was an accident," the stranger fawns, his eyes imploring me to believe him.

"Sure it was," I quip.

"Really," he retorts. "I don't make a habit of feeling up beautiful women on the subway."

I'm beautiful!

"Oh, that's what they all say," I reply—trying not to bat my eyelashes.

"This happens to you a lot, does it?"

"Why else would I be riding the subway at rush hour?"

He laughs, and I giggle in an appropriately girly way (read: victim of goofy yet uncontrollable female reflex).

My mother whispers behind me, "Good catch. And you-know-who seems to be annoyed."

I turn my head, all the better to glare at her and indicate with a lot of staring and blinking that she should shut up.

Turning back to the handsome stranger, I inadvertently make eye contact with the lady in the white uniform.

She gapes up at me with a broad smile. She must have heard us talking. I return her smile.

The lady grins back, but not in that disinterested yet friendly way that strangers do when on the subway. She's looking at me like she knows me—like she's waiting for me to recognize her. How do I know her? A source maybe?

I don't think I know her. But if I don't, why is she looking at me like that? I suppose she could be a random crackpot. Probably best not to stare.

I'll just pretend to be examining my shoes.

I let my eyes drift casually down to the floor.

. . . her name is embroidered over her left breast: Rosa . . .

. . . a picture of me is in her lap . . .

. . . she has thick, circulation-improving granny hose . . .

Wait—

Oh, no. A copy of *Celeb* is open in her lap. It's the new one, folded back to reveal a picture of me wearing fuzzy ducky slippers and brandishing a baseball bat.

I inadvertently make eye contact again.

The woman looks at the magazine, then up at me.

Magazine. Me. Magazine. Me.

I scan the car for any open space, any little cranny to escape to—but there's nowhere to run. The businesses of lower Manhattan have emptied into the subway lines and all the cars are crammed to capacity.

I turn around abruptly, briefly startling the handsome stranger.

He recovers and croons, "Hi, again."

"Hi," I reply.

Suddenly, a hand pops up between us—bearing *Celeb* magazine and a pen.

A voice below me calls out, "You sign?" in a thick Spanish accent.

"What's this?" asks the hot guy, trying to get a good look at the magazine as the woman's hand sways and bounces with every bump in the train tracks.

"I don't . . . I'm not . . . who you think," I tell her. Not this. Not now. Not in front of Ethan!

I gently push her hand down just as the people around us are getting interested. They surreptitiously stare at me.

"Is this you?" the hot guy asks, while staring at my picture.

"Yes!" the lady responds for me, while shoving her pen at me.

I look toward Ethan. A self-satisfied smirk creeps its way out from under that ridiculous beard. Damn, he can hear me.

I whisper to the lady, "But I'm not—"

"You sign. Thank you," the lady says, rudely snatching the magazine out of the hot guy's hand.

My mother pipes in, "Just sign it, darling. She seems like a lovely lady."

"Gracias," says my oppressor to my mother.

My mother is smiling at the loon who wants my signature. Okay, this is too much. I'm in a new reality show, is that it? They make you believe you're in the Twilight Zone or something, right? Will someone please say, "The tribe has spoken," or "You're fired," or "*Auf Wiedersehen*, you're out." Please?

I try again. "No. I'm not famous, you see. This is a big mistake. This"—for the benefit of the lady, I point at the picture—"is a mistake." I don't think she understands a word I'm saying. I point again. "Bad. Wrong. Lies." Crap, the only Spanish I know I learned from reading in the bathroom—the backs of the tags on my towels—Machine wash cold water. *Laveseantes de usarse.* Tumble dry low. *Secar a temperatura moderada.* No chlorine bleach. *No usar blanqueador.* Unfortunately none of these phrases apply.

The woman just smiles, nods her head, and shoves the magazine farther into my belly.

"You're going out with Duncan Stoke?" the hot guy asks in an excited tone. He chuckles deeply, almost at me, as though he's already working out the best way to tell his frat brothers about touching the ass of Duncan Stoke's girlfriend. When his laughter stops it's replaced by a wide, disturbing grin. He is suddenly the least attractive man I've ever seen.

"Next stop we'll go," my mother says in her best concerned bodyguard whisper.

The people around us are unabashedly staring now. A teenage girl with a white studded belt eyes me with a sneer. A guy with thick glasses peers over the teenager's shoulder to get a look at the magazine. A tall man with long black dreadlocks tries to look nonchalant, though he's obviously examining my face—trying to figure out what famous person I am.

"I'm not famous," I say a little louder this time. "This is a mistake."

The guy with the thick glasses is now ogling me freely, with a smarmy grin—like perhaps he's got a fuzzy duck slipper fetish of some kind.

Finally, the train begins to slow, nearing the Third Street station. I have to get out of here, but I'm totally surrounded. I aim my shoulder for the door and try to push my way out. It's no use; I'm pinned. What am I supposed to do now?

The train slows to a stop. The doors open—but they won't stay open for long.

I try once more to leave, but the woman in white presses her arm against my legs to prevent me.

"Sadie!" my mother says, managing to make a hole from her position to the door.

I'm still stuck. Rosa must work out because her arm is like a rock.

Oh, I give up.

I yank the magazine from the lady's hand, sign my name near the stupid and incredibly embarrassing picture, and hand it back to her.

"Move!" I shout at the man with the dreads as the door to freedom begins to close. "Watch out. Coming through!"

The (formerly) hot guy who touched my rear reaches a hand out and catches a swath of my T-shirt. He groans, "Where you going?" before emitting an obnoxious laugh. I feel his hand glide down toward my backside, again—slipping something into the back pocket of my jeans.

Somehow—through sheer force of will, I suspect—I manage to squirm my way to the exit and slip out just before the doors come to a close.

I reach into my back pocket.

It's his business card. Of all the arrogant, disgusting things! Ugh, he's a junior broker at an investment firm—typical.

"Disgusting!" I moan to no one in particular.

"You get it now?" comes a voice beside me.

I turn to find Ethan Wyatt grinning at me, smug and satisfied.

I snap, "Oh, who died and made you Jiminy-freaking-Cricket?"

Flicking my wrist as hard as I can in the direction of Ethan's head, I chuck the business card into the whirling jetstream of the passing train. I watch it come to rest with the discarded gum, bits of old newspaper, and piles of rat feces on the filthy floor of the subway tunnel—where it belongs.

. . . And then I run for the stairs, and my mother, as fast as I can.

"I really think he might be quite handsome under all that hair," my mother quips as I drag her up the stairs. "What did he have to say for himself?"

I look back to see Ethan following us, snapping pictures of me as I ascend the stairs.

"Nothing," I huff, stomping out to freedom. "Just his usual snappish drivel."

"You know, darling, I think he might be interested in you in a different way than you think."

"What in God's name are you talking about?" I ask before taking a deep breath of aboveground air.

"I was watching him," she says coolly, while sauntering toward the street without even a hint of urgency. "There's something about him, Sadie. . . ." Her voice trails off as she turns around.

Paige stops and watches Ethan as he shuffles out onto the sidewalk and looks for a cab of his own—to follow us, no doubt.

I take her arm. "Yes, mother, he's good-looking. Big deal."

"No, he's enjoying this. Really enjoying it. Like those little boys who used to pester you on the playground. I—"

I cut her off. "I have to get uptown! Come on! We might be able to lose him!"

A cab, with its little numbered light indicating vacancy, pulls up to the curb. I open the door and practically push my mother inside.

"Do you hear me, Sadie, dear? I think he—"

"Drop it," I say sternly. I really don't want to hear any of her theories, especially those that reference my childhood. What the hell does she know about what I did or didn't do on the playground? She wasn't even around.

I tell the driver where to go, but it's no use. We've just been swallowed by gridlock. We're not going anywhere. Naomi Watts will be back in Australia before I make it to the Upper East Side. Damnit!

From somewhere in the depths of my handbag, my Sidekick wails.

I dig it out and answer, "Todd, I—"

Todd's harried voice rings, "Are you there? The girl at the shop says Naomi's just checking out and then heading to her hotel."

"I can't . . . I didn't make it there. I was just . . . the sub-way . . . I—"

"You're not *there?*" he gripes—loudly. "Aw, Sadie. Come on!" He's not calling me Killer anymore. For some reason, that makes my heart ache just a little.

"I know, all right? I was almost molested on the goddamn train, okay?"

"A mugger?" Todd asks, concerned.

"Shewantedanautograph," I mumble.

He groans, before adding, "This isn't working, Sadie—"

"Todd, I'll get it under control. Okay?" I have to, this is more than a job to me. This is my *life*.

Todd gives me a terse good-bye and hangs up.

My mother looks over at me. "Do you really enjoy this stress? What is it about this work, Sadie, that would make you fight this hard?"

Unable to summon the grit necessary to lash out in the way I'd like to, I say, "If I told you, you wouldn't understand."

Her dream was to surrender to Dr. Hank—or whatever wealthy man she might have stumbled upon if he hadn't come along. Mine is to be self-sufficient and maintain some measure of stability in my life. Something she never provided—for me, at least. As insane as this job is, doing it makes me feel safe.

This, not being able to do it, makes me want to scream.

In theory, this plan to ignore Ethan Wyatt makes sense, but it turns out there's one significant downside—it feels remarkably like doing nothing, like he has all the control. I think I'm going to need a plan B.

I push a few buttons on the Sidekick and quickly find the number I'm looking for.

After a few rings I hear, "Donna Herschel."

"Hi, Donna. It's Sadie Price. I need a favor. . . ."

THINGS CHANGE

Hollywood is all about up-to-the-minute cool. Stars rise and fall with the rapidity of a paparazzi's flashbulb. Trends come and go, seemingly carried by the famed winds of Santa Ana. "Nothing about this industry is static," says renowned L.A. publicist Jane Bremel. "When you're talking about celebrities, things can turn on a dime. One minute you're hot, and the next you can't pay people to look at your head shots."

In her new book, "How to Stay on Top: A Guide to Power in Any Profession," Ms. Bremel offers useful advice to everyone—famous and nonfamous alike. "The key to keeping ahead is to lead, not follow. Open your mind, listen to criticism, then implement your ideas. When you add a little bit of luck, and a lot of heart, you'll be the one setting the trends."

CHAPTER 18

just have to shake him for an hour or so," I tell Brooke as we trot out of the elevator.

This summer has been classified by all the weathermen as "Gonna be a hot one!" Just as the phrase "partly sunny" actually means "You will be surrounded by a grayish gloom all day," "Gonna be a hot one!" translates to "You will be smoldering, sticky, and miserable for the foreseeable future." Brooke and I step out of the apartment building and I immediately feel like I need a shower. My tissue-weight T-shirt feels like it's made of wool. I scan the horizon for Ethan Wyatt while fanning myself with a Chinese food menu I picked up in the lobby.

Brooke eyes me skeptically. "And then this random *person* that this freelance *person* hooked you up with—"

"Donna," I correct.

"—that *Donna* hooked you up with is going to give you some horrible story about Ethan that you'll use to blackmail him," Brooke says, her tone reeking of admonition.

"I'm not going to *blackmail* him, I'm going to gently encourage him to stop stalking me." And get definitive proof that he's not the saint he claims to be.

Brooke's green eyes blink at me with suspicion. Clearly, she's unconvinced.

I try another tack. "I can't just sit around waiting for Ethan Wyatt to decide he's finished punishing me. You should have seen that banker guy on the subway. He was so . . . *lecherous*. It was beyond gross—it scared the crap out of me. All right? If I can dig up something juicy enough, I might get Ethan to lay off."

"You know how I love helping you out with these things, Sadie. But—just playing angel's advocate here—that picture at blé hit a nerve with him. What kind of nerve is this going to hit?"

"The one that gets him to back off," I reply. I stare at her, pleading with my eyes. I don't know what else to say to make her understand how important this is to me, that my plan may sound crazy, but I can't stand feeling this helpless.

Brooke shakes her head at me. "I want it noted for the record that I think this is a bad idea," Brooke says sternly. "Furthermore, I reserve the right to say 'I told you so' at any point."

"Noted," I reply. "Thank you."

"Okay, what's your big plan to lose him?" Brooke asks.

"I don't know. I got rid of my mother for the day, didn't I? I'll figure it out."

"Something tells me handing Ethan Wyatt a flyer for the Saks Fifth Avenue semiannual sale isn't going to have the same effect that it had on your mom."

I take several more strides down the sidewalk and quickly survey the street ahead and behind us. No Ethan! "Oh, my God!" I exclaim to Brooke. "You don't think he's given up?"

We turn the corner onto Fourteenth Street.

"Uh, Sadie," Brooke says, pointing ahead.

Damn. Ethan is leaning against his rental car, his feet casually crossed, propped out in front him, his camera and that humongous bag looped loosely around his chest. Oh, and he's wearing that ridiculous beard and sunglasses.

"You know," Brooke says, pulling down her sunglasses like a paparazzi-avoiding pro, "that beard is beginning to grow on me."

"You have serious problems." I would love to outline them for her—including the episode last night when I caught her taking notes while watching the commentary track of a Duncan Stoke movie. (She shushed me, turned up the volume, and then mumbled something about "facts and battle plans.") I'm not exactly sure how to bring that up without getting yelled at . . . or shushed.

Brooke and I keep our eyes forward and shoulders back as we stroll past Ethan without so much as glancing in his direction.

"We have to get him as far away from his car as we can," I whisper to Brooke. "Then we'll make a break for it."

"Well, hello, Ms. Serenity," Ethan says, bounding up beside us—causing me to jump. He flashes a grin at me and continues, "Did you start taking yoga or something?"

Naturally, my first instinct is to pounce on him—rip the camera from his hands and strangle him with the purple guitar

strap he's using to keep the camera around his stupid (yet ridiculously smooth) neck. But I check the visceral, gut-level reaction
to seeing him and take a deep breath. I will not lash out. I will
take charge of this situation.

"You like this, don't you?" I ask Ethan.

"What, driving you nuts? Yeah, I get a certain amount of
pleasure from it. I'm not ashamed to admit that," he says, snapping off a few frames. He shoots me a cocky smirk that makes
his fake beard go slightly askew.

"No, Wyatt. You like being a paparazzi. You enjoy being able
to manipulate any situation to your liking—such as choosing
only the most disgusting pictures of me." Frame them so I look
like a panty sniffer.

He opens his mouth wide, inhales as though forming a sharp
rebuttal—then exhales nothing but air. Ha!

Brooke lets out a giggle.

"So, what does that mean?" I add condescendingly. "It
means you are no better than me, and I am no worse than you.
Except, of course, that I find this whole 'being pursued' thing a
minor nuisance, and you crumble like so many Girl Scout
Cookies under the pressure." All right, so I may be stretching it
with "minor nuisance."

Ethan looks around anxiously. I think he's searching for
some kind of comeback.

"Oh, Girl Scout Cookies—that was *good*," Brooke injects.

I turn to Brooke as we continue to stride arm in arm up First
Avenue. "You think? I thought of it last night. Not too abstract
a metaphor?"

"No, no. Very visual."

Ethan lets out a frustrated huff—just enough to prompt me to stop and wait for an answer. I love to watch him squirm.

"You were going to say? About the Girl Scout Cookies?" I prod him.

Finally, his eyes light up. He says, "Tell me something—why is it that you buy Pop-Tarts in bulk . . . and toilet paper by the roll? What is that about? Who buys *one* roll of toilet paper?"

"Toilet paper? This is your response to my very profound Girl Scout Cookie point? You're obviously trying to avoid the issue, Wyatt. I don't have time for any of your silly arguments this morning," I say, as though I had an incredibly pressing appointment with someone regarding matters of national security.

"Oh!" Ethan says, completely ignoring me. "And another thing . . . what's with carrying a handbag *and* a camera bag? Couldn't you put the handbag *inside* the camera bag?"

Not when the handbag is brand-new and supercute I can't, smart guy. "Do you believe him?" I ask Brooke in as patronizing a tone as I can.

"Still avoiding the real issue," Brooke says seriously, nodding her head.

I turn to Ethan. "You're one to talk about bags, Wyatt. What do you even have in there? Huh?" I ask impishly, creeping forward and tugging at the top of his camera bag. The top flap is partially unzipped. I catch a glimpse underneath—a five-thousand-or-so-page tome entitled *Photography for Dummies.* Oh, man, that's really pretty cute.

I eye him with a completely uncontrollable smile creeping its way across my face—and he knows why. He quickly zips his bag and resumes snapping my picture.

I roll my eyes and take two great strides away from him.

"And another thing," Ethan begins again, as he continues to click off pictures of Brooke and me. "How many pairs of shoes do you own? Fifty? Ninety? What is it with the *shoes*?"

"I happen to *like* shoes," I say, feeling a strange sort of thrill at the knowledge that he's noticed my shoes.

I smile and toss my hair while continuing my walk uptown. (I thought I'd get him in the eye, but I missed.)

As if on cue, Brooke whispers in my ear, "He noticed your shoes, Sadie. I think he might *like* you." She pulls away, as her eyes widen with excitement.

"Oh, *whatever!*" I say—remarkably able to quiet the sick, mentally disturbed part of me that wants to giggle and say, "You really think so?"

After a half block of forcing myself not to peer over my shoulder, I hear the distinctive lilt of his highly trained voice. Ethan is not far behind me, shouting the immortal words of Kit De Luca: "Work it baby! Work it! *Own* it!"

Irritating, but not lethal.

Suddenly, he sprints in front of Brooke and me and begins snapping pictures of us while walking backward. "Perfect!" he says, snapping off two shots. "Now just pout for me."

Brooke unconsciously—I hope—begins hamming it up.

"Can I ask you something, Wyatt?" Brooke asks, startling me.

"For you, Brooke, *anything*," he replies with his signature cocky lilt.

"Why Duncan Stoke?" She's obsessed!

"For this, you mean?" he asks, clicking off another couple of pictures.

Brooke tilts her head down for a more flattering angle, and says, "Yeah."

"He spread a rumor about me once," Ethan replies, inadvertently allowing just the tiniest hint of anger to make its way into his voice.

"Oh, *reeeaaally*," Brooke says dramatically. "What about?"

"I was up for the same part as him in *Dereliction of Duty*, and he heard that the casting director had a sweet spot for me. He told the producers that I was unstable and possibly addicted to drugs. I lost the part." Ethan looks up from the camera, measuring Brooke's response.

Brooke squinches up her eyes, studying him—no doubt trying to determine if Ethan is telling the truth. She shakes her head. "He'd never do that," she says with a strident air.

Ethan huffs and then adds, "He did."

"I don't believe it," Brooke whispers to me. "Not at all. *Dereliction of Duty* is the film that made Duncan a household name. Obviously Ethan's jealous."

"*Obviously,*" I concur—completely unconvinced.

I force Brooke to forge ahead. And, doing my best to ignore Ethan, quicken my steps. People are starting to notice us.

"What's the hourly rate, Sweet-cheeks?" Ethan asks—loudly.

I hate to admit it, but a tiny flutter of pleasure squirmed through my midsection at the "sweet" . . . okay, and the "cheeks."

Digging deeper into my well of calm, I stop and flash him an ear-to-ear grin—wide enough to be worthy of Julia Roberts—giving him a glimpse of my amused incredulity. "Comical, Wyatt, but it won't work."

"You're looking tired," he adds smugly. "Should I call some-one? Your parole officer? A psychiatrist maybe?"

I try to smile with flair and ease, but I have a feeling it may actually be more of a grimace.

"Oh, that's *great*," he says, continuing with his act. "More of that, only this time less fangs—more pout."

I pause on the corner of Second Avenue and Sixteenth Street. (Stupid uncooperative lights!) He continues shooting away. His camera, my increasingly fake smile, and Brooke's attempts to follow Heidi Klum's "Tips for Better Snapshots" begin to draw even more attention. Four, maybe five people stop to investigate Ethan's catcalls and inspect Brooke and me, wondering who we are.

A heavyset woman in curlers and a Member's Only jacket ap-proaches Ethan. She points and asks, "Who are they?" Like we're not even here. "What do they do?"

I open my mouth to tell the strange lady to mind her own business, but of course, Mr. Big Mouth beats me to it. He leans over to the curler lady conspiratorially and says—in a stage whisper, "Well, you know . . . *adult films*."

Admirably, I resist my natural instinct to smack Ethan up-side the head. Instead, I turn to him, toss my head back and laugh uproariously. Pulling out my inner flirt, I give him a fresh look at my pearly whites—more fangs than pout—and ask, "What has gotten into you? You are an absolute riot this morn-ing, honey! Now, quit playing around. Go home and find your-self a *job*. Oh, and don't forget to feed your ferrets."

With the "joke" revealed, the crazy lady in the curlers huffs loudly and throws her hands up in disappointment. The other onlookers, however, are not as discouraged. They merely squint their eyes and press in closer.

Ethan gives me a devilish grin, his blue eyes dancing. "You're gonna have to do better than that." He pulls the camera up and resumes shooting.

Just as I'm about to lose my cool, I notice a knot of teenage girls striding down the street toward us. All half-dozen of them are various shades of bottle blonde. Each is clad in a different hue of midriff-bearing pink—bubble gum, ballet, Pepto-Bismol. I gather from the book bags and leisurely pace that they're on their way to school.

I feel an unexpected surge of adrenaline, and a stroke of inspiration that's almost Machiavellian in its poetic depravity. This is it, my chance to lose him.

In a low voice I tell Brooke, "Follow my lead."

She nods her head, and I practically leap on the hood of the first cab to pass by.

I force Brooke (who is still posing) into the cab.

I pause before getting in and lean over the door toward Ethan. I lock eyes with his and give him what I believe approximates a come-hither stare. Well, from my end it feels that way, at least. I do the classic "come here" finger move—curling my finger repeatedly, as if drawing him in by a string.

Stunned, and I think a bit intrigued, he leans toward me. Slowly, carefully, I bring my cheek to his. Barely brushing my lips against his skin, I put a peck on his fuzzy face. I whisper, "You can't beat me. Give it up."

With a quick tug, I pull down a good portion of his poorly affixed fake beard.

Smiling, I scream at the top of my lungs, "Oh, my Gooooood! It's Ethan Wyaaaaatt!"

"Very funny," he says, only slightly perturbed.

I grin a knowing, cocky smile of my own (the first time I've been able to use one of those in a while) and watch as his face begins to show little flashes of panic. Little furrows appear on his forehead. The slight dimple on his left cheek smooths out as his smile slowly curls downward. His blue eyes widen as a shrill, frightening sound assails him.

He hears it, that most terrifying of sounds for the unguarded male celebrity: teenage girls, squealing with delight.

With a wink, I slide into the cab and wave good-bye to my dumbfounded (and amazingly scented) celebrity stalker. Luckily, the cab doesn't spring to life before I get a chance to see Ethan Wyatt being mauled by six extremely enthusiastic young fans.

NOTHING BUT
THE FACTS, MAMA

I have a theory about why so many young actresses are starving themselves to stay thin. The reason? Pregnancy rumors. Some poor unsuspecting young starlet has one gelato scoop too many and suddenly a below-the-belt bulge is the next Baby Brangelina. Tabloid art directors will gleefully circle any old lump in fairly the right place—and, just in case you miss the circle, a giant "BABY!" in bold letters will be added, along with a neon arrow pointing you in the right direction. Who wouldn't want to avoid that?

Truth be told, folks, celebrity mamas in waiting will clue us in when they're preggers. After all, no self-respecting ingenue wants the public to think she's getting fat when she's only knocked up.

When the tabloids say your favorite gal celeb has hitched her wagon to the mommy train, take it with a grain of salt. 'Cause the fact is, she probably just had a few extra grains of salt herself, and she's retaining water.

—Rachel Dewey for Fresh Gossip,
Your Internet Celebrity News Source

CHAPTER 19

Brooke and I step onto the escalator of an Upper East Side Barnes & Noble.

"How are we supposed to recognize her?" Brooke asks, scanning the stacks and café as we're deposited on the second floor.

My eyes flit over the wide mahogany shelves and little placards—Self-Help, Biography, Reference. The sunshine must have coaxed readers outside, because most of the comfy chairs scattered around are empty.

"She told me that she's pregnant, that we'll be able to spot her from a mile away." I return to my visual sweep and notice a very petite, very pregnant woman sifting through a table of bargain books. "That must be her," I say to Brooke, pointing across the room.

"That little thing was Ethan Wyatt's personal assistant?" Brooke says, verbalizing the surprise I'm feeling myself. She adds, "I imagined a Malibu Barbie type." Yeah, so did I.

I survey the room—she seems to be the only pregnant

woman around. With a name as faintly exotic as Jacinta Brown, I really expected her to be sort of . . . well, *exotic*. As it turns out, the only thing truly striking about her is that she's managed to stay vertical. Her belly is enormous, especially given her slim frame and diminutive stature. The fact that she's upright seems to defy the laws of physics.

I approach the woman at the bargain books table. "Jacinta?" I ask.

"Oh, hi! You must be Sadie," she says with a wide engaging smile. Jacinta's auburn, pixie-cut hair shows off her soft, pretty features including, appropriately enough, a peachy sort of glow on her freckled cheeks.

"That's me," I reply, "and this is my associate, Brooke Nolan."

"Associate?" Brooke chides under her breath.

"Would you like to sit down?" I ask Jacinta, indicating the in-store café nearby.

Her shoulders droop while her hand moves to caress her belly. "Oh, that would be great," she replies with a sigh of relief.

Jacinta waddles precariously to a table while Brooke and I bring up the rear—each of us with our hands held out a bit, ready to catch her in case she suddenly loses her epic battle with gravity.

Drinks and Danish are procured, and we settle into a quiet little nook.

I begin. "Thank you so much for meeting with me. I promise that you'll be kept anonymous. I'm sure it must make you a little nervous to break your confidentiality agreement—"

"Confidentiality agreement?" Jacinta interrupts.

Brooke and I look at each other with concern. Oh, no—I've bought a Danish for the wrong pregnant Jacinta.

"Um," I stutter, "you *were* Ethan Wyatt's personal assistant? Yes?"

"I was," she replies brightly.

Wait a second. "He didn't make you sign a confidentiality agreement?"

"No, he doesn't believe in them."

He doesn't *believe* in them? What's there to believe? Nobody has a personal assistant without a confidentiality agreement. If *I* had a personal assistant I'd make them sign a confidentiality agreement, and I don't even have anything to keep confidential.

"You're kidding?" I ask, the only thing approximating a reply that immediately springs to mind.

"No," she says with a smile. "Crazy but true."

Oh, boy.

For the first half hour of our conversation, Jacinta details just how fabulous and fun it was to work for Ethan. The closest thing to a complaint she could come up with was, "Sometimes his schedule was manic." She's done everything but regale us with tales of how he hugs lepers and dries puppy tears in his spare time.

Getting frustrated, I begin a new line of questioning. "I hear Ethan is quite a . . ." How do I say "slut" without using the word *slut*? "I hear he's, um, a bit of a ladies' man." To put it mildly.

Jacinta laughs. "He's lived in L.A. most of his life, and he's a good-looking guy. Of course he's dated a lot. He'd hate me saying this, but . . ." Her voice trails off.

Don't stop now!

"But . . ." I encourage.

"The bad boy image is totally manufactured by the press. He's not like that. He rarely brought women home, didn't really sleep around. I never thought of him as a womanizer or skirt chaser or anything."

"Oh," I say, for lack of anything better.

Jacinta adds, "I suppose he's occasionally fallen into bed with the wrong person, but we've all done that, right?"

I hope that's a rhetorical question, because I'd hate to have to get into that. I mean, do I go chronologically from the beginning? Or start with Todd and work my way backward?

I change the subject. "So, he never hit on you, or . . ."

"No way," she replies with a laugh. "He likes 'em feisty. I'm way too low maintenance for him. That's probably one of the reasons he gets into trouble—high-maintenance women have a tendency to create high drama, if you know what I mean."

I don't know why, but I suddenly feel slightly offended.

Jacinta continues, "I think he likes a challenge."

"Really?" asks Brooke before eyeing me.

What's that look supposed to mean? I shrug my shoulders at her, but she doesn't answer. Brooke simply smiles and takes a gulp of coffee.

Right. This is not going as I'd planned. Let me try again. "But, Jacinta, you quit your job with him. So then, he must have done *something* to make you decide you couldn't take it anymore."

"You're right," she says, "he did." Jacinta looks down to the giant bulge under her Pea in the Pod T-shirt, strokes it gently.

Brooke gapes at me, her eyes widening to the size of dinner plates. She's obviously thinking the same thing I am: *Holy shit!*

"Gordon," Jacinta says sweetly.

"Aw, it's a boy?" Brooke says tenderly.

"What?" Jacinta asks, her nose and eyes squinching up in what appears to be confusion. She adds, "Oh, my God! You thought . . ." before breaking into a fit of riotous laughter.

Several moments pass—Jacinta laughing, Brooke and I looking at each other perplexed.

Finally, as her giggles subside, Jacinta puffs, "Oh! Don't make me laugh. My bladder can't take it." She clasps her hands onto either side of her belly—as if trying to stabilize it. She raises her left hand to show us a small but elegant engagement ring and a thin slip of a gold wedding band. "Gordon—my *husband*. He and Ethan worked together on *Out of Harm*. Gordon played one of the foot soldiers in Ethan's platoon. They became friends, and Ethan set us up on a blind date."

"Ethan introduced you to your husband. The father of your baby," Brooke says, while a smile—with a troublesome "I told you so" look about it—creeps across her face.

"After we got married Gordon wanted to move to New York . . . what he really wants to do is direct. I know, cliché, right? But it's his dream. Anyway, I had to quit my job with Ethan. Oh, and by the way," Jacinta says with a sentimental little gleam in her eye, "it's a girl."

COURTNEY'S WYATT
SHRINE—FORUMS

Post: June 10 Re: Where is Ethan?

Courtney: I've been getting a lot of e-mails regarding Ethan's whereabouts and why he hasn't been seen doing anything around NYC. I've been tapping into my (seriously connected!) sources and nobody seems to know. But I don't think it's a girl. I really don't. Let me repeat that: I am not hearing anything about Ethan Wyatt seeing anybody! We all know Ethan has been trying to get out of the public eye for a while. And he deserves a break. Why don't we all stop freaking out about it and give him his space?

—Courtney Jackson (soon-to-be Wyatt)

"Sometimes you have to put your faith in people. Then let your heart do the rest."

—Ethan Wyatt as "Mason Kapfhammer"
in *Going Nowhere* (2002)

Posted Response: June 10 Re: Where is Ethan?

MistressJC341: OMG, Courtney. You are so deluding yourself.

CHAPTER 20

Turns out Ethan wasn't even angry when Jacinta quit—not even a little peeved. He was the best man at her wedding.

What's worse, when I got home from Barnes & Noble I did a little research online.

I Googled the crap out of his name and, unfortunately, found out loads of very interesting, very exciting, very *nice* things about him. For example, I discovered that the whole business about "Cocoa with an *a* " was a poorly crafted, poorly executed scam. Cocoa had tried the same paternity suit tactic on the CEO of a Fortune 500 company and the erstwhile owner of a chain of Nevada Gas-n-Sips. Ethan was her third—and probably last—attempt at acquiring a handsome child support settlement. As it turns out, all three of her children were fathered by the same man, a gentleman who goes by the name of Lux. (He also happens to be the D.J. at the strip joint she works in.) This story I found buried deep in the archives of the *Las Vegas Sentinel Voice*. When originally printed, the article sat right beside a piece on the proposed rerouting of sewer pipes. Funny, the story about Cocoa *accusing* Ethan was front page news in the same paper. I have to say, even I found that the slightest bit unfair.

With further digging—and carefully sifting out tabloid reports of bar brawls and how Ethan "loves the ladies"—I found dozens of articles about how great he is. Of course, I also found dozens of articles labeling him a sellout and discounting every bit of work he's done since about 1999 as blatant and pathetic bids for money with no regard for artistic merit or, more important, plot. It seems Ethan was expected to be the new indie poster boy—doing good work for next to no pay. He was supposed to be Paul Giamatti, only disturbingly attractive. River Phoenix, only alive. He was to be the rich man's Vincent Gallo. This all ended when he became the rich man's Ethan Wyatt, star of such memorable films as *Loose Girls* and *Felony Charge*. As much as I'd like to defend my own comments about how Ethan has turned into a "plastic action figure," the criticism I'm finding online seems to be overkill. I guess the backlash against him "going Hollywood" probably wouldn't have been so harsh if, in early interviews, he hadn't proclaimed that it was his dream to be a serious actor. He said—repeatedly—that his goal was to "do small but important films" and focus on his "craft." But, come on. I mean, maybe he just saw his first action picture as his one big opportunity to pay off his credit cards. Maybe at first he thought he could do both—one big action flick, followed by one indie. Maybe he just got used to the comfort, and let's face it, joy, of not being beholden to someone else to help pay the rent. Is that really so hard to understand?

Honestly, I don't know how they do it . . . people who really go after their dreams. How do people manage to stick it out and put up with the life of a starving artist? How do they survive the uncertainty of not knowing if the dream will come true or just be a complete waste of time and energy? I can't really blame him for taking a shot at something more stable.

He's a man with a razor-sharp wit that's both self-effacing and charming (and not just in that sort of evil way that I've experienced). And, okay . . . though I wouldn't ever admit to this in public, even if forced to take an oath, I can almost see how someone—not me, mind you but *someone*—might fall for him. In that sort of quixotic way that Brooke has fallen for Duncan Stoke, I mean. If he weren't a phone-thieving stalker, Ethan Wyatt would almost be a bit of a catch—and it's driving me crazy. There has to be *something* wrong with him.

Could he really be this amazing, semisensitive, outrageously good-looking do-gooder? Really?

Would a guy like that stoop to petty vengeance and harassment? I don't think so. There has to be more to him than that. I just have to figure out what.

I turn up the Jason Mraz on the stereo and sing the words into my toothbrush. To stimulate my brainstorming, I polished off an entire box of Chocolate Fudge Frosted Pop-Tarts. To prevent stimulating myself straight to Jenny Craig, I must now stand before my full-length mirror and lunge to the beat.

I lunge at the sinister Brown Box in the corner and raise my voice, hoping to frighten the thing out of existence using only my horrible Jason Mraz impersonation. No dice.

Damn, I have the windows open, no less than three fans

going, and am wearing only panties and a tank top; still, my bedroom feels hot enough to slowly roast a chicken. I position myself in front of the box fan on my windowsill, spreading my arms wide, doing mini arm curls. The mintiness of the toothpaste and the sharp blast of air combine to mimic passably the feeling of a chilly breeze. Lovely.

A shrill clang somewhere outside my window interrupts my brushing and curling. It almost sounds like rusty metal being bent or—oh no. The fire escape.

Jason Mraz sings, "Say it isn't so / How she easily come, how she easy go . . ."

Oh, God, it's getting closer. And, by *it* I mean some evil nightcrawler that will no doubt make me prime pickings for a "ripped from the headlines" episode of *CSI: NY*. I can see it now, the rubber-gloved hands pawing my dainty underthings, big burly men examining my medicine cabinet for overused prescription drugs, that chick from *Providence* flirtatiously swinging her curly hair over my headless corpse.

Man, I wish I had that baseball bat now. Unfortunately, since I ambushed Ethan Wyatt, Brooke has refiled it under a completely different category. It could be in her frighteningly large box of hair accessories, for all I know.

What do I do? I mean, besides panic?

Okay, what am I freaking out about? It's probably some drunk guy who forgot his keys (hopefully not the sicko who lost the four-foot rubber penis in the alley). Or, a really ambitious window cleaner (with a knife fetish and a collection of spy cameras). Or, I am totally hallucinating . . . because I think I see Ethan Wyatt on my fire escape.

"Hey," he says, his voice sounding quivery and comical as it comes through the fan on my windowsill.

I approach the window in silence, clenching the toothbrush in my mouth, and blinking my eyes repeatedly in the hopes that this bizarre 3-D mirage will dematerialize without several thousands of dollars of intensive therapy.

"You didn't play fair before," he adds smugly.

I slowly remove the fan from the window. I inhale deeply and poke my index finger in the direction of the hallucination.

My nail jabs into a soft cotton T-shirt and then beyond, pressing into actual, tangible human flesh.

The hallucination speaks. "Ouch."

Oh, he's really here.

He's really here!

Crap—and I am in my underwear.

I quickly back away so that he can't see the cottage cheesyness of my thighs. "Ever hear of a telephone?" I mumble, spitting bits of toothpaste all over the floor. "I'm in my underwear here," I add.

"Yeah, you are," he says dumbly, staring at me with a strangely blank expression on his face.

"Well, turn your head!" I demand while backing myself to the nearest pair of clean pajama shorts. Oh, God, where would that be? Drawer? Closet?

I switch off the stereo and look behind it for any signs of wayward clothing. Then I freeze as something disturbing occurs to me. "Do you have a camera?" "Have" sounded more like "hab" through the toothpaste, but whatever.

"Naturally," he says, suddenly sounding like Cary Grant.

Coincidentally enough, he also has Grant's signature mischievous grin.

"Don't you dare!" I command, while searching for something to put on. I have literally seventeen pairs of shorts—where are they?

Behind me, I hear the click of a shutter.

"Ahhhhh!" I scream. "Stop! This is illegal! You're on—" Oh, I was going to say private property but that sounds vaguely familiar.

"What?" Ethan asks, his eyebrows rising dramatically. He puts his hand to his ear. "What was that? I'm on *what*?"

"Ugh!" I groan while going ass first in three directions before stopping altogether. I have no idea where clean shorts are—pathetic.

I grab a small but heavy ceramic cat figurine that sits on my bookshelf—another gift from Paige (Needed. Gift for: female. Age: thirteen. Likes: kittens and Scott Baio). I raise the cat over my head. "Get out of here!"

"Hold on!" Ethan says, letting the camera swing down on the strap around his neck. "Okay, relax." He puts his hands up like bullets might shoot out of the cat's beady little glass eyes. "I shot at the ground just now. I swear."

"That better be true, Wyatt," I say, sending bits of bubbly toothpaste dribbling down my chin.

I lower the cat slowly to the bed. He lowers his hands slowly to the windowsill.

At my feet, I spot a semiclean pair of shorts crumpled in a pile. I slip them on and race to the bathroom. While rinsing my mouth out, I double-check my wilt factor. Pretty repulsive.

I whip my hair into a quick ponytail, dab the perspiration and Pop-Tart dust from my face. . . . Oh my God, I'm trying to make myself look presentable for a man who just climbed up my fire escape to torment me. I drop the hairbrush and calmly saunter back into the bedroom.

"Okay, now what the hell are you doing here?" I try to display the proper level of gruff obstinacy, but sitting in my window with that stupid camera around his neck, Ethan Wyatt suddenly looks like a schoolboy on a field trip. I try to keep a smile from creeping onto my face.

"You didn't play fair today," he says gravely.

A tight knot forms in my throat. Oh, God, he knows about Jacinta. He knows about Jacinta, and my plan B, and now I'm sure he thinks I'm a horrible person.

Ethan continues, "I *liked* that shirt."

Oh! I exhale, relieved. Trying to act casual, I ask, "Which one was it?"

"You know, with the little plastic Army guys going across the front."

"Oh, right." It does look good on him.

"Yeah, well, it's now a wife-beater."

I can't help it, a smile makes its way to the surface. "You are *so* exaggerating."

"Fine. But, seriously, though, how do you get hot pink lipstick out of cotton?"

Before I can check the impulse, I'm laughing.

"It's not funny," he gripes.

"Uh, yeah, it is," I reply.

I am laughing with my stalker.

Right. Remember, Sadie, you hate him.

Okay. I clear my throat and wipe the grin from my face. "Couldn't this have waited till—oh, I don't know—dawn? Or, um . . . *never?*"

He replies nervously, "I saw your light on."

What the hell was he doing looking at my lights? And climbing up six flights of rickety fire escape? I guess it shouldn't surprise me. Actors live by a whole different set of rules than the rest of the universe. "Wait, how did you know it was *my* light?" I ask.

My question catches him off-guard. He tips his head and raises an eyebrow with boyish charm—the charm of a *guilty* boy. He stutters, "Binoculars and . . ." He points to the little arch-shaped nook over my bed. "The Galella print over your bed. I took a chance."

"What were you going to do if it wasn't me?" I ask—out of unquenchable curiosity.

"Sign an autograph?" he says goofily, while shrugging his shoulders.

"Interesting . . ."

The room falls under an uncomfortable hush.

Suspecting that he could sit here being uncomfortable for all eternity, I say, "I, uh, don't do laundry. So, is there something else I can do for you?"

"Well, now that you mention it—I had a question," he says, regaining that Cary Grant cockiness. "Were you just brushing your teeth with a Yoda toothbrush?"

"Oh, no," I retort immediately.

"Oh, no—what?"

"I'm not going to let you sucker me into saying something that you can blab about in the papers. You can't use those tricks on me—"

"What tricks?" he asks, a smile spreading across his face.

"Those tricks!" I point at him.

He looks over his shoulder. "What are you talking about?"

"That little . . . sexy, charming, debonair thing you've got going on, with all your smiling and twinkling and . . . whatnot."

"Whatnot?"

"Exactly!"

Ethan laughs, takes off his Red Sox hat, and scratches his head. "Just answer the question. What am I going to say, Duncan Stoke's secret girlfriend is a Yoda fan?"

You'd be surprised how mundane a thing has to be to make it into the papers. I tip my nose down and stare at him, glaring at him like my dad used to glare at me when I was a teenager.

Ethan just laughs. "Come on. It's a simple question. What was on the toothbrush that you were singing into before?"

Singing into? "How long were you standing down there with those binoculars, you sicko?"

"Long enough." He pauses for effect. "The running man, I thought, was a particularly nice touch."

I feel my cheeks go red, my heart begin to pound. "Do you have a telephoto lens for that thing?" I ask frantically.

"Unfortunately, no." He sounds genuinely disappointed in himself. "Answer the question. Was that, or was that not, a Yoda toothbrush?"

I try to be stern and authoritarian. "Uh, yes. As a matter of fact, it was. You got a problem with that?" The only problem is, the topic at hand is a Yoda toothbrush.

"No," he chuckles. "Not at all."

"I happen to consider the fight against tooth decay a fundamental battle of good versus evil," I say, planting my hands on my hips.

He looks at me with a smile. It's wide and unprejudiced. He is looking at me not with bitterness or disdain, but in a normal man/woman, boy/girl sort of way—a deeply perplexing, almost *flirtatious* way. It's almost like he's amused by me . . . interested.

Ethan continues to grin, thinking something to himself. The only clues to his thoughts are the subtle shifts of expression around his eyes and mouth, barely perceptible—but so powerful. It almost makes me want to grab my camera. Not because he should be plastered on the gaudy pages of a weekly glossy, but because it is an extraordinary and intangible thing he has. It should be documented, made solid—to remind me later that it was real.

I wonder if I've ever looked at anybody that way. If I have, it hasn't been for quite some time. Unless, well, I might just be doing it now. Not sure.

I shake my head and try to restore a look of blithe indifference to my face.

"Do you hate it yet?" he asks. "Tired of never knowing where I'll be next, with you on the subway . . . outside your apartment . . . on your fire escape? You haven't been working much lately—my fault?"

"I'm doing just fine, thank you," I reply.

"Sure you are—"

"I could do this for ages. You could sleep out there for all I care."

"Uh-huh—"

"You're failing!" I say, feeling a warm rush of adrenaline. "You think I'm miserable?" I add, gaining momentum. "Do I look miserable to you? Go ahead, take a picture now! Go on! I'm not afraid!"

Ethan lifts his camera and shoots off a half-dozen frames. He looks at me, trying not to laugh—he's not having such an easy time of it.

Against my own will, my eyes drop and I glance at myself. There's a Pop-Tart stain on my tank top, I'm wearing Strawberry Shortcake sleeper shorts—backward. My left knee is swollen and purple, and I'm pretty sure that's toothpaste on my right arm.

My hands clench and I groan with unparalleled frustration.

I stomp over to the window and slam it shut—right on Ethan's camera strap.

I yank roughly on the cord to the miniblinds and then twist them closed.

A rough clang startles me—the window being opened.

"Bye," Ethan says quietly through a hail of laughter. "See you tomorrow."

The window slams shut again, just before I bury my head in a pillow and scream.

STOKE'S "NORMAL" GAL PAL
REALLY IN THE BIZ?

Sources close to Duncan Stoke's new gal pal, Sadie Price, say that the talk swirling around about her is just untrue—she's not such a regular girl after all. The pretty and, some say, notoriously clumsy new glamour-puss on Duncan Stoke's arm isn't any ordinary New York photog. She isn't snapping bedazzled bridesmaids and tipsy tuxedoed ushers. Unless, that is, the Usher in question is the megahot Grammy-winning recording artist. Price is actually a celebrity photographer (that means paparazzi for all of you not up on the lingo). She spends her nights cruising NYC for the latest in celebrity gossip. Our source says the pair met at a glam New York fete attended by Duncan and photographed by Sadie. Sorry, normal girls—better luck next time.

CHAPTER 21

Todd," I say, my tone inching dangerously close to begging. "Please, I may not be able to chase Owen Wilson around Manhattan, but I can do something. I'll do anything. I can't take this time off, it's driving me insane." I haven't taken a single photograph of anyone since that thing with Ethan Wyatt and Lori Dunn—and Ethan Wyatt is getting some sort of amusement from it.

Not to mention my mother just got the brilliant idea that we should all go to lunch . . . and a matinee. To be followed, if possible, by shopping. She'll force me to buy a suite of perfectly boring little twin sets and age-appropriate pearls. Honestly, being eaten alive by birds sounds like a more pleasant alternative. If Todd says no, that's my next stop.

He stares at me while fiddling with a tattered issue of the *Robb Report*. "All right, nothing heavy, though. That thing with Naomi Watts cost me thousands," Todd says before pausing—mulling it over. He continues, "How about this: the premiere

for the new Ashton Kutcher flick is tonight at the Ziegfeld The-
atre. You'll be in the pen, but it could be worth a little cash."

"Fine. Great," I say, heading for the office door.

"Hey, Sadie, I need the old you back. You got me?"

"Yeah," I say solemnly. So do I.

These days, even straight, supposedly highbrow newspapers and
magazines are gagging for photos of the beautiful people dis-
playing their borrowed clothes and jewels. Publications from
Cosmo to, completely serious here, the *Wall Street Journal* routinely feature Adler's red carpet stuff. And let me tell you, it's no
picnic getting it. These parties and premieres may look glamorous on *Access Hollywood,* but they're not. They are loud, either
too hot or too cold, and involve hours of standing around
yelling. I suppose if you're the one walking down the red carpet
it's not so bad. It is, after all, just walking. Most people do it all
day long with very little trouble—I am, at least currently, one
notable exception.

My leg is killing me—I think I overdid it last night with the
lunges. This is what happens when I deviate from lotions and
potions and attempt random acts of exercise. The throbbing
pain of the original injury has subsided, but it's been replaced by
a burning sensation and a strange (and rather disconcerting)
clicking noise emanating from my kneecap. One good thing has
come of all this, though. I have arrived at the conclusion that
giant handbags, especially those filled with rocks, are a clear and
present danger to the health and well-being of the public at
large. I'm going to petition the mayor for a ban. I think it'll go
through without a problem; that guy just loves to ban things.

I shuffle toward the photo pen, my gear and gimpy leg trailing behind in my wake. As I go, I quietly nurture the small hope that all of this has been one very elaborate *Punk'd,* and that Ashton will tell me so himself when he glides past me on the red carpet.

The photo pen is the small, stockadelike structure that keeps the photographers from soiling the expensive rented red carpet. Like farm animals, we are corralled behind barricades and forced to work for our supper. Within its flimsy confines we elbow, crane, muscle, and stretch to get the shots the celebrities and their "people" need to keep this whole business humming. I've always found it a bit ironic that the ones preening, clucking, and strutting around with their feathers and furs are the ones allowed *outside* the pen. Shouldn't the photographers be the ones taking a leisurely stroll while the stars are made to squawk and stumble around in a paddock?

I step onto the red carpet just as the searchlights rev up. Giant swaths of light swish back and forth across the sky. With this, the crowd of extremely chipper Ashton-loving tweens begins to pulsate with anticipation. Their chattering becomes screaming, every emotion exaggerated by the promise of celebrity sightings, autographs, and maybe—just maybe—a quick peck on the cheek from the man himself. Several of the tweens, each with a thick layer of glitter on her eyelids, carry signs that say "Marry me, Ashton!" and "I'm the one you're looking for!" One says, "Choose me! Dump Demi!" I'd say they're about thirty years premature, and woefully uninformed about Kabbalah.

A flock of flustered PR people and security personnel marches up and down the red carpet, talking into tiny microphones and listening to even tinier earpieces. One of them is a source of mine; he slips me tips from time to time. I called him, cashed in a favor, and had him reserve me a spot on the line—front and center. This means I can *sit* on my collapsible stool-slash-ladder instead of standing atop it at the back of the pack like I usually have to when I do this kind of thing.

I force my way into the gathering throng of photographers, waving to the few familiar faces already assembled, and settle in between two guys, Mark and Gary, who consider themselves legit photojournalists.

They're an interesting pair, an Ambiguously Gay Duo of sorts, both frail, spindly little things who only work with each other. I can't tell if they're a couple or what, but they seem to enjoy each other's company enormously. Unfortunately, I also can't tell them apart. Technically, they're paparazzi, too, but unlike me they only work at events like this. And because they're "friendlies" (and New York models and socialites are desperate for publicity), they get invited *into* parties. For some strange reason, this gives them a sense of superiority, false though it may be.

I nod to each of them in turn. They instantly begin snickering like schoolgirls.

Oh, great.

"So, Duncan Stoke?" poses Mark (or Gary), examining me up and down.

Gary (or Mark) chimes in, "Shouldn't you be on the other side of the ropes there?"

"You two should know better than to believe what you read in the tabloids."

"She sure sounds like she should be on the other side of the ropes," Mark quips to Gary (or Gary quips to Mark).

I could break them like twigs. I'd probably do it, too—if I could stand properly. "It's just some demented person's idea of a joke. Either of you recognize the work?" I ask. Pretending not to know who did it seems my best defense at this point.

"Nah, they're some pretty shitty shots," Mark/Gary says before quickly adding, "No offense." Yeah, right.

"None taken," I reply, before turning to Gary/Mark with a silent query.

"No. No idea," he answers. He adds smugly, "Not one of ours, obviously."

"Yeah, obviously." Photojournalists, my ass. Exactly what about standing around with a camera and waiting for people to walk by constitutes journalism? If the walkers in question weren't Demi Moore and Ashton Kutcher, it'd just be loitering—with film.

The first arrivals begin, as the C-listers (the Hasselhoffs, Guttenbergs, and stars of VH1 list shows like *100 Greatest Wardrobe Malfunctions* and *I Love the 00's*) funnel out of cabs and limos onto the red carpet. Camera flashes trickle to a start, and the screaming begins.

"Steve! Steve, over here!"

"David, this way!"

"Smile for the camera, Michael Ian Black!"

"Guttenberg, where's your little lady?"

"Hey, Hasselhoff, you ever beat that DUI rap?"

That last little gem stings my right ear. Both the volume and the familiarity of the voice make me cringe—Phil.

"Ah," Phil grumbles to me above the din of the surrounding photographers. "If it isn't Sleeps with the Enemy."

I reply, "Oh, you've converted to Native American—fascinating. Tell me, Walks with Pitchfork, shouldn't you be digging around in De Niro's garbage right now?"

"Touchy, touchy."

I'm just going to pretend that Phil doesn't exist, that I can't smell his slightly rancid Eternity for Men, and instead focus on the task at hand. A-list celebrities have finally begun to arrive.

A comfortable, soothing rush of excitement washes over me as I click off dozens of frames.

Jamie-Lynn Sigler is ravishing in shades of pink and lilac.

Mira Sorvino and her hot young hubby are adorable.

. . . P. Diddy . . . Christina Ricci . . . Julia Stiles . . . Donald Trump . . . They all saunter past the photo pen, pausing every couple of steps to pose—and I get all of them.

A lull in the arrivals is the only thing that breaks my stride—some sort of limo pileup, no doubt.

A rather fresh and happy-looking Cindy Crawford makes her way down the line of photographers. Lucky her, she's the only celebrity in sight.

I snap off a few shots of Cindy and pull the camera away from my face—to give my eye and my arm a rest.

"Hey, Sadie!" cries Phil over my shoulder.

What now? I turn. "Yeah—"

A dazzling, scorching light fills my eyes.

I'm blind.

That asshole really did it this time. I am actually blind.

Rubbing my eyes, I scream, "What the fuck, Phil? Watch where you point that thing."

"Just in case," he replies slowly, with a bitter cockiness in his tone.

I open my eyes. Through a haze of purple dots I see Phil smirking over the lens of his camera.

I ask, "Just in case wha—"

Before I know it, I'm staring into a half-dozen wide, black, vacant eyes—deep, hollow, and menacing.

"You guys, seriously," I plead.

In an instant, a half-dozen flashes go off in my face. An instant later, eight more, then ten. Gary/Mark, Mark/Gary, and several other photographers in the vicinity fire away at me with impunity.

"You guys!" I beg once more.

"Sorry, but it's my job," I hear Mark/Gary say. The familiar ring of that phrase causes a knot to form in my throat.

The maelstrom of bright light and shutter clicks sends me into a dizzy spell.

The only thing I see—the only thing I can think about—is the flashing light stinging my eyes. There's no use in turning away—nowhere to go. The flashing light spills out over everything, making the world around me seem pale and overexposed.

I squeeze my eyes shut and wait for the clicking sound to stop. It's the only thing I can think to do.

After several seconds of rubbing my eyes, I manage to peel an eye open and discern that the arrivals have resumed. The idiots around me have, thankfully, turned the black eyes of their cameras back to the red carpet.

A sudden deafening outcry from the fan gallery alerts us all that someone important is here.

From the far end of the photo pen comes, "Ethan! Ethan!"

Great. Perfect. And my heart rate was just returning to normal.

I put the camera back to my eye. Now how am I supposed to take pictures like this? I can't see anything. The whole world is covered in a bluish haze and little black dots are floating all over my field of view. My heart feels like it's pounding against my lungs, forcing me to take short, shallow breaths to keep the oxygen flowing.

The cries for Ethan Wyatt's attention crescendo.

Wyatt saunters coolly past the first ten feet of the photo pen, not deigning to stop and pose. He strides down the carpet, an eerie serenity playing on his face. The crowd is mesmerized by his elegant features and expertly tousled black hair. Those impossibly blue eyes. A tiny bit of skin exposed by a jacket gone askew. They're spellbound, and he knows it.

Oh, boy, that walk is something special.

As he ambles into my general vicinity, he turns, slows his pace. His eyes dart up and down the photo pen, scanning for something—someone. Even against the hail of flashes and screams, he remains unruffled.

Through the tiny rectangle of my viewfinder I see Ethan Wyatt's expression change. He takes three purposeful steps up the red carpet and then stops—in front of me.

His jaw tightens up, shoulders tip slightly farther back, push-

ing his well-defined pectoral muscles against the supple fabric of
his shirt.

He glares directly through my lens and straight between my
eyes, like he's trying to bore into my skull. Just the slightest hint
of a smile slowly spreads across his outrageously handsome face.
It causes my camera to slip out of my hands and slide down the
strap. It comes to rest somewhere near my belly button.

That is a look of pride. Sheer, unadulterated pride.

Ethan puts his finger up. As his eyes lock onto mine, he gives
me the "come here" gesture. The power of it almost knocks me
off my feet.

Amid the confused glances of the other photographers, I lean
slightly forward.

Ethan Wyatt angles toward me, that tiny bit of exposed flesh
just above his belt presses up against the cold metal rail separating *us* from *them*. His lips move closer to my ear; his nose grazes
the top of my earlobe.

He whispers, "I meant to tell you, don't forget you have your
monthly haircut and . . . *ahem* . . . lip wax tomorrow. Two
o'clock."

He pulls away grinning slyly, and I'm left leaning against the
railing with both hands—to keep myself from collapsing. Unfortunately, I don't think my wooziness has anything to do with my
knee. (Though, the words *lip* and *wax* could have a little something to do with it.) I swear, there's some sort of black magic in
all that winking and whispering and general . . . hotness.

Ethan breaks his gaze and resumes posing for the other photographers.

I'd love to shake my fists at him and scream, "You won't beat me!" but I can't. Just now, perched on my one good leg, trying desperately to see past a bluish polka-dotted haze, and contemplating the fact that a wickedly hot man knows I get my lip waxed—I have to say, I feel the slightest bit beaten.

Oh, and guess what . . . I didn't get a single shot of Ethan Wyatt.

I hear a grunt from over my shoulder and turn to identify its source. Phil.

His beady, bloodshot eyes glare directly into mine. One of his eyebrows raises up. He's suspicious. Very suspicious.

I suddenly feel the overwhelming need to defend myself, to deflect his curiosity. "Damn actors," I say, trying to sound venomous. "Threatening me with lawsuits. Huh! *Idiots.*" That was really unconvincing. I may have just cranked his suspicion *up* instead of decreasing it. Shit, I really should have paid more attention in the one acting class I took in college. Unfortunately, as it is, I didn't learn much beyond the lyrics to *Annie Get Your Gun*.

The celebrities are all inside. I think I'm going to go home and take a long hot bath and let Jason Mraz sing me into a bubbly coma.

I lumber down the abandoned red carpet and, almost to the sidewalk, I nearly lose my lunch.

My mother is sitting behind the wheel of her Mercedes, just off to the left of the VIP arrival point.

She rolls down the passenger's side window and leans over the center console. "Hi, darling! I thought I'd surprise you and give you a ride home. Fancy some dinner? My treat!"

My mommy came to pick me up from work.

I'm just about to ask her how she managed to make it through the many blockades that have been set up to keep out the riffraff when Paige looks over my shoulder and gives a flirtatious little wave to someone behind me.

I turn around to see a very large member of the security team wave back at her—and blush. Ah, I see.

"I guess—" Oh, crap. The faint tinkle of electronic ringing issues from inside my bag. I give my mom the "hold on" finger point and quickly retrieve the phone. It's my PR contact from inside.

"Hey," I grumble, trying to sound tired.

"Thought you'd wanna know, Ethan Wyatt is on his way out of the building," comes the voice through the line.

"Which door?"

"Back."

"Good, thanks," I reply.

I turn my attention back to Paige.

"Okay," I say to her. "You stay here. I'll be right back."

"Sadie!" she calls, as I do my best to hobble away quickly. I'm going to get a picture of Ethan Wyatt's face if it kills me—this time, with my eyes open.

Behind me I hear a car door slam and my mother's voice tittering, "Would you be a dear? Won't be a sec, thanks!"

I look back to see her handing her car keys to the burly, blushing security guy and skipping in her Manolos toward me.

I stop dead in my tracks. "Mother, seriously. You need to stay here. I'll only be a minute, I promise. Then you can take me wherever you want. Just stay here."

"You're injured. You need help with those bags," she says

while ripping my camera bag off my shoulder and strong-arming the collapsible stool from my hand. "I'll be your assistant!"

My assistant is wearing three-inch heels and a four-hundred-dollar cashmere sweater.

We make our way to the back of the building just in time to see Ethan Wyatt signing autographs for a couple of cater-waiters.

"Okay, I mean it—you have to stay here. No matter what happens, just don't move. I'll come back for you in a minute. All right?"

"Is that Ethan Wyatt?" Not exactly the response I was looking for.

"Yes. Are you going to stay here or—"

She shoves the camera bag and stool at me and rolls up her sleeves as though preparing for a fight. She marches away—in the direction of Ethan Wyatt.

Since she just claimed to be my assistant, does that mean I can fire her now?

As the waiters trudge back into the theater, eBay fodder in hand, Ethan lights a cigarette and descends a set of concrete steps to street level.

"Paige!" I yell.

She doesn't skip a beat.

"Mother!"

Still heading straight for him.

"Is that you, Price?" he says, shielding his eyes from the stark white light illuminating the side of the theater.

Paige closes in on Ethan's position, and I do my best to increase my speed.

"Hello!" I hear my mother say while holding out her hand. "My name is Paige. I believe we've spoken?"

Ethan takes her hand and smiles at her brightly.

My mother continues, "So, you're the man who's stalking my daughter."

"I am," he says proudly.

Oh, my God, this is humiliating. The next thing you know she'll be asking Ethan for his mother's phone number so they can discuss his inappropriate behavior.

Paige appraises him like you would a dog show entrant, examining his hind quarters, quantifying the luster of his coat. "You don't *look* particularly crazy," she says with a coquettish air.

"Thank you, Mrs.—is it Price?"

"Price-Farmer, actually. But please, call me Paige."

I finally hobble into striking distance. I lean over to my mother and whisper, "What do you think you're doing?"

She lays one of her well-manicured hands on my shoulder and says, "It's fine, sweetheart. Trust your mother."

Yeah, that'll happen. I whisper back, "Are you *crazy*?" (That's number two, if you're counting.)

"Mr. Wyatt, my daughter is a very strong-willed individual."

"I'm aware of that," Ethan replies. With nothing but three cubic feet of humid air between us, his eyes suddenly lock onto mine. His eyes are doing that somewhat breathtaking boy-girl thing again, like I'm not the bane of his existence but just a person—a person that he just might like a little bit.

I do the only thing I can think to do—I look away.

Paige resumes, "I don't have to tell you, then, the sorts of things she would like to do to you in return for this vendetta of yours."

"Mother—" I try again.

"I think I can guess," he says—still smiling at me and not even glancing toward Paige.

"Just stop," I whisper to Paige, begging.

She waves her hand to shush me. "Mr. Wyatt, I completely understand your frustration with Sadie's behavior. The picture of you that recently appeared in *Celeb* was beyond intrusive—"

"Mother!" I yelp, trying to grab her arm as she and Ethan begin calmly strolling toward the sidewalk.

I struggle to keep up. Limping as I am with two armloads of gear.

Paige continues, "To be honest, I have often thought Sadie would have been better off sticking with her first passion . . ."

Oh, no! "Don't!" I hiss to her.

"Art photography. *Portraits,*" she says, raising an eyebrow as though fully expecting Ethan to be impressed. "She did such beautiful work . . . once." Oh, my God. "She had an amazing talent."

Had an amazing talent? What, did my talent just up and walk out the door on me? Desert me like some fickle boyfriend?

"Paige!" I exclaim with venom. "You need to—"

But my words get tangled with Ethan's. With his voice dripping in self-satisfied curiosity, he asks, "Portraits? Really?"

As usual, Paige's attention is completely beyond my grasp. She is arm in arm with a handsome man of wealth and consequence—I don't stand a chance.

"Oh, yes. She has a website. Look it up on the Internet."

This just gets better and better. If I'd been the one to throw that in his face, it'd be one thing. But my mother? With the caveat that my talent has suddenly vanished? With the snarky disapproval of all the work I've done since?

Paige resumes the humiliation. "Sadie has had a few trials in her life that precipitated this—"

"Oh, my God, Mother. What happened to the ignoring plan? You're off point. *Way* off point," I plead.

"As I said, I fully understand your frustration," she continues—completely ignoring me. "But I fail to see what justice or relief hurting my daughter will bring to you or those lovely young ladies you were involved with."

Ethan takes a deep breath. He stops, looks at me—thinking. "Paige, your daughter is . . . unique." He turns to Paige. "She's good at what she does. It just so happens that what she does hurts people—namely *me*. That shot in *Celeb* was—" He cuts himself off and takes a long drag of his cigarette. "It was the last straw, in a very long line of straws." Ethan looks around and exhales silvery smoke into the night air. "I just want Sadie to understand what it feels like to be on the other side of that lens. To see what it really means to do what she does. I'm sure it sounds petty. And, trust me, revenge is not something I do, usually. But giving her a taste of that makes me feel just a little bit better. So, I can't promise you that I'll stop. At least, not now."

My stomach turns, but not because he says he won't stop. It's the thing about how I hurt him—that boyish doe-eyed look about him as he said it. That's what got to me.

Obviously frustrated, but trying to control his emotions,

Ethan aggressively shoves his hands in his pockets. As he flips his jacket back, he again reveals that tiny little patch of flesh above his belt. For some reason I can't take my eyes off it.

"I see, then, that we're at an impasse," replies Paige with a demure little nod of her head. "It was a pleasure to meet you, Mr. Wyatt," she adds, holding her hand out once more.

"No, the pleasure is mine," he replies, shaking her hand.

A pleasure to meet the man who's stalking me? A pleasure to meet Paige? These people are lunatics!

Stunned, and possibly slipping into mortification-induced shock, I stand at the edge of the sidewalk and watch Ethan slide into the back of a waiting limousine.

My heart sinks suddenly, remembering something . . . I didn't get a picture. . . .

The light from the streetlamps stings my eyes, red and dry as they are from the assault in the pen.

Paige comes to my side and caresses my arm. "Well," she says, "that's unfortunate."

"Unfortunate?" I say, shrugging off her caress and dropping my camera bag and stool to the ground. *"Unfortunate?"*

"Sadie, calm down."

"You just completely humiliated me. It may only be about the nine millionth time you've humiliated me in my life, but to him? *Now?* You're a fucking fruitcake, you know that?"

"Language, dear," she says calmly.

"God! And I had talent *once*? How do you always know exactly the worst possible moment to say these things? Did you have to train somewhere for that?"

Her eyes fill with phony concern. It's the same look she used to give me when I'd sulk, and sometimes cry, from her little mother-daughter exhibitions. She tries, "Sadie, I—"

"No. No! You can't manipulate me anymore. Why can't you just stop trying to make me feel bad? God!"

"I came here to help you," Paige exclaims, with what looks alarmingly like real shock. "That's what I'm doing."

"If you really want to help me, you'll let me be!"

I grab my gear from the ground and race out onto Seventh Avenue.

TELLING LIES
IN HOLLYWOOD

Rumors aren't just casual diversions in Tinseltown—they're gold. Faintly whispered conjecture is the very fuel that feeds the Hollywood machine. Because of this, it can sometimes be difficult for the gossip industry to sift the truth from fiction.

"We do our best to ensure the accuracy of our reports," says "Celeb" senior editor Theresa Davish. "It can be quite a feat, too. We cover a lot of individuals who would much rather have their private truths be seen by the public as fiction."

The accountability of gossip publications for the verity of their work has always been a flash point for paparazzi-weary celebrities. More than ever, stars are marching into court to defend themselves. Rumor has it Ethan Wyatt is considering taking "Celeb" to the cleaners for their recent reportage regarding his alleged antics with Maya and Lori Dunn. At press time, we were unable to discern how much of that rumor is fact and how much is fiction.

CHAPTER 22

"My mother has a real talent for turning me back into a bitter, angsty teenager," I tell Luke as we sit on the floor of my bedroom flipping through some of my old portfolios. "For years I've done everything I can think of to keep things relatively nonviolent between us, and then *boom*, one suspiciously giant box and a few little words later and I'm back to screaming at her." And digging through the clutter under my bed to find my old portfolios. Damn, she's sneaky.

Luke turns the page of my sophomore portfolio and stares at a photograph of the chefs in the old restaurant my dad worked in. "Hating your job is, like, the last thing parents are allowed to fight with us about. It's the one thing left that won't get them dragged onto *Dr. Phil* for being bad parents. I promise you, fear of Dr. Phil is a major motivation in my mom's life."

"Please. Paige would chew up Dr. Phil like a stick of gum," I grumble. "I wish I could just crawl inside her head and figure out what her damage is." Actually, on second thought, it'd probably be pretty scary in there—all sequins, and Botox, and dog show statistics.

"Wow, this one's nice," Luke says, opening up my senior portfolio and pointing at a portrait I did of an old roommate.

"You just like it 'cause she's hot," I reply, looking over his shoulder.

"Maybe . . ." he replies sheepishly.

I inspect the portrait. God, I'd forgotten how piercing her eyes were. Staring at her in real life, you always had the sense you were being measured, judged. In the black and white of her photo, her eyes are even more penetrating, and yet, somehow, betray just the tiniest hint of vulnerability.

It's exciting to take a photograph of someone you know—someone whose face is so incredibly familiar to you—and capture that tiny fraction of a moment when they are being utterly themselves. We're used to seeing our friends in color, used to the distraction of their day-to-day armor—jewelry, makeup, fashion. We rely on intonation and hand gestures to tell us what we need to know about their state of mind. Essentially, we rely on *them* to tell us who they are. The beauty of black and white is that it erases all that; all the extraneous clues about emotion and convention are stripped away. It's pure. The pictures I always wanted to take, the ones I tried to take before I got into the paparazzi stuff, were about seeing beyond what people want us to think they are, and somehow capturing a flicker of the truth. I sometimes miss that.

"You know what really pisses me off?" I ask Luke.

"What?" he replies.

"She made it sound like I consciously gave up on the portraits. I mean, what does she think? That I just sat down one day and said, 'I'm not going to do this anymore'?"

Luke says, "I—"

". . . Because I didn't. It just . . . drifted away. It happens. The portraits were eventually this thing that I'm always meaning to do but can never seem to find the time for . . . like clearing old clothes from the closet, or dusting the crown molding in the living room. It happened naturally. . . ."

Luke tries, "Sadie, I—"

But I'm on a roll. ". . . And then, I got comfortable with my life without it. Big deal. Is being comfortable that bad? I like my life. It works. You know? Seriously, . . ."

Luke interjects, "Hey, I just—"

". . . why is my life now any less noble or important because I'm not poor and artistic? Why is following your dream so much more—"

"Sadie!" Luke shouts. "Slow your roll there, Killer." He ogles me with an uneasy sort of grimace. "Who are you trying to convince here? Me . . . or *you*?"

"Uh . . ." I stutter. "I'm not trying to convince anyone." I don't think. "I don't know."

I stare down at the portfolios splayed out on the floor—lying on a small area rug that I bought with my first check from Todd.

Luke blurts, "I'm sorry. I shouldn't have—"

"No, you were right to stop me," I say.

"Are you gonna be all right?" Luke asks, suddenly looking concerned.

"Sure," I reply.

"Are you?" he prods, a little crinkle appearing between his eyes. "You've got that weird, sad, faraway look you get sometimes."

I gawk at him, confused. "I get a weird, sad, faraway look sometimes?"

Luke reaches over to a pile of magazines and newspapers—a chronological stack of my meteoric rise to phony fame. He leafs through the top five or six issues and pulls out a copy of *Celeb* from last week.

He flips through the sheets, finding the page with my picture. With a bit of a sad, faraway look of his own, he hands it over.

It's a picture of me in the subway station after the autograph and the investment banker. I'm walking toward the exit, but my head is turned back—looking over my shoulder toward Ethan and his camera.

Huh. I do look sort of sad.

I didn't know I did that.

"I do that a lot, you say?" I ask Luke, feeling a bit like this picture should be hidden somewhere very dark and dusty.

Luke replies softly, "Yeah."

Luke has left for work, and I've renewed the giant Brown Box inspection process. It's pointless, of course, but I can't help myself.

A knock comes at my bedroom door.

Maybe it's Brooke. Maybe she has food.

I roll off the bed and open the door.

Not Brooke.

"What do you want now?" I ask Paige.

"May I come in?" she asks while maneuvering her slender body past me and entering the room.

"Sure," I say sarcastically, throwing my hands up in defeat.

Paige delicately arranges her hair behind her ears and turns to face me. I watch as her eyes land on the giant box and then self-consciously look to me. "Oh," she says. "You still haven't opened it."

"No, I haven't," I spit—hoping to hurt her.

"Sadie," she begins prodigiously, "I realize that what I did this evening may be perceived as unorthodox, and that it might have been unpalatable to you. But to be frank, this mess you've gotten yourself into isn't exactly the kind of thing Emily Post can prepare you for."

Unable to control myself, I roll my eyes.

She watches my face contort, then continues, "I realize that you're angry with me—"

"I have every right to be. You completely humiliated me tonight—"

As usual, Paige interrupts. "I realize that since you were a *little girl,* you have been angry with me."

Her reference to the past stuns me into absolute silence. She never talks about the past—ever. Paige is not the kind of person who looks back with regret on the things she's done in her life. No, forget regret, she doesn't look back *at all.*

Paige takes a seat on the end of my bed and places her hands on her knees. "I'm trying."

"Trying what, exactly?" I ask, straining to maintain composure.

"I realize that I haven't been the best mother to you. Things between us have never been quite . . . right. I see now that, in large part, it's been my doing."

I have no idea what to say to that. I have never heard her admit to anything so unflattering.

She continues, "I know that I can't make up for the way I treated you. I was so very selfish and insensitive. I also know that it may not be possible for you to forgive me. But I would like—if it's possible—to know you."

"*Know* me?" I ask, genuinely confused.

"Thanks to your father, you are a wonderful person. I would like to know you better. And I was wondering if, perhaps, you might be willing to get to know me a little, too."

I don't know what to say to that. Had this speech come at age eleven or twelve I probably would have leaped into her arms joyously. But at twenty-eight? I mean, is she looking to have someone absolve her guilt?

Apparently sensing my apprehension, she adds, "You don't have to love me. That's not what I'm asking. I want to try and be a better person to you . . . for you. In short, I'm trying."

I don't feel like I can stand any more.

I slump down into the chair by my dresser, nearly knocking over the brown monolith. The room falls silent, with me feeling dizzy and my mother staring at her shoes.

There's a hint of sadness in her eyes that I don't think I've ever seen before. Despite all my better judgment, and all the lessons I learned growing up, it makes me really want to believe her.

"Why now?" I ask.

Paige takes a deep, cleansing breath. "For whatever reason,

Sadie, things become clearer as you get older. And I've realized some things over the last few years." She pauses, turns her attention back to the unopened gift she gave me. "You know that old saying about how it's never too late to turn over a new leaf, to start over? Well, it hit me one day—that's a complete load of *crap*." My mother just said "crap." This is serious. "I always said to myself, 'Someday things will get better between Sadie and me,' 'Someday we'll have a proper relationship,' and then I turned fifty and thought . . . *when*?" Her eyes meet mine. "I am not getting any younger, Sadie. And our time here is finite. It *can* be too late. Sometimes you have to take risks, leap into the unknown. Otherwise questions and regrets will hang over you— like a cloud."

Doesn't she know she's talking to the queen of dark little clouds? The very definition of "When it rains, it pours"?

No. I guess she doesn't. That's sort of her point, isn't it?

My mother raises her head and her eyes lock on the Brown Box. More specifically, they bore into the patch of sticky, fuzzy brown paper left from removing her note. Paige says, "You know, I do worry about you. Doing this job. Not taking the portraits anymore. It's not that I think you've lost your talent, darling. I just think you're not using it to its full potential. I hate it when people aren't giving everything to achieve their full potential—"

My glare hardens and aims somewhere between the bridge of her nose and her left eye. "I love my job!"

"I know you do. I know. But what has it done to you, Sadie? How is it affecting you? What is it, do you think, that Ethan Wyatt is trying to show you?"

"You're on his side now?" I yell. "I thought you—"

"I'm on *your* side!" she roars. She clasps her hands together and grits her teeth, as though forcing herself to be calm. She takes a deep breath. Her tone softens. "I wasn't the best example to you. I was . . ." She looks out the window at my little patch of sky, to the place where the stars should be. "I have made mistakes, regretted the choices I've made. I don't want to see you do the same." Her pale blue eyes lock onto mine. Their characteristic iciness melts away before me. "I get the feeling that you're running away from something instead of toward something better."

"You've always hated what I do," I spit.

"The reasons, Sadie . . . the reasons have changed."

I shake my head. "But it's still all about you, isn't it?"

"Sadie Anne Price," Paige says, in that staccato way that mothers do when they're preparing to administer a stern scolding, "this may be hard for you to hear, but I did not make the decision for you to enter this career. It is not my fault that you are in this mess right now. I take responsibility for what I've done—my part in your . . . your . . . way of looking at the world. But I won't sit back and watch you founder. I'm here for *you*. My methods may occasionally annoy you, and you may disagree with me and my ideas. But I love you. Truly. Do you understand? I worry that what you're doing with your life you may one day look back on with regret. You have so many things to offer the world. So, so many . . ."

A tear falls from my mother's eye and down her cheek. She doesn't touch it. Her makeup is running, her skin is pale and imperfect, and she isn't raising a hand to fix it.

She looks at me again, with her eyes full, and adds, "I wish you would stop hating me. Not because I need you to forgive me, but because it's hurting *you*!"

Paige gets up from her perch on my bed and walks through the door. Moments later, I hear the front door open and close.

I stare at the unopened gift teetering precariously against my rickety old dresser.

My mother wants to know me.

I really didn't see that coming.

THE MAN OF YOUR DREAMS

Mrs. Louise Kenelm of Midbridge, New Jersey, isn't your average matchmaker. Mrs. Kenelm, struck by her clients' constant references to movie stars when describing their requirements for a potential mate, has added what she calls a "celebrity quotient" to her matchmaking service. "Women were always coming in and saying, 'I'd like him to have the face of Brad Pitt and the tush of Duncan Stoke,' and such things," describes Mrs. Kenelm. "It used to bother me a bit that these ladies were setting their sights so high." Then her daughter, Marie (a happily matched wife and mother of four), suggested that her mother embrace the trend. "It's added a whole new dimension to the process," says Mrs. Kenelm. "I can't guarantee that you'll be suited for a Duncan Stoke look-alike, but if I know that's one of your heart's desires, I will do my best to find him."

CHAPTER 23

All right, I know this is going to sound stupid, I know it sounds a bit immature and irrational, but I feel like I have to even the playing field with Ethan. I want to know something deep and dark and personal about him so that we're back on an equal footing. All that crap from my mother about the portraits, and lost talent, and "a few trials" in my life . . . and he's seen that sad, faraway look I apparently get sometimes. I feel so . . . exposed.

Okay, and there might be something else. A teeny-tiny, barely perceptible . . . almost *invisible* part of me might want to know a little more about him. Just for me.

I lie on my bed staring at the ceiling, with the phone to my ear. "You didn't find *anything*?" I say to Donna.

"Sadie, I'm not jerking you around here. He pays his taxes. He's a big tipper. He gives to charity and takes his mom to award shows." Donna heaves a frustrated sigh. "I can't even find a speeding ticket, and the guy used to own an Aston Martin, for

God's sake. About the only thing I did find out is that his agent wanted to set up a reality show for him and he turned it down."

Okay, that might be something. "What was the angle?" I ask.

"The agent was a crackpot, if you ask me . . . wanted to call it *Wyatt Riot* and follow Ethan barhopping or something. Ethan got rid of the guy—switched agencies because of it."

A little smile perks at the corners of my mouth. Yeah, he would have hated that idea. I clear my throat in an attempt to shake off the sudden rush of warm and fuzzy Ethan Wyatt feelings. "So, what you're telling me, then, is that he actually *is* a saint?" I ask Donna.

"Honey, I'm gay and *I* want to sleep with the guy."

Part of me is disappointed by the dearth of juicy gossip. Another part of me sort of wants to turn on Jason Mraz and sing into a toothbrush.

"How many times has she done that so far this morning?" I ask Luke.

"Four," he answers with a hint of concern in his voice.

"Yeah, she was doing it yesterday, too," I say.

Brooke has recently become obsessed with our voice mail. She checks it about once an hour. Checking it when she gets home from work, I understand. After returning from the bodega, I get. But she's at home—if the phone rings she'll hear it.

"Brooke?" I ask, approaching her. "Who are you expecting a call from?"

"No one," she says, doing a bad job of acting casual. I hear the voice on the line say, "Press two for saved messages . . ." before Brooke hangs up.

She grabs a magazine, sinks Indian style into a nearby chair, and begins reading an article on Ashlee Simpson with the same intensity a normal person would read, say, a road map to the Holy Grail.

I look to Luke, questioning him with my eyes. He just shrugs his shoulders at me—clueless.

"Where's your mom?" he asks, patting the seat next to him on the couch, inviting me to sit.

"Broomstick repairs. . . . Having her pointy hats polished. . . . Challenging Glenda the Good Witch to a duel. . . . How should I know?" I slump into the corner of the couch.

"Have you opened the box yet?" he asks.

"No! What does that have to do with anything?" Oops. Snapped a little bit there.

Luke gives me his classic "women are insane" expression—eyes wide and confused, one hand moving defensively to his crotch. "It was just a question—"

"I'm sorry," I say sincerely. "Last night she said she wants to *know* me. It threw me a little."

"Really? She said that?" asks Brooke, looking up from Ashlee.

"What does that mean?" asks Luke.

"It means that she's changing," replies Brooke.

"No, it means that she's had a midlife crisis, and I'm going to pay for it," I correct.

"You might want to consider the possibility that she's not after anything, Sadie," Brooke says in a matter-of-fact sort of tone that makes my hands clench into fists.

"Let me set you straight there," I say, desperately trying to keep my emotions in check. "My mother has never done any-thing that didn't benefit her in some way. Shit, she doesn't even give to charities that don't reward her with swag. Even if she is *changing,* as you call it, it's only because it'll get her something. She only does things that make her feel good. The thing that's important to remember is that someone is always—and I do mean *always*—hurt in the process."

It's like Paige's life is inextricably linked to the universe's sys-tem of checks and balances. To keep the world from spinning off its axis, Paige's pleasure must be counteracted, in equal pro-portion, by someone else's displeasure. If Paige were to win the lottery, somewhere in the world a small, innocent village of happy people would have to be smited.

I turn back to Brooke, only to see her shifting uncomfortably in the chair, adjusting her shirt and pants in an odd way. As she yanks her pants up, I spot a black . . . *thing* attached to her left hip. Oh, my God. It couldn't be . . .

"What was that?" I ask, pointing at her waist.

"What was *what*?" she replies guiltily.

"That black thing on your waistband."

"What black thing?" she asks, her green eyes scrunching up in mock confusion. Feigning innocence, she inspects the right side of her pants—ignores the left.

"Brooke," I begin seriously—trying not to laugh. "Is that a cell phone belt clip that you have attached to your paja-mas?"

"No," she says, watching me, as her left hand twitches closer to her waist.

Luke locks eyes with me and barely—just barely—tips his head up and down. Good, he knows what has to be done.

I try, with all my might, to keep a smile from spreading across my face. "It's *not*?" I ask Brooke, taking one tiny step toward her.

"Noooo," she says slowly, while pressing her back farther into the chair.

Brooke's eyes flit between Luke and me—each of us creeping ever closer.

"What is it, then?" I ask.

"I don't even know what you're talking about," she says, matching my tone.

Brooke drops her feet to the floor suddenly. They smack down on the hardwood with a splat.

Luke yells, "Now!"

We both pounce on her.

Brooke screams and falls into a fit of laughter. She wiggles and squirms, screams, "You guys!"

The chair is a knot of arms and legs as Brooke tries desperately to plaster her left side against the back of the chair.

Through my own laughing fit, I instruct Luke, "Get her hands!"

He complies, pinning her wrists to the arms of the chair, while the lower half of her body writhes to and fro.

I manage to spot the little black item attached to Brooke's pants and snatch it up before it disappears again into the downy fluff of the chair.

"Aha! I got it!" I say, raising my arms in victory.

Luke releases Brooke's arms.

"Give me that!" she demands as a shot of crimson rolls across her cheeks.

I take one look at it. "It *is* a cell phone belt clip! What is wrong with you?" I laugh.

She looks at me with a crooked smile, and no small amount of embarrassment flickering across her perfect features. "I have *clients*, okay? They wanna talk about . . . *things*."

Luke is beside himself, face completely red—laughter echoing through the apartment.

"You have it clipped to your pajamas!" I say.

Brooke's eyes dart around the room nervously. She opens her mouth to speak, then closes it abruptly. Finally she huffs, "Important calls come in . . . and . . . and I can't always be near my purse, you know? So . . ."

"So you bought a cell phone belt clip when (*a*) you hate them, and (*b*) you don't wear belts."

"Yes, okay? I did."

Luke and I can do nothing but stare at each other, shaking our heads in complete and utter confusion.

Out of nowhere, Brooke lets out a squeal—loud, unbridled, seriously disturbing. She hops out of her seat, grabbing the remote control from the coffee table.

She turns to Luke and me and says, "Shhhhhhh!"

Luke, completely confused, shouts, "I didn't even say anything!"

Brooke shoots him a glare that shuts him up immediately. She racks up the volume on the television to roughly two hundred decibels and, fidgeting wildly, returns to her chair.

Duncan Stoke's face appears on the screen. Oh . . . it's a *True Hollywood Story*.

"Okay," I whisper to Luke, "now do you see why I was worried about her?"

A loud harsh buzz suddenly blares from the little security panel by the front door.

Brooke jumps and frantically unhooks the cell phone from her waistband. She flips the phone open and says a remarkably calm and sultry hello. She tries again, "Hello?"

The buzzer echoes through the apartment again.

"Brooke, that's the front door," I say.

She exclaims, "Damn!" before promptly returning her attention to the *True Hollywood Story*.

Luke whispers to me, "Yep, now I'm with you."

I head to the security panel and push the talk button. "Hello?"

Todd's voice blasts into the apartment. "Buzz me in. I've got something on Wyatt."

WE THANK YOU
FOR YOUR BUSINESS

Are you famous? Is your schedule so crazy that you haven't had time to travel the world in search of exotic babies to adopt? Has your exfoliation, peeling, or trussing routine been interrupted because of a scheduling conflict? Do you have difficulty finding time to roll around blissfully in your piles of money?

If you've answered yes to any of these questions, you're obviously spending too much time making personal gestures of thanks and goodwill. At least, the brain trust at Famous Ink thinks so. For the bargain price of ten thousand dollars, the Famous Ink team guarantees to "free your valuable time by managing and maintaining your correspondence." In other words, they will write and send the many thank-you notes, RSVP's, and apologies you, as an A-list celebrity, are obligated to make—but are completely disinterested in doing yourself. Finally, a service for those who care enough to spend the very best.

—Rachel Dewey for Fresh Gossip,
Your Internet Celebrity News Source

CHAPTER 24

I wait at the elevator door for Todd, my stomach churning. This is good news. Isn't it? This could be the thing that gets Ethan off my back—the thing that gets my face out of the papers and Ethan out of my life.

My stomach lurches.

The elevator doors screech open.

Todd bounds out like a bull on a rampage, almost walking right by me.

"What is it?" I ask, startling him.

"Oh, hi. I got a tip that he's going to be meeting up with Lori Dunn tonight."

My heart leaps into my throat. "Oh." Whoops, that sounded a little like disappointment. I clear my throat. "I mean . . . *really*? Excellent."

Todd's caterpillars begin one of their famous bouncing and wiggling routines. "This is what you wanted, right?" he asks.

"Absolutely. Yeah. Sure." Although, I may be experiencing

some minor—barely noticeable—form of slight . . . um . . . jealousy. I imagine the headlines in the next issue of *Celeb*: "Ethan Wyatt's Romantic Reunion with Former Flame," "Wyatt and Dunn Do-Over," "Cheeky Bastard Gets Back with His Ex." I ask, "Is it a solid tip?" in a bit of a whimper. "I mean, you know, I don't want to waste my time on bad information."

"As solid as they get," Todd says. "Hey, you're not getting cold feet on me, are you?"

Okay, get it together, Sadie. "No, of course not. No, this is exactly what I was looking for. Thank you, Todd."

"Don't sound so excited," he says sardonically.

"Oh, I am excited!" I exclaim in a completely unintentional, and fairly creepy, falsetto.

Todd looks at me with an odd mixture of concern and amusement. "Are you all right?"

"Of course. I'm *great*!" I sound like Tony the Tiger. Maybe I should just stop talking altogether.

"Good," Todd says, though clearly unconvinced.

"The thing is, Todd, I'm really going to need a car."

I stare at him, my eyes blinking in what I think is a pity-inducing, alluring sort of way. I blink—and wait for him to get a clue.

He cocks his head at me like a confused puppy. Then slowly it dawns on him. "No!" He says gruffly. "Absolutely not. The Cayenne? No way."

"Todd, it's just for one night. You know how I hate that thing. I promise if I didn't absolutely have to use it, I—"

"No way," he repeats. "Can't the Hungarian give you a loaner, or . . ."

"You know that's not going to happen. And I don't know anybody else with a car, okay. No one."

Todd runs his thick fingers through his already messy hair. He paces around in a little circle, staring at the elevator's down button with longing.

Suddenly his expression shifts from frustrated contemplation to clear, crisp relief. "Uh, Sadie, you do know someone else with a car. . . ."

This was a bad, *bad* idea.

"Mother," I say, doing my best not to grab the steering wheel as we careen ever closer to the Jersey barriers on the FDR Drive. "Why don't you let me drive? I know the city better." And how to drive. "It's pretty dark out tonight." Yeah, there's a brilliant one, Sadie.

"I only agreed to participate in this scheme to keep an eye on you. If I were you, darling, I wouldn't look this particular gift horse in the mouth."

"Okay, fine." I take a deep, cleansing breath. "Another quarter of a mile until our exit."

"Good."

I try, "You could go a little faster if you—"

"There is nothing wrong with going the speed limit."

Unless everyone around you is going twenty miles an hour faster. Something tells me this argument will be lost on her.

"Sadie?" Paige's tone changes, softens. "You don't have to do this, you know."

"Can we please not discuss this?" I plead.

"You're always going, always moving forward—like a . . . like a steamroller. Pushing through, when what you might need to do is step back, darling."

"I'm fine," I retort—a little more defensively than I'd intended. "I know what I'm doing." Sort of.

"You're a strong woman, and that's a wonderful thing. But, Sadie, you're allowed to be confused. To have a time-out. Sometimes people need that time to gain perspective. Are you sure that you're ready for what might happen as a result of getting these pictures?"

"Absolutely," I retort. "There's an excellent chance that I'll be able to ride the subway without being hit on by slimy investment bankers and go to work without being intentionally blinded by my co-workers."

She looks at me. "You know that's not what I meant—"

"Ah, Mother! This is the exit. This is the exit!"

Paige turns her attention back to the road, and with screeching tires and no small amount of luck, we miss running straight into a street sign—or three.

After catching my breath and relaxing my grip on the dashboard, I say, "It should be right up here. A block up on the left."

"I can turn around, you know—"

"No! This is a one-way street!"

"I mean, darling, that I can take you home and you can forget about this."

Instinctively, I groan. "Just drop me off by that bodega up there, please."

She double-parks outside the bodega. I gather my things and open the door.

"You find a place to park somewhere. I'll call you on the cell when I'm done, and we can figure out a place to meet up. All right?"

She nods her head yes, but there's a bit of a devious twinkle in her eye that worries me.

"I'm serious," I say. "No funny business."

She makes a crisscross motion over her chest with her bright red nails.

I slam the door and watch closely as my mother's Mercedes lumbers down the block and disappears around the corner.

Okay, this is it. Ethan and Lori should be seated at the restaurant by now. If my instincts are correct, they'll be seated in the little alfresco/smoking section in the back. I've eaten at this place before. It's low key and private, but not flashy enough to be the sort of place you'd expect to find two celebrities canoodling. The alfresco patio is softly lit and romantic, and on a warm night like this, the jasmine planted along the privacy fence will fill the air with a beautiful scent. I have to commend Ethan on his choice; it's the perfect place for a reconciliation.

Locating the narrow air shaft between the restaurant's three-story brownstone and a seven-floor apartment building, I march in.

I shimmy my way along the side of the building. To keep myself walking in a straight line down the dark pathway, I run my fingers along the wooden privacy fence.

I was right, the air is heavy with the smell of jasmine, intermingled with the aroma of countless steaks being grilled over an open flame. The many lanterns beyond the fence cause thin shafts of light to break through cracks and poorly patched holes.

I sidle up to a particularly bright spot, a dislodged knot in one of the planks, and press my eye to it.

There he is.

He's wearing a lightweight chino blazer, but underneath I see the tiniest slip of his shirt with the little army figurines. If I'm not mistaken there's a smattering of pink by the collar. Lori Dunn is seated across from him with her arms crossed and her body sort of slumped forward—almost self-consciously. Her shoulders positively glisten under the warm lantern light. Her skin looks so perfectly pale and pristine it really borders on criminal.

Quietly, carefully, I ready my camera.

"How have you been?" comes Ethan's voice through the fence.

I look up startled—thinking he's found me out.

"Fine," replies Lori.

"You look nice tonight," he says.

"Thanks," she coos. "So do you."

Blahbeddy blah blah. Everybody's beautiful. Let's get this over with.

I lift the camera to my eye and point the lens through the hole. There's just enough of the fence in the frame to make it look really hidden-camera-ish; the editors will love that. They think it makes the pictures seem more *real*.

I put my finger on the button, ready myself to shoot . . .

. . . and then stop.

A sleek, ginger brown curtain of hair swishes into my frame.

I drop the camera from my eye and smash my face against the fence. Someone else has joined them.

Holy crap, it's Maya Dunn. In contrast to her sister, Maya's skin has a warm golden hue. Amazingly enough, it appears to be a real tan, not the spray-on kind. A thin wisp of a dress hangs off her shoulders, just barely clinging to her body in all the right places—bust, waist, hips. Her legs are so impossibly long, they seem to start somewhere near her chin. How could any mere mortal ever compete with that?

Maya plunks a Mojito on the table and sits down with Ethan and Lori.

"All right," Maya says, a deeply bitter tone marring her voice. "We're both here. Together. What do you want?"

Oh, my God. All three of them. The infamous Wyatt-Dunn love triangle reunited. The editors will scratch each other's eyes out for this. The pictures will go for thousands—thousands upon thousands.

I pull the camera up and rest the very edge of the lens on the hole in the fence.

From my vantage, I can see Ethan's leg begin to thump up and down under the table. Oh, wow—he's nervous.

It makes him look so uncharacteristically . . . *vulnerable*.

He says, "I want to apologize for the misunderstanding that caused all this mess we got into in the press."

Maya crosses her arms defiantly. She sits up a little straighter in her chair. Meanwhile, Lori has slumped so far down she's actually more under the table than over it; her eyes haven't left her place setting since Maya sat down.

Ethan takes a deep breath and a slow gulp of water.

Maya grumbles, "Go on."

Ethan sets his water glass down carefully on the table.

"Maya, I should've been more clear about . . ." He shakes his head, as though shaking off the thought he almost vocalized. "I was . . . I didn't want to hurt your feelings by telling you that I wasn't into you in that way. And, Lori, I shouldn't have asked you out knowing that Maya wasn't really, totally clued in."

Lori finally looks up.

"Now look," Ethan says stridently, his leg finally beginning to still. "You guys shouldn't let me get between you, all right? It was a stupid, fucked-up mistake. And my fault."

Oh, God, that's sweet. It almost makes me want to gag. Can I really take a picture of this?

If this goes to the editors, they'll make it out to be some big drama. They'll probably say they ran into each other by accident and that Maya and Lori bitched him out. Or worse, they'll intimate that it was the beginning of some sleazy three-way thing.

Ethan continues, "You're sisters. You two were inseparable." He smiles. "I feel guilty enough as it is—don't make me carry *that* around."

"Oh, this is all about *you*," Maya snaps.

Lori shakes her head and regains her posture. "It was a joke, Maya."

"Oh," Maya says meekly.

Ethan directs his gaze to Maya. "I really am sorry." He shakes his head, his body language absolutely oozing regret. "It was a dumb move, and I think Lori agrees with me there."

Man, he's so freaking *decent*.

I pull the camera from the fence, quietly open my bag, and slip the camera inside.

It's not that I can't get the shot—I totally could. There are no freaky emotions or strange stomach quivers impeding me. I *won't* get this shot. It would hurt him, and I don't want to do that.

"What a nice young man," murmurs my mother's voice over my right shoulder.

I gasp—louder than you should ever gasp when hiding behind a fence in the dark—and somehow lose my footing. My body careens forward. Instinctively, I brace myself by splaying my hands against the fence.

The acres of jasmine are jarred out of a restful state and rustle disturbingly from one end of the fence to the other. With my hands plastered to the fence, my eye jumps to the hole.

Ethan, Maya, and Lori apprehensively look toward the fence. But it's only Ethan who spots the hole. His eyes lock onto mine.

I quickly push myself off the fence and, slinging my arm through one of Paige's, drag her off toward the sidewalk.

"Did you get what you needed, darling?" my mother clucks in that cloying, all-knowing, irritatingly sarcastic way she does.

"Oh, my God. Just *move!*"

KISS AND TELL

Ethan Wyatt fans take note: the special edition DVD of the cult favorite "Ground-swell" (2001) is about to drop in a video store near you. The special features include a newly remastered director's cut version of the film with seven additional romance-rich minutes, a behind-the-scenes documentary, and commentary track with Ethan Wyatt and director Noel Cambridge. On his love scene with Amy Smart, Ethan Wyatt divulges, "Kissing is never a bad thing. And getting paid for it isn't half bad, either."

"Groundswell" (2001, original version)—****
"Groundswell: Special Edition DVD"—***
Release Date: June 20

CHAPTER 25

He couldn't have spotted me. He couldn't have known it was me. The most he could have made out through that hole in the fence was maybe a tiny bit of an eye. Right? He probably caught a brief glimpse of a random nondescript eye. Definitely not enough to identify me. I think.

Even so, I felt like I had to lie low most of today. But now it's six-thirty, Ethan's feeding time.

I've discovered that though consumed by an unflinching need to make me suffer, he still requires sustenance. Like clock-work, every night at six-thirty, he eats. Sometimes, he even leaves the front of my building to do it. Amazing.

I am taking this opportunity to visit Blockbuster. It sounds simple, right? Stupid, even? Well, it's not. It's one of those silly little things that you miss when you're shadowed twenty-four hours a day and worried that you might be featured renting *Armageddon* in a national publication. (I find watching Ben

Affleck in orange astronaut wear to be extremely soothing. Sue me.) So now I only go to the video store at six-thirty and run there like I'm being chased by a man in a goalie mask. Big deal.

Anyway, I'm here. At Blockbuster. And I have been for the last forty-five minutes. This movie rental process is taking much too long, but I'm having a little problem.

No matter what I do, I always seem to end up in front of an Ethan Wyatt movie. They're everywhere. I've been staring at the back of *The Hager Saga* for the last ten minutes. The cover features a picture of Ethan in a perfectly tailored tuxedo, circa 1925. He's waltzing across an enormous dance floor with Minnie Driver. He's so . . . so . . . oh, who am I kidding? He's just totally fucking amazing-looking. It is an incontrovertible truth: Ethan Wyatt is heartbreakingly beautiful. And, in this film at least, a sensitive and thoughtful (yet alluringly roguish) hero with a bazillion-dollar family fortune. That's the very textbook definition of irresistible.

I mean, I hate him. I do. He's stalking me. At the same time, though, he's sort of adorable. He's goofier than I thought he would be, with a sharp wit, and a smile that grabs you and sucks you in—against your will. Most disturbing, I'm kind of getting used to him being around. Sometimes, I even like talking to him. And last night, I did him a favor—a favor that irked Todd to no end. Worst of all, since Ethan didn't even know I did it, it's a favor that will never be repaid.

I think I may be losing it.

And I really want to rent this movie.

But I can't. I absolutely cannot rent it.

"Ah, one of my favorites," comes a pugnacious male voice from the other side of the shelf.

I look up and see a mop of dark hair that looks suspiciously like . . . oh, Jesus.

Without thinking, I drop *The Hager Saga*.

Trying to catch the case in midair, I elbow one of the flimsy metal shelves, causing a cacophonous noise and sending roughly three dozen DVD cases tumbling into one another. *Hair* covers *Hamburger Hill*, *Hannibal* hits *Hannah and Her Sisters*. Two Blockbuster employees continue to look disinterested and underpaid.

Ethan Wyatt smirks at me over the big blue and yellow Drama sign.

"Oh, *you*," I say, while putting the three *Hamlet*'s back in their proper order from best to worst—Branagh, Gibson, Hawke.

"Yeah, *me*," he says, with that deliciously disarming smile fluttering across his lips.

A sudden sort of otherworldly feeling strikes me, as my eyes tick back and forth between Ethan's face on the cover of a DVD and his smooth, disguise-free face right in front of me. I find myself confused and blankly staring at his rather pouty and alluring lips.

He looks at me puzzled and adds, "What? You're not going to rent *Hager* now?"

Okay. Time to get it together. I cannot let him know he's getting to me, or that I'm sort of . . . a little bit . . . just barely . . . into him, ever so slightly.

I quietly pull the cell phone from the front pocket of my

jeans. I flip it open and set it up for the maximum picture quality. Please, for the love of God, let me finally get a picture of the man's face.

Ethan pads down his aisle while blabbing and turns the corner toward me. "If you haven't seen it, you should. But, if you're in the mood for something a little more relate-able . . . might I suggest *La Dolce Vita* for a start?"

"Oh, I get it. You work here now," I retort, while wondering exactly which sickly shade of green my skin has turned under the harsh fluorescent Blockbuster lights. "Good, could you tell me where I can find *Motion of the Ocean*?"

"Cute," he replies to my little dig.

I roll my eyes and continue, "Do you know what your problem is?"

"I have a problem?" he replies, coming closer.

"Your problem is, you set yourself up for this." I pull the phone up and snap a picture of his face, which has contorted slightly in surprise. Ha! I did it!

"Ah, another *picture* phone," he says, trying to seem nonchalant, but clearly disturbed by the fact that I've captured his image yet again.

I snap off another picture. Oh, this is great.

"Ooh, that was *good*," I say, clicking off another one. "But you might want to smile next time," I add while flipping the phone around to show him his own image, frozen in another horrible expression. I inspect the photo again triumphantly. "You know, you're looking a little tired. Should I call your stylist? Plastic surgeon, perhaps?"

"God, you never stop. You are *always* on—like some photography bot."

"What about you and your Mr. Big attitude?" I mock his voice, "Might I suggest *La Dolce Vita* for a start? You know, for a guy who doesn't like to be photographed, you spend an inordinate amount of time pestering photographers. Hey! Wait a second!" I exclaim, genuinely excited by this new train of thought. "Is this one of those Sean Penn God-complex things?" I mime pulling out a pad and pencil, change tone, and do my best concerned doctor imitation. "Do you, or any members of your entourage, believe you have the power to save the world from itself? Have you gone on any diplomatic missions without State Department approval, or insulted the media while on a promotional *media* tour?"

"I am not like Sean Penn!"

"You may not have married Madonna. Or gone down to Louisiana to save people in a boat too full of photographers to actually *hold* anybody needing rescue, but you do whine an awful lot about the same things," I reply matter-of-factly.

I wait for a response, but he just looks at me blankly. I think I may have rendered him speechless. *Nice.*

"Oh, and another thing!" says Ethan boisterously, with a little gleam in his eye. Another thing? What was the first thing? "Your portraits—"

"What do you know about my portraits?" I ask, as a touch of queasiness grips my belly.

"I found the website." He pauses for effect. "It hasn't been updated lately, I noticed . . . but it's all there."

"So now you know my deep dark secret. I am, in fact, a legitimate photographer."

"No, correction," Ethan says, moving closer to me. "You were *once* a legitimate photographer."

I can't think of a single thing to say, a single insult to throw at him. The only word I can form is "Humph."

He smiles at me . . . waiting. I got *nothing*.

I click off another picture. Damn, I think he might look pretty stunning in that one.

"When did you sell out?" Ethan asks pointedly.

"*I'm* a sellout?" I bite back.

"You're joking, right? You're taking pictures on a cell phone . . . right now. Again."

Oh, that's rich. "*You* of all people are calling me a sellout?" I grab two of his DVD covers and say, "How did you go from this"—I hold up the cover of *Junkies,* a highly praised indie that resulted in his one and only Oscar nomination—"to *this*?" I hold up *Going Nowhere,* an incredibly lame explosion-filled popcorn flick that the critics rightfully panned.

He stares at me, a look of stunned disbelief flickering across his eyes and extending down to his open mouth. Aggravated, he raises his voice. "But you're this . . . smart, quick . . . reasonably easy to look at woman . . . with an amazing talent. Those portraits are good. Really good!"

"Oh, and you're not talented, I suppose?" My voice rises to match his. "You were incredible in this film!" I say, pointing at the back cover of *Junkies* and a picture of Ethan, ugly and emaciated, acting his ass off. "You weren't a movie star in this. You were an actor. A *great* actor!"

We both stand stock-still and stare at one another—both of us, I believe, coming to realize that we've just been insulting each other with compliments.

His bright blue eyes dance nervously over my face. He inhales, as if to speak, but doesn't say anything.

"Ugh!" I say finally, turning on my heels and stomping toward the exit. "You are so *frustrating*!"

And what the hell is "reasonably easy to look at" supposed to mean?

I march out of the store and head back downtown toward my apartment.

"Hey! Sadie!" comes a loud male voice behind me.

I look over my shoulder to see Ethan headed in my direction. He races toward me, while shoving his camera into its bag. I increase my pace and make a sudden left in an attempt to lose him.

"And another thing!" he shouts, catching up to me.

"Why do you always say 'and another thing' when nothing has been said before it? What is that *about*?" I ask, stopping suddenly in front of a kosher deli and startling a trio of Hassidic men eating at the counter that faces the street.

"Why do you always change the subject when I'm about to make a point?" he fires back. "I know why you're not taking the portraits anymore!"

"Oh, yeah?" I ask haughtily.

"Yeah!" A little smile creeps onto his lips. "You're too scared!" he says definitively, as though I'm now supposed to break down or beat him up or something.

"What am I so scared of, then?" I ask.

He rolls his eyes and huffs, "I've been trying to figure that part out for about the last three days but . . . (*a*) your mother has stopped taking my calls, and (*b*) well . . . there is no *b*." He forces himself to stand straighter. "But I know you're scared of something!"

"Genius!" I reply. "Now, can you tell me why I can't get my VCR to stop blinking?"

"Will you just drop the act?" he says firmly. "I saw you last night, all right?" My heart feels like it's just stopped beating. He continues, "I saw you behind that fence. And I know you didn't take any film on it."

"What fence?" I ask, dumbly.

His arms fly up in the air with frustration. He slaps a hand to his forehead and grits his teeth, before exclaiming, "Come on!"

Losing a bit of my steam, and genuinely curious, I ask, "How do you know I didn't take anything?"

His body language softens suddenly. He replies, "I asked around."

Ethan's eyes lock onto mine, really begging for an answer. But it feels too raw, too guileless and pure of a look to be wasted on me.

"I don't know what you're talking about," I say finally, before turning to walk away.

He grabs my arm, forcing me to turn around and face him.

"Why do you always deflect? Why don't you listen, Sadie?" Ethan exclaims, letting go of me and flinging his hands around like a windmill. "Why are you holding on to this so damn tight?"

"Holding on to what?" I shout right back.

"This paparazzi thing, this act you've got going—being tough and not caring about things. That's not you! You're better than that. God, you're stubborn—"

"*I'm* stubborn?" I ask, amused. "Why can't you just leave me alone?"

"Why can't you just let me speak?" he says with a scowl.

Oh, good, an easy one. "Because you're a pompous hypocrite! You call *me* a sellout?" Curious, he's moving toward me. I continue louder, "You are the clearest-cut case of selling out that I've ever seen. *Articles* have been written about it!" Ah! He's moving even *closer*. My voice rises a touch higher. "*Rolling Stone . . . Entertainment Weekly . . . Max*—"

He puts his hands on either side of my face and kisses me.

I'm kissing Ethan Wyatt.

Ethan Wyatt is kissing me.

It's a kiss that comes from his whole body, every single cell concentrating on me—wanting me. It's the kind of kiss that forces my hands to clutch the strap of the bag on his shoulder, to dig my nails into the nylon and hold on. I suddenly feel like I'm falling.

I break away to catch my breath. "Why did you *do* that?" I ask, trying not to notice that the three Hassidic gentlemen in the window are now smiling and chuckling with one another.

"To shut you up?" Ethan replies sheepishly.

Well, it worked. I have no idea what to say. Especially since I think I might have liked it. I may, in fact, really want him to do that again. Soon.

"You're . . . you're a sellout!" I say, trying desperately to recapture the anger that was in my voice just seconds ago, and hoping to somehow banish the strange fluttering in my midsection that reminds me so much of the feeling I had when I first laid eyes on him at the airport.

"I know," he says gently. "And so are you."

Ethan adjusts his camera bag, and simply—far too simply—walks away.

———

WYATT'S NEW ATTITUDE

Word on the H-wood grapevine is that Ethan Wyatt is about to embark on an image overhaul. A friend of Wyatt's, speaking on the condition of anonymity, worries about his sanity. "He's not himself," the pal says. "He barely goes out, and keeps talking about not becoming Sean Penn. I was, like, dude, the guy's got an Oscar. We're all worried about Ethan." The young actor has apparently vowed to his reps and the honchos at Miramax that he's going to clean up his act. Though an inside source says it was all Wyatt's idea, others say the attitude reversal is undoubtedly a result of the industry flak he received for his most recent tabloid escapades. Others think it's a simple case of studio intervention. Speculation is, the suits feared Wyatt's upcoming "Charming Samantha" (in which he costars with ex Maya Dunn) would fall victim to the dreaded "'Gigli' Effect" and told him to nix the inkworthy hijinks. No word yet on whether or not this is a permanent shunning of Ethan's bad-boy image or a temporary media stunt. (As of press time, there is no indication which Tinseltown spin firm will be hired for consultation.)

CHAPTER 26

'm not a sellout. *Am I?*

No.

Yes?

No. How can you be a sellout when you were never really "in" in the first place?

Ethan Wyatt was in. He's the sellout.

I'm not ashamed of what I do . . . most of the time. I didn't abandon my artistic principles just for money. Well, I didn't exactly pursue them in spite of the *lack* of money either.

In a perfect world, I would have been able to make enough money to survive on my portraits alone. I would have gotten a gallery to show my work straight out of art school. I wouldn't have had my father's debt hanging around my neck like a millstone. I wouldn't have been petrified of poverty. In a perfect world, I would have been able to remind myself not to give up— or maybe there would have been somebody there to remind me. Anyway you look at it, though, this is not a perfect world.

And, even if I am a sellout, so what? Who am I selling out? *Me.* What business is it of Ethan's? Why does he care? Is he just trying to hurt me? One last stab at retribution?

I stagger into the apartment, not knowing exactly what to do. In the living room are Brooke, Luke, and Paige.

All three of their heads turn to me. Luke smiles, Brooke and Paige look concerned.

"What happened out there? You look upset," asks Brooke, while pulling her chestnut mane into a taut ponytail.

"Are you all right, darling?" adds Paige.

Luke chimes in with "What'd you rent?"

"I just need . . . some time . . . alone," I say, before shutting myself into the bedroom.

So, what did he mean by that kiss? Was it just another way to manipulate me? Does he plan on suckering me into thinking he likes me and then dumping on me as part of his revenge?

Could he possibly *feel* something for me?

There's a quiet tap on the door. Brooke pops her head in. "Did something happen? I knew we shouldn't let you go alone. Did he do something to you?" Brooke says—sounding more and more like my mother by the minute.

I nod my head yes.

She tiptoes into the room and gingerly closes the door behind her.

Brooke pulls my one little chair closer to the bed and sits down facing me. "Those celebrities are such assholes!" she spits. "What happened?"

"I think I have a little problem," I tell her.

"Okay, what is it?" she asks, giving me her undivided attention.

"I think I might . . . like him."

"Ethan?" she asks, bravely trying to mask the shock cascading down her face.

"Yeah," I reply guiltily.

"Huh," she says before taking a deep breath. "Do you like him, or do you *like* him like him?"

"What are we, in tenth grade?" I huff. I look to the Brown Box for support. "I think I might *like* him like him." I am now reduced to speaking high school riddles with my best friend.

"Well," Brooke says with finality, "that takes care of that." She reaches into the back pocket of her pants and pulls out a very slim pink leather notebook. Its onionskin pages rustle as she grabs a pen off my dresser, flips some pages, and marks something down.

"What are you doing?"

"Crossing him off," she says, returning the notebook to her pocket.

"You have an actual *list*?"

"Organization is not a hobby, Sadie. It's a lifestyle choice."

"You're a little sick, you know that?" I kid.

"*I'm* sick? You're the one falling for a man who's stalking you."

"You may have a point there."

"What are you going to do?" Brooke asks.

"I have no idea. I don't know if he's still stalking me or what. I don't know . . . anything. . . ."

"Wait, what happened, exactly?" asks Brooke.

"Well, he complimented me. And then he kissed me. And then, he called me a sellout—"

"He kissed you?" Brooke asks, startled.

"Yeah," I say, looking to her with the hope that she'll have some idea what's going on.

"He *kissed* you?" she tries again, her eyes widening.

"Yeah . . . that's what I . . . just said."

"Ethan Wyatt *kissed* you?" she says once more, while slamming her fists into her own thighs.

"Brooke—breathe."

"I'm sorry," she says, just a hair away from hyperventilation and anger rising in her voice. "Excuse me, he *kissed* you?" I don't think she's even talking to me. She seems to be talking to the Brown Box. All the muscles in her face are tensing up—simultaneously. Her eyes instantly become puffy. Her cheeks drain of color.

"Are you all right?" I ask, hoping not to set her off.

"Ethan Wyatt kisses you, the woman he supposedly hates. Meanwhile, I . . . I . . ." She struggles against a wave of tears.

"You what? Brooke—"

My mother flies into the room, no doubt drawn by the volume of Brooke's rant.

"What is going on in here?" Paige asks, worried.

"Well, let's see," Brooke exclaims, recovering herself. "Ethan Wyatt kissed her. And Duncan Stoke doesn't remember me! God, and you were warning me about these guys," she says, pointing at me.

"What the hell are you talking about?" I yell.

Paige shakes her head and then takes a deep breath. "Let's

get this all sorted out. Sadie, what is this about Ethan Wyatt?"

"He kissed me," I say matter-of-factly, staring at Brooke and wondering what the hell just happened here.

Paige looks away, trying to hide the self-satisfied, knowing sort of smile that is creeping out from under her Chanel lip gloss. "Well," she says to me calmly, before pursing her lips, "that is a development."

"Why do you say it like that?" I ask her.

Paige shakes her head at me, silently telling me to drop it, as she gently places a hand on Brooke's shoulder. "Now, Brooke. What is bothering you, sweetheart? Do you feel comfortable talking about it?"

Does she feel comfortable talking about it? She was just screaming about it.

Brooke closes her eyes and takes three deep harried breaths like a person preparing to dive into icy water. "When we met with Duncan Stoke . . . after Sadie went running off into Central Park . . . I was flirting—"

Excuse me? "You were *flirting* while I was hobbling through the streets—"

Paige gives me a stern glare. "Sadie, it's Brooke's turn."

Brooke continues, "We flirted. I gave him my number and he said he would call. . . ."

Well, I guess that explains the running and shushing and general mania of the last couple of weeks.

"But he didn't call." My mother finishes Brooke's sentence.

Brooke shakes her head no. "And then I called him this afternoon. I finally tracked down his number. I had to pretend I was the sponsor of a charity softball tournament," she says, the shame evident in her eyes. "And he didn't remember me."

"Oh, Brooke." I lay a hand on her knee. "I'm so sorry."

"Are you really? You *kissed* Ethan Wyatt!" she shouts.

"I didn't mean to!" I shout back. "He kissed *me*, okay? I was just standing there!"

"But you kissed him back! And you liked it!" She points a finger at me. "Don't lie. I can see on your face that you liked it."

My mouth drops open. I whisper, "My mother is in the room. Will you please—" I tell Paige, "He also called me a sell-out." As if somehow that will temper the "I can see on your face that you liked it" comment.

"Is everything okay in here?" asks Luke, darting into the room. He looks slightly like a man who's just been jolted out of a nap. He scratches his forehead and rubs at his cheeks.

"Well, let's see," says Brooke again, "Sadie kissed Ethan Wyatt. And she liked it. *A lot.*"

"Really?" says Luke. "Cool. Do you think you could get him to sign a few dozen—"

"Luke!" shouts Brooke.

"Well . . ." he says, shrugging his shoulders.

"Now, Brooke," interjects my mother. "You know how hard relationships are for Sadie—"

"Mother!"

"It's true, darling," she says, way too easily for my liking, then turns back to Brooke. "As I was saying, Brooke . . . if she enjoyed this kiss . . ."

Oh, my God. Shoot me. Somebody shoot me.

". . . we should be happy for her. Don't you think? I think

she would be happy for you, if the shoe were on the other foot. Wouldn't you?" my mother asks me.

"How the hell am I supposed to—" Paige cuts me off by giving me a look so filled with motherly admonishing that I suddenly feel like I'm about to be grounded. I say, "Sure. Absolutely, I'd be happy for her."

Paige coos, "See there, Brooke."

"Oh, God, you're right. Of course, you're right," she whimpers to Paige. "I'm sorry, Sadie."

"Okay . . ." I reply.

"All right, then," Paige declares. "Now come on, Brooke. I'll make you a cup of tea."

Paige takes Brooke by the arm and leads her out of the bedroom. Luke trudges out behind them.

What the hell just happened here?

"Hello?" I yell to my bedroom door. "Girl with a problem here! Anyone?"

Luke opens the door. "What's the problem?" he asks dumbly.

"Um, let me recap. Kissed the man who's stalking me. Might have liked it. Not sure what to do next. Any ideas?"

Luke tugs on the bottom of his T-shirt, twists the fabric around his index finger, and stares at the floor.

Finally, he looks up. "Uh, no. I got nothing." Luke turns right back around and walks out.

Well, that makes two of us.

SPOTTED

. . . Ethan Wyatt kissing a mystery blonde outside A-1 Kosher Deli on Avenue A in the East Village in New York City . . .

CHAPTER 27

The bright sunshine of early morning streams through the windows of the living room. I tiptoe past Luke, who is sacked out on the sofa, his long limbs knotted up at odd angles so that every part of his body is covered by one little throw blanket. I shut the curtains to improve his sleeping conditions, then move to the kitchen to make some coffee.

The phone rings, loud and jarring.

But I am not going to answer. And on second thought, I'm going out to get myself a coffee and an egg sandwich—without bodyguards. I turn off the ringer so Luke and Brooke can sleep, then head out of the apartment.

I don't know what to think about Ethan Wyatt. I don't know what to think of the things he said to me, and the way I reacted. I don't know what to think about anything anymore. So, I'm going to stick with what I do know. I'm hungry, it's a gorgeous New York day, and for whatever reason, the memory of Ethan Wyatt kissing me makes me happy.

*   *   *

Bounding out of the lobby door, I'm immediately engulfed by warm, refreshing, sweet city air. Tainted as it is with exhaust fumes and a hint of rotting garbage, it's still the smell of a fresh summer morning.

I stroll three blocks toward my favorite deli.

The sharp pounding of feet on pavement is my first indication that something is not quite right. It's a stampede, the unpleasant sound of many rubber soles slapping down on concrete. My heart leaps into my throat as the slapping gives way to a strange rumbling noise, braying. A vaguely human prattle. It's muffled, though—harsh and dissonant, incomprehensible. I think it could be that my ears are ringing and distorting the sound.

I can't count them all . . . the wide black eyes in my face. Ten, fifteen maybe. Maybe more. I hardly recognize my reflection in their convex glass. I think that's my mouth that is hanging agape, my stunned blue eyes, my nose made to appear three times too big for my face by the curve of the lens.

The light, bubbly, summer-induced sensation from just moments ago is replaced by a surge of fear and anger swelling up from somewhere in my midsection.

I turn to go back to the apartment, but there are too many bodies in my way. I look up the street and my feet begin moving toward the deli. Egg sandwich. It's the last place my legs were told to go. They haven't yet received the message that I'm under attack.

The swell of anger quickly crests. It smooths out over my entire body, not hot and violent, but tepid like bathwater. It feels almost like calm—born of recognition and understanding. I don't know why I didn't see this coming.

Voices erupt behind me as my feet move more quickly.

"Sadie! Wait up!"

"Where you going?"

"Come on, you know me!"

"Stop running, *bitch*!"

My head turns on that last one, much to the delight of the clicking, mashing crowd of photographers. Behind one of the lenses I see the suspiciously slimy head of Phil Grambs. He looks at me with a nauseating kind of grin—it's not even self-satisfied, just joyous. Absolute bliss.

I slip into the deli and race toward a man who looks to be in charge, an older guy with a thick five-o'clock shadow and black horn-rimmed glasses. When I see "Manager" printed on his name tag, I tell him that the photographers will try to come in unless he tells them not to. He takes one look outside at the disruption, the many legs, feet, and arms tangled up with one another. He then surveys his tiny shop with all of its odd angles, precarious food displays, and freshly mopped floor. He barely bats an eyelash before running to the entrance and peeking his head out.

"Get outta my doorway!" he shouts. "Stay on the freakin' sidewalk!"

"Thank you," I say breathlessly.

"Are you all right?" the manager asks kindly.

"Yeah, I—" I stop short when I notice the manager's staff of two looking back and forth between the newsstand and me.

When I turn around, my heart sinks and a heavy knot forms in my throat.

On the cover of *Celeb* is an enormous picture of Ethan and me kissing on the sidewalk yesterday. There's a smaller inset picture of Duncan Stoke, probably taken years ago, looking distressed. On the other side of that is Ethan's picture of Duncan with his hands on my shoulders. The headline reads: "Steamy Love Triangle Has Stoke Heartbroken." The subhead: "Wyatt Strikes Again!"

Similar layouts appear on *Star, Us Weekly,* and *People.*

To recap, I am on the cover of *Celeb, Star, Us Weekly,* and *People.*

"I just wanted an egg sandwich" comes out of my mouth before I have the sense to stop it.

The manager snaps his fingers at one of his employees, and she instantly begins cracking eggs and frying bacon.

What am I going to do now? I'm trapped in a deli. I guess the good news is I could gorge myself on salami for at least three weeks. But then what?

"Do you have a back door?" I ask the manager, who has just picked up a copy of *Celeb* and is reading the article inside.

He glances up. "Nope. That's it," he says, pointing to the front door.

My cell phone rings—Todd.

"Todd, I—"

Todd's voice rings out, sort of. He sounds out of breath. "It's huge, Sadie. Stopped the presses. Went back to design. Cover was supposed to be Oprah, more weight loss. Then you with Wyatt—"

"Trust me, I know."

"You're bigger than Bennifer."

Please, God, don't let that be true.

Looking out the front window of the deli, I say, "Todd, uh . . . I don't think I'll be able to work today."

The animals are getting restless. Two photographers are arguing over a position near the window. A small cluster of onlookers has gathered around the fringes of the photographers. I see heads bobbing and weaving over the commotion, trying to get a look inside the deli.

I feel a tap on my shoulder. The manager hands me my egg sandwich, wrapped in a plastic bag. "On the house," he says uncomfortably—as though this is the first time those words have ever passed his lips. He looks at me sheepishly. "Well . . . uh, look, lady. We like celebrities here, same as anybody else and all, but we shoulda had about fifteen customers by now. My regulars can't get in."

I guess that means I shouldn't be blowing up the air mattress? I take a deep breath. "Okay . . ."

"Todd, I have to go," I say into my phone.

"Where are you?"

"That deli I like—off First Avenue, but I'm going home."

"No!" he shouts. "Wait for me. I'll be there in a few minutes."

"No, Todd. I'm fine. I'll be fine."

I hang up the phone and take a deep breath.

No. Okay. Right. I can do this. I've been in packs like this before. I've done it a million times. Of course, I've been on the other side, but it couldn't be too bad, right? A few moments of discomfort, a few assholes yelling my name. If I can put up with Ethan Wyatt on my tail for a couple of weeks, how much harder could this be? I just have to block out the noise and the struggle and walk home. I just have to walk home. It's just walking. Easy.

Turning to the deli manager, I point to *Celeb* and ask, "Can I see that?"

Just as I thought. The photo credit for the layout says "Phil Grambs."

There are seven pictures, a perfectly captured sequence of events. Ethan saying something to me, wildly gesturing, his face still so very handsome and striking even when contorted a bit in frustration. Ethan putting his hands on my face. Ethan moving in. Ethan kissing me. Me standing there dumbstruck, and yet with a slightly elated look on my face. Ethan walking away, his sooty black hair flopping into his eyes. Then, me standing there, confused and watching him get in a cab.

My heart thumps like a drum in my chest as I look at the sequence over and over again.

I feel . . . violated, like something personal and private has been taken away. Like all the meaning and significance that I'm just now beginning to understand has suddenly been completely stripped away. It hurts, and fills me with a profound sort of sadness for the loss of it. Those seven moments were important to me, they were special.

I sling the bag with my egg sandwich over my arm and hike up my pants—seems the sort of thing I should do.

With three strong, defiant strides, I step out of the deli and into the fray.

Assholes, I silently repeat to myself, you can have that piece of time, but you're not going to beat me here.

The second my feet hit pavement, I'm swallowed by the

pack. Elbows and hands fly this way and that. I duck to avoid being decapitated by a wayward camera.

The voices around me are loud and belligerent. "Look here, damnit!" "Sadie, why Wyatt?" "Are you going to his place now?"

I wait for the adrenaline to kick in, for its smooth warm glow to wash over me. I wait, but it doesn't come.

My feet won't move on their own; I have to will them forward. I tussle and push just to get past the deli's windows. People keep randomly careening into me as I try to press my way through the crowd. I end up elbowing a French guy and a Swede to try and reach fresh air—to spot a slice of the street up ahead so I know where I'm going.

The air around me suddenly feels heavy, too many people exhaling. I feel like I can't breathe.

I feel a sharp jab to my back, then my rib cage, as the pack begins to stagger farther down the sidewalk. I'm pinned between a morbidly obese photographer and the wall of a copy shop. My face just inches from the glass, I startle a woman inside who looks to be preparing a photocopier for the day ahead. She looks stunned, then smiles when she notices the camera flashes and general mayhem. I put my head down and plow forward as best I can, guided only by the grooves of the sidewalk.

I try to craft my facial features into the very incarnation of defiance, but my shoulders are beginning to slump under the weight of the task ahead. How many blocks did I walk? Should I go left at the next street, or go forward? What on earth am I doing here?

The shouting around me increases, causing all the cries of "This way" and "Slow down" to run into one another and sound like the indecipherable barking of wild dogs.

After a half block, we do a complex formation turn and head uptown. As the walkway widens, the tight knot of the pack dissolves. I can finally see uninterrupted daylight.

Photographers stagger and stumble over one another, getting ahead of me to resume shooting. They perform that famed paparazzi dance—blindly walking backward down the sidewalk with cameras to their eyes.

The screaming quiets. Most of my cohorts can't walk and chew gum simultaneously, let alone speak while walking *backward*. A few of them, I imagine, are simply out of shape and out of breath.

My heart leaps as I feel a brief opportunity for escape.

I hustle to the edge of the street and stick my arm out for a cab. Several groans of "Come on!" and "You're not getting away that easy!" pierce my ears before the pack, unwilling to see me go, springs to action and surrounds me.

Excellent. I think I've just managed to piss them off.

Using only my egg sandwich and my forearms, I push my way free of the pack. I do the only thing I can think to do— keep marching as briskly as I can without it seeming like an all-out sprint. In no time, the pack is back in front of me, their worn-out Vans and Nikes tapping out a feverish rhythm, in slight discord to the clicking of their shutters.

Did I comb my hair this morning? Did I brush my teeth? Why didn't I change my T-shirt?

Phil moves up to the front of the crowd. I can hear his wheezing and the labored shuffling of his feet on the uneven pavement.

"Look up, you. For fuck's sake, girl," a man shouts in a thick French accent somewhere ahead of me.

"Give us your face—we go away," chimes another.

Funny, I didn't realize I was looking down.

"You fucking him?" cries an American.

"Come on, Sadie. Give us the whole ugly truth and we'll let you walk home," shouts Phil. "You gonna marry that asshole or what?"

That's my life they're talking about. That's *my* life.

Don't pick your head up. Don't look up. Don't let them see you crack—they feed on it.

I can feel the tingling sensation of a cringe, an angry glare desperately trying to surface on my face. I inhale deeply, and when I exhale, a barely audible groan escapes my lips.

And my heart sinks.

The verbal assault gains momentum. A hail of insults and obscenities are tossed my way.

Finally regaining the strength of his abrasive voice, Phil screams, "Are you loving this or what? Huh, Miss Fucking Perfect? Your career is so fucking over."

At this, I look up. I can feel my face reddening, my teeth clenching, my fists just begging to go through Phil's lens and deep into his skull. What did I ever do to him? What did I do that was so awful it deserves this in return?

Glancing at my surroundings, I see that we're now drawing an audience. Pedestrians have stopped to watch us pass. They point and smile like they are gazing up at the SpongeBob SquarePants balloon in the Thanksgiving Day Parade. A wide array of faces are plastered to the expanse of huge windows at Starbucks. Traffic slows as passengers and cabbies rubberneck while going past. This is a spectacle, a show for all who are here—an amusement. These men will frame some souvenir snapshots, cutting out the chaos of the other photographers and extraneous passersby, and create a tiny little world where a girl who should be happy, who should be smiling—a girl who kissed a movie star—walks home from the deli looking deeply upset.

When the pictures are on the printed page they'll only tell the story each of these guys wants them to tell. Those crisp glossy images will leave out the bit about how this girl, vulnerable and unprotected, was ambushed by a dozen people who clawed at her and pushed her around while screaming obscenities. The people who see the images won't know that the only reason she looked up from the pavement was the cruelty of one disgusting photographer. And, I suppose, when people look into the pages of *Celeb* and see these astoundingly pointless shots of a woman walking home, they won't notice that I am shaking a little and trying to keep myself from crying. They won't notice that I'm scared or comprehend how lost and lonely I feel right now. They won't know how overwhelming it is to be completely powerless in the face of the scrutiny and the aggression, or that the printed pictures aren't nearly as agonizing as the experience of having them taken. People will probably just glance at the shot and move on, flip the page to a layout of *American Idol* contestants or something equally ridiculous. So I will have been hurt, insulted . . . I will have gone through all this . . . for *what*?

I'm just trying to walk home. All I want to do is go home! This is what Ethan wanted to show me. This is it.

Oh, God, I made people feel this way. I made *Ethan* feel this way. When I followed him that night at the airport, when I walked into that stupid restaurant . . . I did *this*.

No wonder people hate me.

I feel the tears, only after they begin trickling down my face. The passersby don't look concerned. They just point. The rapid-fire *click-click-click* of the cameras increases steadily, capturing each and every drop as it rolls over my cheek.

Suddenly, there's an abrupt, unceremonious tug at my shirt—from behind. The force of it propels me back, compelling my feet to move with it, or risk being tipped backward and dragged like a tree that's just been felled.

A pair of strong hands grip my waist and force me toward the street.

"What—?" I yelp.

A slow, soothing voice says, "I've got you, Sadie."

ONCE MORE, WITH FEELING

What Ethan Wyatt says, Ethan Wyatt does. Recent reports have Tinseltown's hottest bachelor slowing down and assessing his priorities. Wyatt is said to be taking steps to more elaborately protect his privacy and keep the rumor mill from grinding his every move into tabloid fodder. To this end, Wyatt has turned down several possibly lucrative (and unquestionably high-profile) movie roles on the left coast and is opting to apply some patience and await a plum gig on the Great White Way. Wyatt's publicist commented, "Ethan is looking to put down roots in Manhattan. He is confident that the industry will support his branching out to new areas and welcome his commitment to the craft."

CHAPTER 28

I expect to see Todd sitting next to me in the cab, but instead it's a disheveled mop of sooty black hair and deep beautiful blue eyes.

"I tried to call you," Ethan says, touching my hand. "I'm sorry I didn't make it in time."

I look out the dirty window of the cab, trying hard not to let my emotions get the better of me.

Watching the city go by, I say the only thing that I can think to say, "You win."

I get it now. I understand it completely. How it hurts to be in the middle of all that, the way that I hurt Ethan, the way that I hurt a million other people. I drew a line in the sand, a line I would not cross, but it was so arbitrary and pointless. It was a mirage. Every time I pointed my lens at someone, I compromised a little part of myself, weakened what few bonds I had with the part of me that believed in unveiling the truth.

All those pictures in those magazines, all those pictures

Ethan took of me . . . they were like mirrors. Showing me that I'm not the person I thought I was. Showing me just how far removed I am from the person I once wanted to be.

Do you know what it felt like being in that pack, having all those people stare at me as I fought and willed my way down the sidewalk? It felt just like when I was little and my mother paraded me around to her friends. All those eyes drilling into me. I swear, I could feel what they were thinking. Just like when I was playing the part of Paige's darling daughter. I've been running from that, but all the while I was slowly becoming just like her. It was like slapping salve on an old wound—masking it, but not healing it. I was oblivious or just unconcerned by how my job—my choices—affected other people. Just like Paige.

I walk into the apartment to a jumble of greetings and apologies, and worry. Brooke and Luke look sleepy and startled, while my mother appears to have been primped and polished by a team of stylists. Beside her slick beauty, Todd looks like a rough-hewn caricature. His caterpillars bounce and wiggle as he—and the rest of them—spot my unlikely rescuer.

"Hi," Ethan says, self-consciously lifting his hand by way of a greeting.

"Hi," the peanut gallery says in time.

"Sadie, are you—" Brooke tries.

"Not. Yet." I say, staggering into my bedroom.

I drop the squished egg sandwich on my bed and race to the giant Brown Box. Gripping the torn outer edge of the paper, I wrench it down. I rip through the cardboard, shredding it into a thousand little pieces, and finally understand what my mother meant in her note.

Sometimes the things we run away from should be given a chance to catch up. A reminder of things past—and perhaps future.

The contents of the box, quite literally, takes my breath away.

It's a self-portrait I took my last year of college. The self-portrait that earned me the title of Graduate with the Most Potential. Originally a modest eight-by-ten, it's now larger than life.

In the photograph, I'm sitting on a simple wooden stool, wearing a worn-in old white T-shirt and tattered jeans. My hair was shorter then, pulled off my face. In the warm, grayish sepia tones of the photograph, you can see the tension in my muscles, the way my teeth are slightly clenched—defiant. My posture is straight and proud—shoulders back, chest out. My eyes are wide open, piercing through the lens. All I can think now is, *That girl has courage.*

I looked so happy then, so determined. I was so sure of my future, of what I was going to do with my life. I *knew* that I would be a success. I *knew* that I could make it. Then, two weeks later, my father died. My father died, and I got scared. My father followed his dream straight to the grave, and my mother followed hers straight out of my life. I blamed my choices—to abandon art photography, to abandon my dream— on my father's debt and my mother's unwillingness to help me. But it was my fault. I let go of the portraits because I didn't want to end up like my parents. I didn't want my dream to swallow me up like their dreams swallowed them.

The tears begin again, unstoppable.

A noise over my left shoulder startles me.

"I had it blown up," my mother says quietly, approaching me.

"Why?"

"So you couldn't ignore it." She puts her hand on my back, rubs it gently from side to side.

"I've been trying to tell you . . . in my way," she says. "Perhaps I haven't said it as well as I should."

I stutter, "I wouldn't have believed you anyway."

She puts her hands on my shoulders, forces me to turn toward her, to look her in the eye. "I didn't send this because I'm not already proud of you, Sadie. Portraits, or no portraits, I am proud of you." She takes a deep breath and exhales by way of a sigh. "Your dad was a good man—kind, loving, generous to a fault—but I know that in some ways he was just as selfish as I was. We both neglected you for these *things* we were so determined to have. Our priorities were completely off," she says with regret. "I sent this because I don't want you to give up. You survived the chaos your father and I put you through. You can do *anything*. And that includes not repeating our mistakes. Do you understand?"

I nod yes.

My mother gives me a squeeze and then rises to leave.

"Hey, Mom?" I say through my tears. "Thank you."

She blows me a kiss and slips out, leaving only a hint of rose water behind her.

After an hour of staring at my self-portrait, and one long hot shower, I feel strong enough to face the masses.

I step out into the living room. What had been a quiet but steady chatter drops off to complete and utter silence.

"I'm not dying, people," I say, trying to lighten the mood. "Oh, but Todd?"

"Yeah," he replies sheepishly.

"I quit."

He nods. "Sort of saw that coming."

"All right. I need a drink."

Standing in the divot by the window, I look down on First Avenue at the troupe of photographers staking out the entrance to the building.

"Hey," says Brooke, pressing her head against the window beside me and staring down to the street. "I really am sorry about yesterday."

"I know," I reply, trying to see the make and model of a suspicious black SUV double-parked across the street.

"Seriously, Sadie," she presses, turning around and staring across the room at our motley collection of friends, relatives, and the odd celebrity.

I turn around and join her, leaning my back against the window.

"I did some digging last night," Brooke says. "I looked into that story Ethan told us about when they were both after the part in *Dereliction of Duty*. I'm pretty sure he was telling the truth. Right after that, Ethan started getting the bad press and rumors of drug use and all that. Duncan Stoke is an asshole."

"You're over him then?" I pose gently.

"I guess," she says, shrugging her shoulders.

A hail of rambunctious laughter erupts from Ethan, Todd, and Luke.

Brooke gazes at Ethan and adds, "You know, I think you might have a decent guy there."

"He's not *my* guy . . ." Yet.

"Are you worried about the celebrity stuff or . . ."

I take a deep breath. "No. I don't think so. Not anymore." I'm not afraid of what any new pictures might reveal. If I can get a good handle on who *I* think I am, I'm pretty sure the opinions of everyone else won't be a problem.

"Good," Brooke enjoins. " 'Cause I think he's a keeper."

Hmmm . . . a keeper. I've never had one of those.

I open the fridge for another beer, and when I turn around Ethan is standing in the entryway smiling at me. He's pink and warm from the heat, and the beer, and a lot of very boisterous conversation with Luke and Todd.

I smile back, not knowing exactly what else to do.

His face suddenly goes all serious, his eyes doing that world-weary brooding thing they do so well. "I'm sorry," Ethan says.

"For what?" I ask, taken aback.

"Uh . . ." he says, "the stalking . . . criticizing . . . general *mayhem*."

"Don't apologize," I reply immediately. "I should thank you."

"Oh, please. No problem. Anytime," he jokes.

"Once might be enough, actually."

He retorts, "The Yoda toothbrush still hasn't been captured properly . . . for posterity, I mean. So . . ."

"Cute."

"Thanks," he replies.

"I think we have a problem though," I say softly. "How do we . . . uh . . ." I try to read the tiny movement of his eyes over my face, the little wisp of a smile that seems to be perking at the corners of his mouth. I don't know how much I can say without completely screwing this up. I'm used to *situations*. This is the first time I've ever been interested in having an actual relationship with someone. "How do we make it stop?"

"Make what stop?" he asks, eyeing me with a roguish grin.

"Kissing in front of a kosher deli . . . torrid love triangle . . . you and I dating . . . Any of these things ringing a bell?"

He replies immediately, "You want to stop the stories?"

"Wouldn't *not* stopping them be kind of *inconvenient* for you?"

"Not if it's the truth," he counters matter-of-factly.

I wait for him to elaborate, clarify, *something* . . . but he just stares at me with those big blue eyes.

"Help me out here," I say. "Was that you just saying you want to date?" Ah, must be more specific! "Me, I mean. Date me?" I am like the biggest dork ever.

"Yeah," he replies sweetly, dropping the roguish thing.

I let the tingling this inspires wash over me and settle in. "Oh," I say, as an enormous smile bursts to the surface.

"Does that mean you want to? Date? Me, I mean," he asks teasingly.

I crinkle my nose up dramatically, teasing right back. "Eh," I grunt. "I don't know. I just quit my job and all. . . . I've got to get back into the legit photography. I think I might try celebrity portraits. Like Annie Leibovitz . . . only, you know, not as amazing. Something like that. I'm probably going to be really busy."

"I have to tell you, Sadie," Ethan says, inching toward me, "it would probably be best if you lie low for a while."

"Oh, *really*?" I ask, playing along.

"And the place I'm staying is pretty fantastic."

"Is it?"

"The room service is outrageous. There's a concierge . . . maid"—his right eyebrow arches wryly—"in-room *massage* . . . It's a veritable *who's who* of minions. We could probably survive—I don't know—ten, twelve days without ever leaving the bed." He smiles at me, practically beaming—his eyes doing that amazing, irresistible sparkling thing they do.

"*Really*," I reply wryly, "never leaving the bed?"

"And you know, I'm something of a celebrity myself," he says.

"You don't say . . ."

He edges toward me, wraps one arm around my waist and slides the other slowly up to my neck. "Maybe you could use me . . ."

"Are you getting fresh with me?"

"You've got a dirty mind, girl. I mean, you could use me to practice your *photography*."

He tips his head down and his lips meet mine. It's a kiss so slow, soft, and intense that it's almost paralyzing.

Ethan pulls away. "Did I mention there's a minibar? If we play our cards right, we might not have to leave till fall."

I'm beginning to think he doesn't hate me anymore. . . .

Epilogue

ETHAN WYATT GETTING A
SLICE OF THE APPLE

Recently reformed bad boy Ethan Wyatt is finally putting down roots in the Big Apple. He's come out of hiding to sign on for the Broadway debut of *My Favorite Wife*. He'll fill the role made famous by James Garner in the film *Move Over, Darling*, with Doris Day. He must think it's a winner, too. He's been seen tooling around Manhattan in a fully restored 1979 Camaro, going from one prospective apartment to another with his girlfriend of five months, Sadie Price. There's no official word on whether the duo will be cohabiting in Wyatt's new digs. Wyatt and his reps have been tight-lipped about the pair since their splashy beginnings. But psychiatrist and love expert Dr. Abigail Dalton gave us her two cents: "Soliciting consultation from a significant other on big-ticket purchases, such as a home or car, clearly indicates that the couple is taking things to the next level."

Up Close and Personal
With the Authors

(Or, Sarah Bushweller and Emily Morris sit down and force themselves to discuss their latest work instead of what they just read in *Us Weekly*.)

EMILY: Hmmm. So we're really not allowed to discuss Tom & Katie, Nick & Jessica, or Brad & Angelina, is that it?

SARAH: Correct. We must only discuss *Accidental It Girl*.

EMILY: Well, then . . .

SARAH: Yes. Well, then . . .

EMILY: Can we talk about what they were wearing in the pages of *Us Weekly*?

SARAH: No.

EMILY: Oh.

SARAH: How about this: How did you first get the idea for Sadie and the unusual situation she gets herself into?

EMILY: Oh good, an easy one. Thanks.

SARAH: No problem.

EMILY: Okay, it started many years ago when I caught a report on *Entertainment Tonight* about JFK Jr. getting ticked off at a photographer who was following him around Central Park. JFK Jr. went and got himself a camera, followed the photographer's car, and hounded the paparazzi right back. I started to wonder about what would happen if a celebrity really took this to the extreme and tried to get back at a photographer who'd wronged him. Like I always do, I sort of filed the idea away in the back of my mind—and in my master book of ungerminated ideas. Finally, a couple of years after the initial spark (sometime around 1999 or 2000, I think), I was doing a screenwriting workshop with Lew Hunter as part of my college coursework and I developed the idea further.

SARAH: You started a screenplay but didn't finish.

EMILY: Thanks for reminding me.

SARAH: No, I just mean that the plot was a lot different from the one we developed into *Accidental It Girl*.

EMILY: Yeah, originally it was much more of a farce. It was a sort of morality play exploring the silliness of Hollywood culture and the American obsession with celebrities.

SARAH: That's why we decided to develop it into a novel. We're both completely obsessed with the famous and infamous—and a bit confused as to why.

EMILY: It's fascinating. On the one hand, we say, "Of *course* celebrities are just people, there's nothing really special about them."

SARAH: And yet my favorite tabloid section is the "Stars— They're Just Like Us" page. I laugh about how the magazines say "They walk their dogs!" and "They try on shoes!" like we should all be shocked that famous people also have feet and need to try on their shoes. The tabloids treat celebrities like they're these aliens who don't eat, sleep, or breathe like the rest of us.

EMILY: Right. We laugh and say how silly it is. Yet, that's the section of the magazine we turn to first. What's even more intriguing is that you and I, having researched and written all about Sadie and Ethan, have really delved into what it feels like to be followed and watched twenty-four hours a day. We've come to the conclusion that it's infinitely harder than it looks in the magazines, and just as frustrating and frightening as the celebrities claim.

SARAH: But we still buy the magazines, and delight in the fact that we get to see those images.

EMILY: Right. The whole thing is just beyond complex, and still totally fascinates me—on a personal level (in relationship to my own questionable sanity) and when looking at the culture as a whole. I mean, I don't think we solve the mystery of these phenomena with Sadie or anything, but . . .

SARAH: The thing with Sadie is that she gets an entirely new perspective on just how similar the famous and unfamous are—how celebrities really are "just like us." She and Ethan have led parallel lives, in a way. They both set out to have a career—a life—that meant something, and slowly lost touch with that.

EMILY: In a way they're both paralyzed by a public image, Sadie as a tough, no-nonsense paparazzi, and Ethan as Hollywood's hottest bad-boy action hero. It's like that old adage: "Don't believe your own press." Really, Sadie and Ethan both have. Deep down, each of them knows that they are more than the image they've been stuck with, but neither of them has done anything about it. Sadie resigns herself to the fact that people hate her, and Ethan has resigned himself to being a walking, talking action figure.

SARAH: Until Ethan's big scheme puts Sadie back in touch with the person she always hoped she'd be. And Sadie sees the kind of person Ethan really is—and how she's helped to perpetuate this ridiculous bad-boy image he has.

EMILY: Man, I love Ethan.

SARAH: Me, too.

EMILY: Oooh, here's a question I get asked a lot: Is Ethan Wyatt based on any particular celebrity?

SARAH: Nope. Unless you count the many idealized versions of celebrities we've concocted in our heads.

EMILY: Yeah, Ethan could be any number of famous guys you and I have had a crush on over the years, I guess. Successful, debonair, perfectly imperfect.

SARAH: Outrageously good-looking.

EMILY: Yeah.

SARAH: Okay, let's close this on a fun one. What would you say is your favorite movie about the movies?

EMILY: Hmmm, that's a toughie. Oh, you know what movie I love? Albert Brooks's *The Muse* with Sharon Stone. I think I probably love it so much because I can relate to the main character's frustration as a writer. The movie is freaking hilarious, and shows all too accurately how being a writer can make a person go completely nutso. How about you?

SARAH: I really like *The Player*. You have to love a movie that makes you root for such an evil main character. It's just so . . . Hollywood. But my favorite movie about the movies has to be *Singing in the Rain*—love all that singing and dancing. Or, it could be because Gene Kelly was a total fox.

EMILY: Oh, Gene Kelly. He was dreamy.

SARAH: Yeah.

EMILY: Hey, Sarah, are we, uh, done interviewing now, because, for some reason, I really feel like going to Blockbuster.

SARAH: Let's go. I've got the pickles and popcorn!

Life is always a little sweeter with a book from Downtown Press!

ENSLAVE ME SWEETLY
Gena Showalter

She has the heart of a killer…
and the body of an angel.

CARPOOL CONFIDENTIAL
Jessica Benson

You'll be amazed what you
can learn riding shotgun.

THE MAN SHE THOUGHT SHE KNEW
Shari Shattuck

What kind of secrets is
her lover keeping?
The deadly kind…

INVISIBLE LIVES
Anjali Banerjee

She can sense your heart's
desire. But what does *her*
heart desire?

LOOKING FOR MR. GOODBUNNY
Kathleen O'Reilly

Fixing other people's problems
is easy. It's fixing your own
that's hard.

SEX AND THE SOUTH BEACH CHICAS
Caridad Piñeiro

Shake things up with four
girls who know how to spice
things up…

WHY MOMS ARE WEIRD
Pamela Ribon

And you thought *your* family
was weird.

Whether you're a Good Girl or a Naughty Girl, Downtown Press has the books you love!

Look for these Good Girls...

The Ex-Wife's Survival Guide
DEBBY HOLT
Essential items: 1. Alcohol.
2. A sense of humor.
3. A sexy new love interest.

Suburbanistas
PAMELA REDMOND SATRAN
From A-list to Volvo in sixty seconds flat.

Un-Bridaled
EILEEN RENDAHL
She turned the walk down the aisle into the hundred-meter dash...in the other direction.

The Starter Wife
GIGI LEVANGIE GRAZER
She's done the starter home and the starter job...but she never thought she'd be a starter wife.

The New York Times bestseller!

I Did (But I Wouldn't Now)
CARA LOCKWOOD
Hindsight is a girl's best friend.

Everyone Worth Knowing
LAUREN WEISBERGER
The devil wore Prada— but the bouncer wears Dolce.

The New York Times bestseller!

And don't miss these Naughty Girls...

The Manolo Matrix
JULIE KENNER
If you thought finding the perfect pair of shoes was hard—try staying alive in them.

Enslave Me Sweetly
An Alien Huntress Novel
GENA SHOWALTER
She has the body of a killer... and the heart of a killer.

Great storytelling just got a new address.

DOWNTOWN PRESS
A Division of Simon & Schuster
A CBS COMPANY

Naughty Girls

Available wherever books are sold or at www.downtownpress.com.

15067-2